THE LAST WEEKEND IN WONDERLAND

To Robin
All the best
S. L.

SIMON LYONS

Published by Starblack Press (a division of Blackstar Promotions Ltd)

www.blackstarpromotions.org
www.simonlyonsauthor.com

Cover by Julia Durman.
Edited by Mairi Mayfield

Final edit and publishing by Alan Galaxy who when not promoting gigs and publishing books is the drummer for the legendary Spizzenergi

ISBN 978-1-915787-09-9

Printed in United Kingdom

First Edition

DEDICATION

To all those talented and brave enough to stand on a stage (or sit, if you're a drummer).

PROLOGUE

I sat with my back resting against a random tree. Eric and his mates were gathered around sharing a joint.

"Sid and his mate Jimmy were at the Weeley festival that my brother is always banging on about"

Eric informed his troops who collectively nodded their approval, offering me their respect.

"Sid saw a man get hacked to death there, didn't you Sid" Eric proudly proclaimed giving his new pal a friendly pat on his shoulder.

"I did indeed Eric, and a few bands"

"Tell the boys about the toilets Sid"

I laughed and thought back to those Spartan days of the early seventies.

"There's not much to tell to be honest" I replied before adding

"That's because basically there wasn't any".

The Assembled crowd laughed as one, I saw Jimmy in the distance carrying the beers. The sun was setting behind him, I saw Jimmy was smiling as he got closer. The boys were still laughing, we could hear music throbbing from a nearby stage. This truly was a wonderland.

THE 'TO DO' LIST

1) Preparation
   a) Research suffocation (with a pillow).
   b) How long will it take?
   c) How traceable is it?

2) The night before
   a) 9.00 to 10.00pm - engage with carer (She/he leaves apartment 10.00pm sharp).
   b) 10.10pm - check pillow in top cupboard above bed.
   c) 10.20pm - set phone alarm for 6.00am.
   d) 10.25pm - try and sleep in armchair beside bed.

3) The execution (exact timings to be confirmed depending on result of 1a)
   a) 6.00am - wake up.
   b) Go to bathroom wash face etc.
   c) Remove pillow from top cupboard.
   d) 6.10am suffocation (Allow 20 minutes?)

4) The clean up
   a) 6.20am-ish - remove pillowcase from pillow, put pillow back in top cupboard.

b)   Place pillowcase in black sack with contents of bin in kitchen, exit apartment and put sack down communal rubbish chute
c)   Make sure death looks completely natural.
d)   6.50am prompt - go back to sleep in armchair beside bed.
e)   7.00am - carer let's herself in and finds me asleep next to the deceased. She will wake me and inform of the sad news. I will ask for a few moments alone. She will likely go to kitchen and put kettle on.
f)   7.10am - join carer and thank her for everything. Tell her I'll start to make the necessary calls and suggest she goes.

5) Phone calls
    a)   7.20am - call doctor's surgery to report death.
    b)   7.22am - call Mark.
    c)   7.24am - call Warden.
    d)   7.26am - call Rab.
    e)   7.30am - call funeral directors.
    f)   7.35am - call Leo and Tara.
    g)   7.40am - call Trudie (Maybe I should call her first?)
    h)   7.50am - call Jimmy.

6) Wait for doctor to come and certify death.

7) Liaise with Mark.

8) Liaise with Rab/funeral directors.

9) Once funeral arranged wait for Mark/Trudie/kids to arrive and get them to contact all on separate 'guest' list.

10) Confirm logistics with Jimmy re. festival.

11) Destroy (Burn?)

1

THE LAST MOSH PIT

(2018)

"SO, YOU COLLAPSED in a 'mosh pit', Mr. Levinson?" The young Indian doctor asked whilst perusing my notes.

"Apparently." I tried to recall my exact situation from when I passed out.

"And your date of birth is the twenty sixth of the eleventh, nineteen fifty-six?" the doctor read aloud, whilst adopting a wry smile.

"Yep. I'm sixty-two tomorrow," I confirmed.

"And you were in a mosh pit?" he asked mockingly.

"Yep. I don't think I was the eldest either!"

"Who were you 'moshing' to?" he enquired, whilst checking my blood pressure.

"The Damned." I nodded towards the black, blood-soaked t-shirt on the back of the adjacent chair with *Damned Damned Damned* printed in red letters on the back. "Although, technically I was 'pogoing' rather than moshing."

"Don't know them," the doctor confessed. "I've only been to one concert to be honest, Coldplay. They were very good, lots of singing along. No mosh pit though."

"No, I don't suppose there was." I groaned, feeling a spasm of pain in my big toe.

"So, I guess they're a heavy metal band?" The doctor noted my blood pressure.

"Punk, punks pogo, metal heads mosh," I confirmed. "So, what's wrong with me doctor?"

"You sustained a nasty blow to the back of your head causing a concussion. You've also got small fractures in your big toe and a couple of metatarsal bones on your left foot. You've got very high blood pressure. Other than that, you're fine."

"So, I'll live then?"

"I think so, but clearly you've had a warning. I suggest a change of lifestyle, such as a healthy diet, moderate exercise and Coldplay," Dr Shah stated cheekily.

"Diet and exercise are doable, the other thing is out of the question."

Our conversation was interrupted by Trudie entering the room with a bag of fresh clothes and assorted goodies. "How is my idiot husband, doctor?" she enquired.

"He's hopefully going to start acting his age, Mrs. Levinson."

Trudie sniggered. "Would that be his physical or mental age doctor?"

"I've recommended that your husband enjoy the delightful melodies of the likes of Coldplay."

"Sid quite likes Coldplay, don't you dear?"

It didn't take long for Trudie to embarrass me.

"Arghh your guilty pleasure, Mr. Levinson! The truth is out."

"As it happens, I saw Coldplay open the second stage at V festival in nineteen-ninety-nine when they'd just brought out *Yellow*, and yes, I could see they were going to be big and, I confess, I bought the first two albums." I felt no shame in this revelation and I could have brought up my liking for

Travis, Snow Patrol and The Beautiful South but I suddenly felt exhausted.

"So, no more 'moshing', Mr. Levinson," Dr. Shah ordered as he left the room, "polite, even enthusiastic, applause in future please."

I closed my eyes thinking about Jimmy, if he'd been there, he'd have had my back. I thought about my next gig, Sham 69. *'Polite applause, I don't think so.'* Then my mind drifted back to my first gig, almost forty-eight years ago.

2

THE ART OF DECEPTION

(1971)

I'M NOT SURE what the average age is when an adolescent forms the ability to lie. I don't mean boasting, fibbing, little white lies, I mean deceit, manipulative misinformation. Proper lying.

I guess I was around fourteen when I started my apprenticeship in the dark art. Looking back it wouldn't have been just a matter of my maturing and the hormones surging through my body. There was a more practical reason for me trying to bend the truth. My father, like many of his generation that fought and won the Second World War, ruled us with iron discipline. As my cultural horizons widened, so did my desire to venture further from the suburban bubble I lived in. This meant permission from my parents, which of course meant me asking my mother first. Her reply to everything was, "Ask your father." My father's reply to any question that involved either money or travel was a stock, "Don't even think about it." So, I gave up asking and explored other means to escape to the wonderland of football, music, and then less wholesome pursuits.

In the winter of 1970, I started to hone my skills by dabbling with the odd day of truancy from my sink comprehensive school, which I hated with a vengeance. It was two buses away and there was an equally poor school within walking distance. The reason for my parents sending me to hell for five years, when purgatory was just around the corner, has still never properly been explained to me. The school all my friends went to (around the corner) had girls in it. Yes, there were also psychopaths from the local council estate, but the boy's school they sent me to had double the psychopaths and absolutely no Jews. The Jew business I will come to, it's relevant to *the list*.

It was early June, just after the Whitsun holiday. I was on the second bus, having avoided any bullying on the first, when I ran into my co-conspirator Jimmy Faulkner. He was pleased to see me and show off the fruits of his shoplifting at the local newsagent. I didn't have the nerve to indulge in this delinquent pastime. As with most forms of early teenage skulduggery, I feared the consequences if my father found out. Jimmy was lucky. His father had died two years earlier, so he had free rein to do as he pleased. Alice, his mum, was too busy working to be arsed if her boy was naughty. Besides, they weren't his real parents (that's how I saw it back then, not now obviously), as he was adopted. No dad, adopted, the world was his oyster. I actually *envied* his situation.

He offered me a spangle and a square of Big Fry chocolate. Not my favourite but it would be ungracious to be fussy and ask him to nick Mars bars on demand. He then produced a pristine copy of that week's *Melody Maker,* which we studied as if a holy script. Led Zep' and ELP were the cover headlines. We stared at the photos of Jimmy Page and Keith Emerson as if they were Moses and the Lord Jesus almighty. I was desperate for Jimmy to turn the pages, but he told me I could buy it for half price, a three-penny piece. Fair enough, seeing as he'd risked a clout from Mr. Bradley, who owned the newsagent. We used to call him Hood Head as he looked like the baddie in *Thunderbirds*. As it transpired, I exchanged a copy of *Shoot* magazine for Jimmy's *Melody Maker* and that evening I studied every page, every word, instead of doing my maths homework.

I particularly poured over the adverts for forthcoming gigs, I loved discovering the names of new bands and venues. I was familiar with some of them as my brother Mark, who was six years older than me, was a regular at the Marquee Club and the Lyceum Ballroom. When he wasn't getting on my nerves, which was most of the time, he was useful for purchasing records and providing information that would impress my peers.

Mum shouted that supper was ready. I was perusing the list of bands due to appear at the *Hope and Anchor*. My cousin Trevor had tried to get in to see a band there but was refused entry for being under eighteen. He was two years older than me and had started shaving! What chance would I have?

"Sid, your supper will get cold!" Mum bellowed.

She was generally a very elegant woman but would turn completely mental around mealtimes. I was about to place the oracle under my maths exercise book, a security measure in case my father came in my room, when I saw the advert that would change mine and Jimmy's lives.

I wolfed down the Spam fritters, chips, and peas and rushed back to my room to return to the advert. I searched my craft drawer for scissors and carefully cut out the object of my curiosity, placing it in my maths book. I spent the night plotting and planning, getting very little sleep. I wanted to make sure I got on the same bus as Jimmy, which wasn't an exact science. I wished I could phone him but that would mean asking my father's permission, which would raise suspicions.

The next morning, I managed to get the front seat on the top deck. As the bus pulled up at the stop by the Jackson estate, I saw Jimmy arguing with Ink Bat. I knocked on the window to get his attention. He came scurrying up, threatening Ink Bat to stay downstairs.

"What a prize wanker that Ink Bat is," he exclaimed, handing me a corner of the chocolate bar he'd just nicked. "Fuck it, it's dark chocolate," he said, apologising. "The Hood almost saw me as well."

I removed the ad from my exercise book and showed it to Jimmy. He read the names of the bands aloud with the same excitement as I did.

"T. Rex, The Faces, Rory Gallagher," he paused before slapping me on the back and shouting "King Crimson!" in pure joy. Just then a ball of scrunched up newspaper hit him on the head. "Fucking Ink Bat!" he hollered. "Let's study this properly at lunchtime, I'm going to get that wanker!"

He got up and disappeared down the stairs in pursuit of that idiot.

At lunch, we sat with our backs to the concrete wall of the gymnasium, studying the advert in silence for a couple of minutes before both of us shouted, "Mott the Hoople!" in unison.

I can recall exactly when and why Jimmy and I fell in love with Mott the Hoople. We'd flirted with metal bands like Zep, Purple and Sabbath but they were too huge for us to contemplate following. Mott on the other hand played small venues in towns like Hereford (their hometown), Stafford, Scunthorpe and, most interestingly, Aylesbury. Jimmy reckoned he had an uncle in Aylesbury, and it wasn't that far from our North London suburb. We had discussed the possibility of going to a Mott gig there in September, but now we had bigger fish to fry.

"Where the fuck is Weeley?" Jimmy asked.

I pointed to the address on the advert and read aloud. "The Weeley Festival of Progressive Rock, Weeley, near Clacton on Sea, Essex."

"I've been to Essex!" Jimmy yelled. "It's in Southend, it's by the sea," he confirmed.

"Look, Jimmy, travel info," I said, pointing to the small print on the bottom left hand corner. "Trains, Liverpool Street to Weeley (station adjacent to site)."

"Liverpool's fucking hundreds of miles away mate, forget it," Jimmy said seriously.

"No Jimmy, there's a station in London called Liverpool Street. My brother gets off there every day, he works near there."

"So, what's the plan, Sid? How much will it all cost?" Jimmy asked.

"I'll make a list, Jimmy. I'll meet you tomorrow ten o'clock at the Third Tree Club," I confirmed.

* * *

From the moment I mastered the art of writing, I loved making lists. After supper I retreated to my 'cave', opened my school rough book at a clean page and wrote:

WEELEY FESTIVAL OF PROGRESSIVE ROCK - AUGUST BANK HOLIDAY

1) *MONEY*

I sat back chewing my pencil wondering how two working class fourteen-year-olds could raise the necessary funds for such an adventure. I wrote down:

2) *ADMISSION £2*

You could save 50p by ordering in advance, but this seemed risky and would involve envelopes, stamps etc. I guesstimated that the train fare would be around 50p return. Then there was spending money. We could take our own sandwiches and pop but there were going to be refreshment stalls, so I factored in another £1. That made the running total £3.50, which I rounded up to a fiver just to be safe.

3) *EXCUSE*

We needed a rock-solid alibi, a realistic reason for two fourteen-year-olds to have a weekend away. The part of my adolescent brain that was devious enough to embrace truancy was now working overtime, I soon had the answer. It would also be the answer to number four on my list:

4) *ACCOMMODATION*

I hated going to Scouts but my father insisted on it. I struggled with the practical stuff, the knots, climbing, Bunsen burners, that sort of stuff. I'd recently, as the weather improved, taken to playing hookie from Friday night Scouts. I preferred hanging about with other assorted oiks in the local station car park. My father loved the paramilitary ethos of the scouts, I despised it. Having suddenly discovered free will, I was on the verge of teenage rebellion. However, there was a pending summer camping trip to Jersey, which would mean a week away from home. Worth hanging on for. *Now,* I was engineering another benefit.

* * *

We'd formed the Third Tree Club the previous summer, the first time our gang had been allowed over the park (or anywhere) without parental supervision. There was a small grassy alcove beside the rugby pitches with four large trees, which we used as goals for three-a-side, as toilets, and more recently for ambushing Ink Bat and his inbred mates.

We tended to sit under the third tree, which was great for both climbing and sheltering from passing showers. Two weeks into the summer holiday our game of three-a-side was interrupted by this tall pasty-faced boy who'd asked if he could join us. Smithy told him no and then told him to fuck

13

off. Threats were exchanged, and the stranger insisted to meet the next day (mid-day) to have a 'one to one'.

"That's a bit strong, Smithy," I tried to object. "He could have taken my place for ten minutes."

"Fuck him, he's just moved into the estate from South London somewhere. Lots of rumours about him and his family."

I'd never met anyone from South London but assumed from Smithy it was not good. I'd heard my father call anywhere south of the Thames 'bandit country'. Maybe Smithy was right.

The next day I got to the third tree just before noon. Perry was already there, his first name was actually Neville, but everyone called him Perry because his surname was Mason. The South Londoner was next to turn up.

"Where's your mate, has he bottled it?" he asked aggressively.

"He'll be here," Perry replied.

"I'm having a one to one, don't you get involved," he demanded.

"We're not bullies, it's just you and Smithy, mate," I confirmed.

Right on time, Smithy strode up with a couple of other friends.

"I thought you'd bottled it!" the lanky stranger teased.

Smithy was never one for fancy words, he was happiest playing football or terrorising the park keeper with his creative home-made weapons. We called him the 'Scientist' because he was forging a fearsome reputation for his homemade fireworks/incendiary devices. To my surprise he tossed his opponent a football. "Wanna play, mate?" he offered, and then watched as the ball was smashed as far away as possible.

"Fuck off, I wanted to play yesterday! Today I want to fight! You bottling out?"

I stepped forward and politely offered him some friendly advice. "I'd join us for a game if I were you, believe me, you don't want to fight Smithy, he's indestructible and full of surprises."

He smiled at me and then got in Smithy's face. "So you are bottling it."

"My dad said I should welcome the new family, give you a chance, you really don't want to fight me," Smithy said with a smirk.

"Oh, I do." The new boy spat and gave Smithy a provocative slap round the face.

Smithy wore a fixed smile as he walked slowly backwards away from his attacker who continued to slap him.

"Don't be a girl, mate, come on, hit me!" he teased, dropping his hands and beckoning Smithy to hit him.

Smithy got to the park fence still retreating, still smiling. Suddenly he received a proper punch on the jaw. He never flinched or changed his mad stare, he nonchalantly reached into his inside pocket. The rest of us had been following them a few feet behind, I glanced at Perry as we both saw the glint of metal and instantly guessed this was another lethal homemade weapon. Smithy wielded what looked like a medieval star and chain and smashed it round the South Londoner's head. We heard the yelp and stood motionless as he collapsed, clutching his bleeding skull, semi-conscious, as Smithy climbed over the fence and legged it towards the estate.

"What the fuck did he hit me with?" the new kid in town yelped, feeling his head.

"I did warn you, mate!" I reminded him, relieved he was still alive.

"I'm off to my aunts in Frinton for a week, when I get back, you're all dead!" he threatened as he got up and staggered off.

* * *

A couple of weeks later I indulged in my first real serious deception involving my parents. It was more

15

misinformation, then deceit, I told them I was going over the park all day to watch Smithy's older brother play cricket. We actually met at our local underground station with the intention of going to see our beloved Chelsea play Arsenal. We were both fairly certain our fathers would say no if we'd told them the truth. In hindsight, we wouldn't have blamed them.

Hooliganism was commonplace back then and we had to navigate the tube network right through enemy territory to our north London suburb. Smithy was the only other Chelsea fan I knew, as it was the norm to support your local team. I followed them because I'd stayed with Uncle Fred in Battersea when I was seven, when my father had his mysterious virus. He walked me to Stamford Bridge with strict instructions I was not to support either team (Chelsea or West Ham), as he would take me to see his team Spurs as soon as possible. However, by then, it was too late. I saw the blue shirts, smelt the hot dogs and was hooked for life. Smithy supported Chelsea because, whilst he was a scientist, he was shit at geography.

"Oh shit," he muttered, as the train moved out the station, nodding towards the seat diagonally behind me.

I looked round and saw the object of Smithy's attention. The South Londoner he'd almost killed over the park boy sat staring at us. He had a knitted blue and white scarf round his neck, disappearing into his black 'Harrington'.

"Should have told us you were a Chelsea fan, come and join us, mate," Smithy said, gesturing him over.

"What's your name, mate?" I asked him, as he casually sat opposite us.

"Jimmy, Jimmy Faulkner. Where's your scarves?" he asked.

"We don't wear colours, got to go through enemy territory," I explained.

"Take it you're tooled up?" he asked Smithy.

"Fireworks, homemade fireworks," Smithy stated with a proud smirk.

By the time we got to Chelsea we were firm friends. I discovered there was no room for Jimmy at the local shithole school, so he'd be going to my two buses away shithole. Another Chelsea fan, great news. Before entering the famous 'Shed' terrace, Jimmy told us he wanted to nick a programme. He said he'd meet us by the white wall, a random landmark on the giant terrace.

Just before kick-off, he found us leaning against what was to be our crash barrier for the next ten years. He presented us with not just a programme each but also a silk scarf, which was all the rage at London grounds. This was our first taste of Jimmy's prolific shoplifting skills. We tied the scarves around our wrists, the trend of the day, loving the camaraderie, as we would for years to follow.

We found three seats together on the train for the return journey. Just before the doors shut, three skinheads, probably a year older, sat in the seats directly opposite us. They wore red and white scarves tucked into their Crombie coats. Their red Doc Martins looked lethal. We sat staring at each other all the way from Earls Court to Kings Cross, where they got up and made to exit the carriage. The lad who'd sat opposite me suddenly turned and grabbed the scarf off my wrist and ran off the train. The doors shut, but then for some reason opened again and Smithy was up.

"Come on, let's have the bastards!" he shouted, as he and Jimmy jumped onto the platform.

I wasn't too keen on getting a kicking over a scarf, but it was too late to jib out. We chased them through the station and round St. Pancras. They legged it into the infamous Somers Town estate, where they lived. They knew every nook and cranny. We were lost.

I found myself one-to-one with the skinhead who'd been sitting opposite me. I turned and ran as his steel-toe capped boot kicked me up the arse. I sprinted back to the entrance of Kings Cross Station, wondering how the boys were.

Ten minutes later, Smithy came around the corner sporting a bloodied nose. "You all right, Smithy?" I enquired, relieved to see him.

"Fine. The bugger got a punch in, whilst I lit the fuse to one of my fireworks. Almost blew his head off!" he boasted.

"Any sign of Jimmy?" I asked.

"Lost him. Let's give him ten minutes, but we'd better head home soon before our mums start worrying."

We waited fifteen minutes and were about to head underground when Jimmy came limping around the corner. He had a black eye and a split lip.

"Shit! Jimmy, you ok, mate?" Smithy asked, as he put his hand on Jimmy's shoulder.

"I was ambushed. Come on, let's get going before they get reinforcements."

We had just got back on the tube when Smithy opened his coat, which had been buttoned up to the top, and revealed a bloodied red and white scarf. "A souvenir," he stated with pride.

We patted him on the back.

Jimmy, the new boy, sang his praises like they were lifelong buddies. I felt a pang of jealousy. I'd known Smithy since forever, at least since we moved from Stoke Newington to the suburbs. There seemed to be an instant bond between them, which made me feel uneasy.

We reached Arsenal station and once the doors were shut, we made gestures at the people on the platform. Jimmy then turned to me and playfully punched me in the upper arm. "I've got a present for you, mate," he said. He put his hand in his inside pocket and pulled out my silk scarf.

I took it thankfully but felt guilty he'd taken a battering on my behalf. Thirteen-year-olds can't see the future and seldom think about it. I knew I'd found a new mate, I wouldn't have realised though that we'd be best mates for the rest of our lives.

* * *

A year on and Jimmy and I were not just fellow football fans, we had discovered popular music. I had generally had a liking for crooners and can recall pleading with my mum to buy me my very first single, *That Girl Belongs to Yesterday* by Gene Pitney, but then I saw one of my brother's latest purchases and fell in love with the psychedelic cover. *Disraeli Gears* by Cream was a game changer for me.

Meanwhile, Jimmy invited me round and showed me a couple of albums he'd stolen from the new local record store (there were at least two on every high street back then). The first was by the most marvellously named Tyrannosaurus Rex and the title had us gripped, *My People Were Fair and Had Sky in Their Hair... But Now They're Content to Wear Stars on Their Brows*. The second, which he gave to me, was self-titled, *Mott the Hoople* by Mott the Hoople. Once again, the cover intrigued me, it was a piece of art. I would later discover it was a copy of a drawing by the Dutch graphic artist MC Escher. Our only source of information on these new discoveries were the music papers and the John Peel radio show. It wasn't long before I saved enough pocket money to buy more recent Mott albums.

In the meantime, Tyrannosaurus Rex had become T.Rex and Marc Bolan was all over the TV. Their first big hit was *Hot Love* and the 'Shed End' at Chelsea adapted the chorus into a terrace anthem. Jimmy and I sang the loudest.

We'd discovered Mott played smaller venues and were never likely to appear on Top of the Pops, hence the dream of seeing them in Aylesbury.

* * *

I was sat against the third tree at 10.00am sharp, armed with my 'Weeley' plan of action. Ten minutes later there was no sign of Jimmy.

Suddenly Ink Bat came roaring along the path on his bike and skidded to a halt.

"If you're waiting for Jimmy, forget it. He's been grounded for a week!" he exclaimed, seeming pleased about the situation.

"What for?" I asked.

"Julie O'Neill on our estate came home with a love bite! Her dad went 'round to Jimmy's and had a go at his mum."

I wasn't sure what a love bite was but pretended to understand. In the year since he arrived, Jimmy had built up a reputation for fighting (badly) and flirting with girls (successfully). Rumours abounded about his exploits with Julie O'Neill, and others. I was yet to experience my first proper snog.

I exchanged some abuse with Ink Bat, the most annoying boy in the whole universe, and looked at my list forlornly.

"Sorry I'm late, Sid!" a voice called out, as Jimmy crept into view.

"I thought you were grounded, mate!" I responded.

"Blimey, bad news travels quick 'round here. I escaped whilst Mum was at the launderette. So, what's the plan of action?"

Jimmy sat down next to me peeking at the list.

"Ok, number one: Money." I started to give him the details: train, entry cost, etc.

"What's the total?" he interrupted.

"Approx. three-pound-fifty for everything," I guesstimated.

"Call it two-pound, Sid. We can definitely sneak onto the train for nothing and it will be no trouble getting into the festival free like your brother at the Isle of Wight."

I was immediately concerned about sharing Jimmy's criminal intentions, though I understood his comment about what happened at the Isle of Wight festival the year before. So many people turned up the fence got knocked down and it was declared a free festival. My brother being so high maintenance hated the whole experience and vowed never to go to another festival or camp again. He never has.

"Ok," I agreed, knowing I'd take the whole three-pound fifty. Moving on, I explained that number two, *Excuse,* and number four, *Accommodation,* were linked. "Scouts," I explained, in one word.

"Scouts?" Jimmy repeated, intrigued.

"Yes. Scouts."

"But I'm expelled," Jimmy protested.

"Doesn't matter, Jimmy, leave it all to me. You just have to tell your mum you're allowed back." Jimmy told everyone he'd been thrown out for foul and abusive language to Skipper Ron. Skipper Ron told his mum he'd been thrown out for stealing. Both were plausible, but I recently discovered that they were both lies. The truth was far more sinister. I went on to explain that we were to tell our parents that we were going to do the Scout camping badge over the August bank holiday at a farm the Scouts used in Hertfordshire. I suggested we tell them an older Scouter would take us and pick us up from the Scout hut. Meanwhile, I'd tell Skipper Ron my dad is taking us and ask if it's okay to take a tent home the night before.

"But I'm excluded," Jimmy reminded me.

"That's where Ink Bat comes in," I confirmed. "Oi, Ink Bat!" I bellowed across the green to the pasty-faced cretin who was doing wheelies on his bike. Nobody was really sure where he got his strange nickname from and he certainly was a strange boy. Looking back, we were unnecessarily cruel to him. He was different. Nowadays difference is celebrated, back then it was ridiculed. It was Ink Bat's manner that ground our gears, he was sarcastic and a stirrer. But right now, I needed his help for our plan to come together. He skidded to a halt next to us, curious to why he'd been summoned.

"What do you two gay boys want?" he smirked, in his usual annoying manner.

"Do you want to join the Third Tree Club?" I offered. I'm not sure who was the most taken aback, Ink Bat or Jimmy.

"What's the catch?" he asked.

"You have to do us a favour and in return you get all the club benefits, like tree football and any spare treats that Jimmy nicks from Bradley's newsagents."

"Is that it?" he replied, without enthusiasm.

"Our motto is 'All for one and one for all', like the musketeers, so if anyone picks on you, we'll all have your back," Jimmy intervened.

"Does the back-up include Smithy's homemade bombs? If so, I'm in. What favour do you want?"

3

GRAND FUNK RAILROAD

WHILST I STARTED to plot, plan and lie, Jimmy acquired another music paper, *Sounds*. In it, we spotted two items of interest. First, the Isle of Wight festival had been cancelled due to the organisers having their license revoked because of the previous year's chaos. This was to have a major impact on our plans further down the line. Secondly, a free festival at Hyde Park was announced for early July. The headliners were a band nobody in the UK had heard of, Grand Funk Railroad. The music press hyped them up as America's answer to Led Zep. We decided to make this a dry run. It would be our first taste of live music and it was free!

To help consolidate my reluctant but necessary relationship with Ink Bat, we decided to invite him. We all chanced our arm and asked our parents for permission. Ink Bat's mum came around and spoke to mine about the logistics. Initially, my father squashed the idea but relented when he heard it was free and that half my class were going (misinformation).

Jimmy went on another shoplifting raid at the record shop, acquiring a Humble Pie album. They were the support band and we were excited by the noise they made. My brother had bigged up Steve Marriott for his work with the Small Faces, whilst Peter Frampton would find stardom a year or two later.

Around this time, there was a lot of friction at home between my brother and my father. I assumed it was because my brother had issues with his job in the menswear department of a big store up west. This was good timing though, as it took me off the old man's radar. I'd worshiped my father up to the age of around nine. He was my hero, the strongest man on the planet. But suddenly he changed. He was made redundant just after his mystery illness, soon after the rows with my mum started, along with the shouting/smacking of my brother and me. Yet I still respected him, possibly loved him, up until the Rattín incident during the '66 World Cup.

* * *

Smithy joined us for our first ever gig. He would have been up for Weeley but was going to be on holiday in Margate with his mad family. The weekend before the trip to Hyde Park, my brother surprisingly decided I needed some decent clobber and took me to Carnaby Street. Although we lived in the same house, we hardly engaged at all, mainly due to the age difference. Mark, like my father, had no interest in sport, but he seemed quite pleased that he'd had some influence on my musical taste. I knew nothing about fashion, still don't, but Mark was a clothes fanatic. He seemed to spend all his wages on dapper suits and flowery shirts. "You're not a bleeding queer," my dad remarked, more than once.

So, I met the boys at the station, regaled in a purple corduroy jacket, yellow Grandad vest and purple loon trousers. Jimmy had his Doc Martins on, as if we were off to football. Smithy was always wearing a heavy coat to conceal his weaponry, and Ink Bat looked like he was off to school.

The concert was a mesmerising experience. We'd been on crowded terraces, but nothing prepared us for being amongst over one hundred thousand people in a field. Heads Hands & Feet became the first band we ever saw live. Their guitarist was amazing, I later discovered his name was Albert Lee.

As Humble Pie took to the stage, we attempted to get right to the front. In the crush we lost Ink Bat and, although secretly pleased, I felt responsible for him and needed him onside as he was integral to the successful planning of the Weeley mission.

I weaved through the crowd but, as I was probably the smallest boy there, it was a futile effort. Meanwhile, Humble Pie had the crowd going wild. I couldn't see a thing, but I could certainly hear them. They finished with *Walk on Gilded Splinters*, I was enthralled as the crowd called for more, but there was a strict timescale and no encore. Twenty minutes later, Grand Funk took to the stage and within seconds the crowd was calling for Humble Pie back. They were truly shocking. Although that was my first gig, they remain the worst headliners I've ever seen.

I continued searching for Ink Bat, suddenly I heard a mini explosion near the stage. The crowd cheered as a plume of white smoke obscured the overhyped rubbish on stage. I was pretty certain who and what the source of the explosion was and made my way towards it. As the crowd dispersed, I saw Smithy and Jimmy standing in the vacated space, handkerchiefs tied around their faces. I congratulated Smithy on his good work, he smiled and produced a couple of 'bangers'.

"Get ready to leg it!" he cried, as he lit the fuses and threw them onto the stage.

There was pandemonium as the fireworks exploded beside the bass guitarist. Security men jumped into the baying mob. We legged it to Hyde Park Corner station, where we fled underground and headed home, minus Ink Bat.

Seems strange now, but back then open-air gigs finished before it got dark. Well, Hyde Park ones certainly did. Grand Funk Railroad fled without even doing an encore, it wasn't even 7pm yet. They were likely driven straight to Heathrow for the flight back to LA, never to return and disturb British eardrums again.

We'd told our parents we'd be home by eight-ish and we were. Well, I thought we all were but at nine o'clock the phone rang. My father was incandescent. "Who the hell would be phoning at this time of night?! Please tell me it is not one of Mark's stupid friends!" he bellowed up the stairs. "Mark! The bloody phone's ringing, it must be for you!"

My brother, when not out with his 'weird friends' (as my father called them) would spend all his time in his room. The friction between him and my father got worse every day. This secretly pleased me, it was a double whammy, not only was my brother no longer the golden boy but this would help divert my father's attention away from my devious plans.

Eventually, my mother reluctantly got up and answered the phone, whilst my father continued to curse the mystery caller. "Gone nine, Saturday night, bleeding idiot."

A minute later Mum came into the room and addressed me. "It's Mrs. James, Michael isn't home yet. She's very worried. Didn't he come home with you?"

It took a moment for me to compute who she was talking about. I always referred to mums as so and so's mum, not Mrs. James. Also, nobody had called Ink Bat by his real name for years. "Michael?" I repeated.

"Michael James. Didn't he come back with you and your friends Sid?"

I then mumbled that we'd lost him in the crowd, he'd kept wandering off and we'd spent the whole concert looking for him, which was half true…well one-tenth true.

My father put in his two pence, ranting on about friends always sticking together.

I wanted to explain that Ink Bat was not in any way a friend but that would have killed off any chance of my Weeley plot coming into fruition.

My mum was on the phone to Ink Bat's mum for a few more minutes. All we could hear was Mum answering, "Oh dear," repeatedly.

My father rolled his eyes. "Women," he muttered.

Eventually there was silence. Then my mum exclaiming, "Thank the lord for that!"

Mrs. James' idiot son was home.

I'd experienced my first gig. I wanted more, lots more.

4

THE MAGIC BUS

UNFORTUNATELY, FOR THE plan to work, I had to start taking scouts more seriously. First, I actually had to attend rather than play truant, and secondly, I had to show some enthusiasm, particularly when skipper Ron was about.

With seven weeks to go I wrote another list:

OPERATION BANK HOLIDAY

1) *Ask skipper Ron if Ink Bat and me can do camping badge*

2) *Tell mum and dad Ink Bat and me doing camping badge August bank holiday weekend*

3) *Jimmy to tell his mum he's allowed back in the Scouts*

4) Jimmy to tell his mum he's going to do camping badge with me

5) Sort money

6) Make list for trip i.e. Borrow Mark's rucksack, pick up tent from scouts etc.

It was a week before the long summer break, and I was counting the hours until the bell on Friday. Ink Bat got on the bus and sat next to me. *Why did my parents send me to the shithole two buses away where the only boy I knew was bloody Michael James?* One day he would tell me, and lots more besides, but for now, I was stuck with him on the Monday morning journey. I reminded him that I was going to tell my parents that I was going to do my camping badge with him and that if he wanted to continue to enjoy the privileges of being a member of the Third Tree Club, he'd better play along.

I couldn't tell my parents I was going with Jimmy for two reasons; they knew he'd been excluded and would be suspicious if I said he'd been reinstated, *and* my dad reckoned a pound note was stolen from his jacket pocket whilst Jimmy was round my house.

Ink Bat told me he was okay with his task and mentioned that Jimmy was taking the week off, but he didn't know why. I presumed it was pre-holiday truancy. One thing I quickly learned when I started secondary school is that boys and buses are a lethal combination.

I survived the Monday without a whack or detention. The teachers seemed as desperate as us for Friday to come, a glorious seven-week break lay ahead.

I was waiting for the second bus en-route home, Ink Bat was muttering on about me taking him to a gig again. Suddenly, Grant Bishop, aka Mad Bish, came towards us. He was two years older and a huge lump. "What time's the next bus, Levinson?" he growled.

I was taken aback as he'd never ever spoken to me before. It was probably not a good thing that I'd recently discovered insolence (as well as deceit). I told him to look at the timetable.

He looked at me as if I'd asked him the meaning of life, which in truth would be easier to work out than the bus timetable. Back then it was a secret mathematical code embedded in the concrete pillar behind glass. A few seconds later his big fat fist smashed into my right ear.

I saw stars and then heard nothing but ringing, which took a good minute to subside. I tried to keep my composure, without Jimmy about that was my only weapon against this bully. I badly wanted to touch my swelling lobe but pretended I wasn't bothered, which seemed to really irk him.

"Tomorrow, Levinson, I want exact information when I ask for it," he demanded.

I nodded without making eye contact. I made a tactical decision to sit downstairs, as at least eighty percent of incidents seemed to take place on the top deck. Ink Bat came and sat in front of me and spent the journey making sarcastic comments about my swollen ear. He had broken the golden rule of our club, 'All for one, one for all', but I remembered the list, so I let it go.

As I got off the bus, a feeling of utter dread consumed me. My father! He'd want to know who'd hit me and what I did to my attacker in return. I was, in truth, more fearful of my father than Mad Bish.

I sought sanctuary in my room until I reluctantly came down for dinner after my mum's third cry of, "Sid, your dinner's ready!"

I ate with my fork, my right elbow on the table and hand covering my ear. After a couple of moments my fears were realised.

"Eat properly boy, use your knife."

He noticed instantly as I obeyed his command.

"What the hell happened to your ear? Who hit you?"

"No one, Dad, I played rugby in games, I was in the scrum."

"Well don't forget what I told you boy, if someone hits you, you smash them in the nose."

'*Roll on Friday*', I thought and then made a few hints about doing the camping badge, which my father seemed to react to positively.

"I like that Michael, he's a sensible boy," my mother added, as I got points one and two out the way.

* * *

Tuesday dragged, it always did, but maths and double geography were out the way. I'd broken the back of the school week, everyone would be thinking about the break from now on.

I got to the second bus stop early so I could study the timetable carefully. Ink Bat emerged, he laughed as I ran my ruler over the confusing numbers.

"Better hurry up, here comes Mad Bish," he said.

"What time's the next bus, Levinson?" Mad Bish sniggered.

"Sixteen eighteen," I replied promptly.

"That's better Levinson, well done." He patted me on the back. I felt flushed with relief, but he then whispered in my ear, "You'd better be right Levinson or I'm going to punch you in your great big Jewish nose."

I waited and hoped, trying not to show any fear. At precisely 16:17 the bus came around the corner. It was the first time I'd considered that there may actually be a God. It came to within fifty feet of the bus stop when a refuse truck reversed out of a side road blocking the bus's way. It took a good two minutes for the bus to get to us.

At 16:19 sharp Mad Bish took the gaze away from his expensive watch and came for me. I held my hands up in front of my face in a defensive position as he tried to hit me. He turned to Ink Bat and growled, "Hold his arms or you're next."

My fellow member of the Third Tree Club dutifully grabbed my arms and I felt the massive fist smash into my nose.

Looking back, it was the second most painful experience a human can endure. I'll come to first later. The stinging sensation between the eyes is indescribable, it seemed to go on forever. Then there's the blood, which took an age to stop. I got on the bus holding a handkerchief to my nose and took a seat downstairs. Ink Bat followed my attacker upstairs as if he was his bestie.

I vowed revenge on both of them. Ink Bat would be sorted after I got back from the festival. The Mad Bish, well, I considered one of Smithy's bombs.

The stinging was replaced by a dull, continuous, bruising ache. I suddenly realised there was no God after all, I felt dread in the pit of my stomach. *My father.* Shit.

5

JIMMY'S GOOD EYE

(2013)

JIMMY'S TEXT MADE no sense whatsoever. It wasn't a case of predictive text gone wrong, it was simply an incoherent collection of letters. Still, it was good to have at least some form of contact from him, as he had slipped off the radar for months. I knew this meant he was in a bad place. I left a voicemail telling him I was here twenty-four seven if he needed me. What more could I do.

A couple of days later another indecipherable text arrived. There was at least a clue I could just about make out, *LEMO TRE ARMS* stood in the middle of random letters. We'd been to the Lemon Tree Arms three times, 1978 (the Yorkshire business), 1993 (discovering Molly) and 1997 (Heena finding herself). Three crisis meetings. Jimmy's crises, not mine. It couldn't be trivial if the Lemon Tree was involved, I wondered.

I discussed my concerns with Trudie, but she thought I should let him contact me when he was ready.

The call came unexpectedly a few days later, early on a Wednesday evening. The Lemon Tree wasn't mentioned, there was a more immediate problem.

"Sid, it's Jimmy," he said when I picked up the phone.

"You alright, mate?"

"I'm at a cash point, I can't get any money out!" Jimmy shouted.

"Where are you?"

"Kings Cross. I can't get any cash out, I'm stuck."

"Stuck?" I asked.

"I've got no money and only got a debit card with me."

"When d'you last use it?" I wasn't really computing what he was telling me. I assumed he'd either forgotten his PIN number or had insufficient funds.

"Yesterday."

His answer worried me. "Ok, Jimmy, go and wait in the Parcel Yard pub over by platform 9, just past the Harry Potter shop. I'm on my way."

I repeated the highlights of the conversation to Trudie as she drove me to the nearest tube station. Forty minutes later, I found Jimmy sitting on the steps leading up to the Parcel Yard. I went to the bar and got him a beer and sat him down at a discrete table.

He looked like shit. "I'm in trouble, Sid," he said, with tears in his eyes. He looked desperate and was physically shaking.

"Did you forget your PIN number, Jimmy?" I asked, naively hoping that was all it was.

"No, mate, I couldn't see the keypad."

"What do you mean, Jimmy?"

"I'm going blind Sid." He pointed to his good eye.

"Slow down, Jimmy, take a sip of lager, mate." I put a reassuring hand on his. "When did this start happening?"

"I'm not sure, but it's getting worse. I'm making mistakes at work, Heena wants me to move out."

"Heena wants you to leave?!" I was livid.

"She says I'm not the man she married."

"Thank fuck for that!" I exclaimed. "You were a liability back then, you're a much better man now."

"There's something wrong with my good eye, Sid, I know it. I've not told anyone, I'm going blind, mate, I'm getting crippling headaches."

"It's probably stress, Jimmy."

"No, mate, there's something wrong, I know it," he replied.

"Well in that case, you should see a doctor ASAP, get checked out. But I guarantee its stress related," I said, trying to reassure him. "In the meantime, here's some cash for you. I'll get you home, but you have to tell Heena and see the doctor tomorrow."

* * *

Heena is not my greatest fan, and vice versa, but Trudie was right as usual, I needed to speak to her about Jimmy's problem. I procrastinated for a couple of days, undecided whether to phone her or pop round. Both options worried me, but the problem was solved when out of the blue, she called me.

I was unsure of how much she knew of what Jimmy had told me, but I soon discovered it was everything. She explained how he'd been coming home from work and not bothering to change, he'd just sit and stare at the ceiling, not engaging at all. She mentioned that he wasn't bothering with personal hygiene, which shocked me. I'd never known a man who spent so much time in the shower. As usual with Heena, the conversation was about her, well, about how his behaviour impacted on her lifestyle. He does nothing in the house, he shows no interest in her at all, she was particularly disappointed that he didn't engage in any way with her latest work of art.

I asked her if she thought he might be depressed and, whilst she didn't rule out the possibility, she rambled on about how it was affecting her mental state. She did say that she wouldn't do anything rash until he'd been to the doctors.

"At the end of the day, Sid, I think he's just a cunt!" she offered in conclusion.

I tried to analyse the half hour conversation but had to bear in mind we had no time for each other. I'm certain she secretly hated the fact that I was always going to be a fly in the ointment in her effort to totally tame him, and she was the constant barrier between me and my best mate.

As usual, I found honesty difficult and skirted around the issue with both of them. I wanted to tell Jimmy that under no circumstances must he let her throw him out. But if he did leave, he'd end up the winner, he'd find himself a MILF (or GILF) who he'd go to gigs with, get pissed with, eat meat with, and have sex with! I, of course, said none of those things. I also didn't tell her *she* was the (selfish) cunt who'd driven him to the state he was clearly in. She was the one who went walk about in the early noughties to fucking find herself, which was definitely a contributing factor in Jimmy's mindset. She'd always been on my kill list, and maybe the time had come to act.

* * *

I was wrong with my diagnosis. I had convinced myself Jimmy's sight problems were a temporary blip and that a few drops of Optrex would sort out his good eye. As it turned out, Jimmy had a disease, which whilst it triggered his depression and anger, it wasn't the cause of it.

I had no contact from him for three weeks until he called me on Heena's phone. He told me the doctor had referred him to a specialist at Moorfields Eye Hospital and that he was going to have a brain scan and all manner of tests. He was scared and so was I. I offered whatever help was needed to Heena and waited for news.

A couple of months later I received a text, '*Sid I've got eye melanoma. Meet Lemon Tree Arms tomorrow night. 7ish*'.

Trudie was away for a couple of days with her sister, I sat in my chair and googled 'Eye Melanoma'. I was terrified, my mind went back forty-seven years to Jimmy's accident. Fuck. My best mate could be totally blind within weeks.

* * *

I recalled the three previous crisis meetings in the Lemon Tree. At the time, I didn't know what Jimmy was going to spring on me. This time I did but being prepared didn't help at all. I spent too much time researching the disease on the net. I wrote a list of questions, but selfishly only really concerned myself with one. Would Jimmy still be a best mate? Would he still be up for gigs and football and how long for?

I got there dead on time and brought myself a large scotch and lemonade. l looked for a quiet table, like most pubs it was now basically a restaurant, but I didn't think Jimmy was planning to eat. Point number six on my list of questions was 'alcohol'. I was halfway through my drink and there was still no sign of him. I tried ringing but, as usual, his phone went straight to voicemail. Had he decided it was too dark and difficult to come? Perhaps I should just call round and knock on his door, but that would mean possibly engaging with Heena.

It had been at least two years since I'd actually seen her in person and, bearing in mind she is one of only two women to make my kill list, it was best we had as little engagement as possible. Her description of my best mate, "I think he's just a cunt", hadn't done anything to help the animosity I harboured. I never considered her to be evil, just fucking annoying, which when all said and done is not really grounds for killing someone. The other woman to make the list, Erika, she was evil, a demon seed, she fully deserved to die.

"Hello, Sid."

I was shocked by the voice and the hand on my shoulder, disturbing my dark thoughts.

"Heena, hi, you okay? Where's Jimmy?" I stuttered, gesturing for the most annoying woman in the world to sit down. "What do you want to drink?" I asked, knowing the answer would be complicated.

"I know this is a bit strange, Sid, but do you think they have soya milk?"

"I can ask." I smiled through gritted teeth and unsurprisingly returned with a glass of semi skimmed and a glass of tap water. I then had to sit and listen to her go on for five minutes about her latest dietary fad.

"So, where and how is Jimmy?" I interrupted.

"Not great today, Sid. He showered and changed and was about to come down here when he started ranting about how the Lemon Tree wasn't the pub it was, how they expect you to eat now. He started swearing about it being dark so early since the clocks went back, so I calmed him down and told him I'll come and bring you up to speed. Probably best if you pop by one morning. He's good in the mornings."

I went through my list of questions, which Heena tried to answer, but I would discover all the answers in the next few months. I rephrased the last one, number twelve, '*Does Heena still want you to leave?*'. "How do you feel about the situation, Heena? I know you two have had your ups and downs, must be really tough on you," I asked diplomatically.

"Now I know Jimmy is ill, of course I will stick by him no matter what," she answered sincerely. She was off the kill list.

* * *

Two weeks later, I met Jimmy for breakfast in our usual cafe. He'd lost weight since I last saw him and looked pale. Nevertheless, I watched him devour a 'Mega breakfast'. I prompted him gently through some practicalities of his condition. He was relieved not to be able to work and drive, but I could tell he was terrified about the road ahead and was seriously depressed. Heena had reminded him that the consultant had told him he needs a routine and had given him a daily list of chores to carry out. Hoovering, ironing, general cleaning. "So, you're basically a sex slave, without the sex!" I tried at humour.

He didn't laugh, he looked confused.

"What can I do to help, Jimmy?" I asked.

He demolished the remains of his black pudding and smiled. "Music. The consultant asked when I'm most relaxed. I said listening to music."

He seemed far away. Just then his mobile rung, he looked at the screen, fiddled about. I realised he couldn't see the screen clear enough to answer. This was a complicated disease and Jimmy was a complicated person. We sat in silence for a few minutes with our thoughts, Jimmy seemed lost.

"Weeley. Jimmy, remember Weeley?!" I suddenly mentioned.

"Yep, I remember your fucking tent. If only I hadn't got involved with you know what." He had a tear in his eye, he struggled for a minute.

"Heena's going to look after you, mate," I said, placing my hand on his.

"I know, Sid."

"Let's do it again," I thought aloud.

"Do what, Sid?"

"A festival, let's do a festival next summer."

"I'll have to clear it with Heena."

He didn't seem too keen and appeared preoccupied. "What ever happened to that cunt James?" he said a bit too loudly.

"Who's James, Jimmy?"

"You know that cunt, Michael James."

"Ink Bat?!" I confirmed.

"Yeah, Ink Bat. Cunt," he growled.

"Who knows, guess he's upsetting someone somewhere Jimmy."

"Where'd you reckon he ran off to, Sid?"

"Who knows, Jimmy. Spain, Ireland, who cares."

"If I ever run into the cunt, I would fucking kill him, I'd fucking kill him."

I had to quiet him down as other diners turned their heads. I looked at my mate and thought to myself, '*Don't worry, Jimmy, he's already on my list. I've got it covered*'.

6

THREE STRIKES AND YOU'RE OUT

(2013)

I GAVE UP trying to communicate with Jimmy by phone, as all my calls went straight to voicemail. Two weeks went by and I was in a dilemma about what to do. I didn't want to patronise him but at the same time I wanted him to know I was there for him. I reluctantly called Heena a couple of times but got her answerphone too.

In the end, I decided to take Trudie's advice and call round his house. She also suggested I pop in and see my father as it was on the way. I made a bit of a drama out of it but Trudie rightfully reminded me, "He *is* your father, Sid."

My father had lived in a small two bedroom flat in a warden-controlled block for the last four years. My mum passed a couple of years ago, a week before her eighty-sixth birthday. It was a blessing to be honest, she'd been ill for years but was hanging on to keep an eye on my father. God knows why, the cantankerous old git. They'd been married sixty-nine years and were completely co-dependent. Two stubborn East Enders, though my mum's clothes were strictly West End. She was an elegant lady to her last breath, whilst my father lived permanently in his string vest. I never ever heard her swear, whereas my father struggled to complete a sentence without an expletive.

We assumed he'd have to go into a nursing home after Mum died but decided that we'd try and keep him where he was happy, with the help of twenty-four-hour carers. To be honest, although Trudie, Mark and I wouldn't admit it, this option was the better of two financial evils. A nursing home would mean selling the flat and watching our future inheritance disappear. If my father had gone first, I'd have not considered the money aspect and would have done whatever was best for Mum.

My first mission on entering the main entrance was to avoid the warden Ms. O'Hara who ran a very tight ship and I knew my father was not exactly her favourite. I skipped past her office and started to open the door that led to the stairs. "Excuse me, Mr. Levinson, can I have a word please?" Fuhrer O'Hara's strong Northern Irish accent stopped me in my tracks and I reluctantly retreated to her office.

She pointed to the chair opposite her desk and glared at me. "You will recall the 'Three strikes and you're out' rule, Mr. Levinson. Well, unfortunately, your father has far exceeded the rule. Since his second warning, I've turned a blind eye to several misdemeanours but I'm afraid his latest shenanigans gives me no choice but to report him to the management team," she said.

"And what will they do?" I queried.

"They will give you three months to sell up and find your father alternative accommodation. Don't you want to know what he's done?" she asked.

* * *

My mind drifted back to his two previous warnings, both before my mum passed. The first was only a couple of weeks after they moved in. The actual move had been a nightmare for Trudie and I. Mark, as usual, had escaped the stressful practicalities of sorting our parents. They'd been in the same house for forty years and had accumulated forty years of absolute shite. They needed to get rid of the lot and I told them to put yellow post-it notes on anything they absolutely had to keep. I knew there was going to be trouble when my mum phoned me and told me they'd run out of post-it notes. Rows ensued as I tried to get them to see sense. Mark called me from the safety of his Los Angeles home, chastising me as Mum had called him and said I was being cruel. I told him he should come over and see for himself. He sent me a curt email giving me a precise list of the shite he wanted to keep. "You will have to get it shipped over to your place then!" I demanded. The conversation deteriorated, and I didn't speak to him again until Mum fell ill.

The move nearly killed them, and I was driven to drink. I decorated their new home, personally arranged the removal from their house, but my father wouldn't stop moaning and driving my mum to tears.

There was entertainment in the communal lounge every Wednesday afternoon. Two weeks after the move, my mum phoned me and told me my father had been involved in an incident during the entertainment. Mum explained that he'd spent the two previous days sulking and had hardly uttered a word. That evening there was a magician performing to a large crowd of residents. Halfway through the act, my father stood up and shouted, "You're no fucking Tommy Cooper are you!"

The magician laughed him off and replied, "I'd say I was more Paul Daniels to be honest."

"More like a big cunt!" my father bellowed, and stormed back to his room, leaving my mum in tears and the fellow residents in shock. The first warning was swiftly administered.

Looking back this was quite an amusing story but sadly his second official warning was anything but funny. It was almost exactly two years since the first incident. Things were beginning to fall apart physically and mentally for my parents, particularly my mum. Her health issues, along with coping with my father's increasingly irrational behaviour, sent her into a spiral of depression. She told me she was only hanging on because she couldn't trust my father to look after himself. After a lifetime of putting up with his boorish behaviour she started to belittle him, often humiliating him. I should have seen the explosive situation coming, but I had my own problems.

I was at a meeting with an insolvency lawyer trying to salvage what I could from my dying business. My phone buzzed, I shouldn't have looked but I saw a missed call from my mum. I saw she'd left a voice message. I guessed she was phoning to say the 'meals on wheels' man was late again. If he was a minute late with lunch, she'd phone me in a state asking me to find out where it was. "Excuse me, message from my elderly mother," I said gesturing to my phone, "I'd better check her lunch has arrived."

I played the message. "Sid, Sid help me! You've got to help me, it's your father! He's attacked me! I'm bleeding, help me."

I stood up in shock and panic. "Sorry fellas, I've got to go. My mum's been taken ill," I sort of lied. I tried to contact Trudie but only got her voicemail, I remembered she was having a pub lunch with a couple of friends.

Forty minutes later I rushed into their flat. I could immediately hear sobbing coming from the lounge. My mum was on the sofa curled up in the foetal position. "Sid!" She wailed, and then started to rant incoherently.

I went to the kitchen, fetched a glass of water and tried to calm her down. I could see her ripped paper-thin flesh hanging off both her upper arms where my father had grabbed her. Between sobs she explained she'd sent him out to get the paper, he'd bought *The Times* instead of the *Mail*. She'd obviously chastised him, and he'd flipped.

"Where's Dad now?" I asked. I only ever called him Dad when I was with Mum.

"He swore at me and stormed off, slamming the door behind him. But that was ages ago. I hope he's dead!" she wailed.

Trudie arrived, having got my SOS, but unfortunately bad news travels fast and Ms O'Hara also gate-crashed the party. There was a conference as to whether to call the doctor, but we decided Mum would only get more stressed. So, Trudie and the warden patched her up, whilst I went looking for my father.

I found him sitting on a bench between home and the corner shop. He'd obviously gone back to swap the newspaper. "What the fuck you been up to?" I snapped at him.

He looked up casually. "Hello son, just gone to get your mum's paper."

"So I heard, what the fuck did you do, Dad?"

"Pardon?" He offered his ninety-year-old ear.

"You attacked Mum!" I shouted.

"Don't be ridiculous, I would never harm your mother, she fell over."

His lying reminded me of myself when I was fourteen. I sat down next to him and grabbed him by his jacket lapels, my face in his. "Now listen carefully, Dad. I could call the police. If this ever happens again, I'm going to do one of two things. Either put you in a home or fucking kill you."

He never touched her again in the last two years of her life. The warden gave him his second warning.

* * *

"Don't you want to know what your father did, Mr. Levinson?" The warden asked, bringing me back to the present.

"The radio," I offered.

"Exactly, you know about the radio then, Mr. Levinson?"

"The lady above is completely deaf and had her radio on top volume at four in the morning, it was driving my dad mad. I told you about this, Ms. O'Hara," I replied.

"Yes, you did, Mr. Levinson, but that doesn't give your father the right to enter her room whilst she was napping and throw the radio out of the window. She reported it stolen, caused a right ruckus, and then the gardeners found it in bits behind a rose bush. I'll have to report him I'm afraid, Mr. Levinson, and sadly there will be consequences."

I glared at the Fuhrer for a second and then replied, "No, you won't report it, Ms. O'Hara, because he didn't do it," I confirmed.

She looked confused. "Mr. Levinson, it's obvious he did it. He told me the day before '*if*', and I quote, '*the old bat keeps me awake again with her fucking wireless I'm going to throw it out the fucking window*'. They were his exact words, Mr. Levinson."

"I don't doubt it, Ms. O'Hara, he said the same to me, but he didn't throw the deaf old bat's radio out of the window," I corrected her.

"Then who the hell did?" she protested.

"I did," I confirmed.

"You did, Mr. Levinson?" She was taken aback.

"My father phoned me at five in the morning, three days in a row, out of his mind. Ranting about the radio keeping him awake. I'd had enough of him waking us up, I've got my own problems, Ms. O'Hara, I'm in the middle of going bankrupt, sleep is hard enough already. I came around and stood by my dad's bed, I couldn't believe how loud the bloody thing was. I went upstairs and knocked gently, the door was unlocked, she was in bed snoring. The radio was so loud I couldn't hear myself think, the window was open and..."

* * *

My father's carer was watching Jeremy Kyle with her feet
up. "Where's my father?" I said, startling her.
"Sorry, Sid, he's napping." Suzi sprang up trying to
make herself busy.
My father had almost regressed to being a baby again.
Sleeping, eating, shitting. That was his routine. I related the
radio story to Suzi, who found it very amusing. I then went
into the bedroom, the old man was snoring so loud it
sounded like an early Metallica song. *'Why can't the sad old
fucker just die in his sleep,'* I pondered darkly.

* * *

Heena opened the door, she looked harassed. I soon
discovered why. The house was bedlam, screaming children
and a general state of chaos.
"Everything okay, Heena? I've been trying to contact
Jimmy for weeks."
"Sorry, Sid, been a bit of a difficult time. Come into the
lounge, Jimmy's feeding Max."
"Max?" I queried.
"Jimmy's latest grandchild." Heena rolled her eyes.
We entered the lounge, normally a calm sanctuary of
peace and tranquility, festooned with Heena's spiritual
paraphernalia. Today it was full of kids' toys, bags of
nappies and was a complete mess.
"Sid!" Jimmy bellowed in a friendly greeting. He was
sitting in his usual chair with a tiny baby on his lap guzzling
a bottle of milk. "Say hello to Max, grandchild number
four!" The baby screamed in fright as Jimmy shouted.
Heena came and took him off Jimmy's knee, she was
already attending to a toddler.
"That's Nessa," Jimmy nodded, expecting me to
remember her.
"The last time I saw her, she was Max's age," I
confirmed.
Jimmy led me to the box room, which now seemed to
be his world. There was a single bed, a small chest of

drawers with a tiny record player on it, the most basic I've ever seen. "I've been relegated to this bedroom since the invasion force arrived."

I'd studied hours of info on Jimmy's condition on the net. I'd been expecting a lot worse than the slightly thinner version of Jimmy that stood against the wardrobe, whilst I sat on the bed. He removed his sunglasses, I noticed his eye looked a little glazed and lacking its usual mischievous sparkle. He explained that his daughter Molly had struggled since the new arrival, which had been a complete surprise to Jimmy, and she'd ended back in rehab. The older two kids were in Coventry with her half-sister and the younger two were dumped with Heena. To my surprise she'd not only committed herself to looking after Jimmy, but Molly's latest 'mistakes' as well.

I wanted to know how Jimmy was feeling but thought it best to keep the conversation light whilst he was in a good place. "Nice record player," I nodded towards it, "you need to get some of your vinyl down from the loft."

Jimmy opened the top drawer of the white melamine chest and pulled out a single album.

"King Crimson," I confirmed, despite their being no info on the cover.

"You're correct, Sid, *In the Wake of Poseidon*, great cover, shit music." He laughed and for a moment seemed just like my old mate.

"Well, put it on, mate," I suggested.

He suddenly looked agitated. "Fucking record player's shit, it won't work. Not surprising seeing as it was a so-called present from that fucker Beck."

"Beck?" I interrupted, noticing he had instantly become very agitated.

"Yeah, that cunt Beck, he knew it was fucked."

"Do you mean Tony Beck?"

"Yeah, the fucking arsehole," he confirmed.

"When did you see him? I haven't seen him since we were at school. Why would he give you a duff record player?"

"His missus is a friend of Heena's, they came 'round for dinner. I don't know why he gave me this heap of shit, fucking cunt." Jimmy was now shouting and his eyes were wild.

"Fancy going to Chelsea next week?" I quickly changed the subject. It had the desired effect.

"Love to, Sid, who they playing?"

"Bournemouth, got a couple of tickets off Fester."

"Nice one, how is the mad fucker?"

"Still mad, Jimmy. I'll call round one-ish Saturday week."

"I'll look forward to it, Sid. I'm really looking forward to Glastonbury as well."

"Glastonbury?" I was thrown by this.

"Yeah Glastonbury, you said we were going to Glastonbury, Sid, remember?"

"No, Jimmy, I mentioned us doing a festival next summer, I didn't specify which one. It's nigh on impossible to get to Glastonbury…but I can try."

"You definitely told me we were going to Glastonbury, Sid, I've told everyone I'm going. I've got to go, mate. I told that cunt Beck, don't let me down."

7

ANTONIO UBALDO RATTÍN

(1966)

IT WAS AROUND 3.35pm on the afternoon of the 22nd of July that I realised I no longer loved, respected, or even liked my father. He'd been my hero, but the illness and the redundancy had made him a bitter, angry man. There were other issues which I'd later discover, but all that mattered as a nine-year-old boy was I loved sport and he had no interest at all. I watched with envy as many of my friends told of their Saturday afternoons spent on the terraces with their fathers and sometimes brothers. Mark, like my father, had no interest in anything sporty. He was obsessed with the Beatles. At this stage, I was still stuck on Gene Pitney.

By the time June arrived I was busy collecting World Cup coins and studying a wall chart Uncle Fred had given me. On the morning of the opening game, my class was bursting with anticipation. Our teacher Mr. Redmond, a fearsome dour Yorkshireman, tried to keep us focused. Someone shouted out, "Will England win tonight, Sir?"

Redmond walked to the blackboard and wrote URAGUAY in capital letters. "Does anyone know where Uruguay is?" he growled.

As far as we were concerned it could have been a planet in a faraway galaxy.

He drew a crude map of America and stuck what looked like a pear on the bottom. He put a spot where we assumed this mysterious country to be.

"Are they any good at football, sir?" Melanie 'Flea Pit' Andrews enquired.

"Can we win the World Cup, sir?" someone shouted.

Mr. Redmond put the chalk down. "I'm sorry to dampen your enthusiasm but I can confirm that even though Uruguay has a population smaller than Scotland, they have won the World Cup twice. Are they good at football? No, but what they are good at is winning! Winning by any means possible. Fouling, spitting, diving, any form of cheating, that's what the continentals do. We have no chance tonight and absolutely no chance of winning the World Cup."

We were crushed. I sat in front of the TV that night and watched England struggle to a 0-0 draw.

* * *

Two weeks later Mr. Redmond's predictions had been proved wrong. On a hot afternoon England faced Argentina in the quarter final. The whole country was gathered in front of TVs and radios, except for my father of course. He was preparing his car for the annual family trip to Devon the next morning. Mum was busy ironing, Mark had been in his room for days after yet another blazing row with the old man.

In those pre-PC days, the commentator basically described the Argies in the same tones as my teacher. The first thirty minutes were a litany of fouls and badgering the referee. The main protagonist was the colossus that was the Argentinian captain, Antonio Ubaldo Rattín, who in the 31st minute became the first player ever to be sent off at Wembley Stadium. I sat transfixed in disbelief as he refused to leave the field, then, when he did, the rest of his teammates followed him off. Kenneth Wolstenholme, the commentator, was apoplectic as the pandemonium unfolded. I ran out the living room, through the hallway and out the front door, shouting at my father who was washing the bonnet of his Maxi 7.

"Dad, Dad!" I screamed. "You've got to come and see this. Rattín, the Argentinian captain, has been sent off! They've all walked off!" I was so excited, I was struggling to get the words out.

"Son, this car won't wash itself," he muttered, without even looking up.

Argentina had lost their captain and ultimately the match. I'd lost my father.

* * *

Holidays are supposed to be enjoyed, but a seven-hour drive with my father at the wheel meant our family holidays were to be endured rather than enjoyed. We stayed at a relative's holiday flat. This particular vacation would be memorable for two reasons: a Russian linesman and because it was to be my brother's last trip with us.

Mark told my parents he was going for a walk to the pier after tea. He didn't return until the small hours. I was woken by my father hooting and hollering, then my mother sobbing. A couple of days later, it was my turn to cry when on the Sunday morning my father announced we were having a day out. I immediately burst into tears.

"What's up with you?" he snapped.

"It's the World Cup final at three o'clock," I pleaded.

"We'll be back well before then," he claimed.

I spent the day frantically clock watching and when we got back at five-past-three I was convinced my father's car was the only one driving in the entire world! As I switched on the tiny black and white TV, the Germans opened the scoring. I was distraught and was shocked to see my father celebrating, as he assumed England were playing in white.

I felt better as England went 2-1 ahead and enjoyed the only time I would watch the game I loved with my family. I felt sick when the Germans equalised with the last kick of the game.

"Not a bloody replay," huffed my brother.

I explained the concept of extra time.

"Half an hour, bloody hell, how tedious," he whined.

Geoff Hurst shot against the underside of the bar. *Was the ball over the line?* Time stood still as the Russian referee and linesman conferred.

"Goal!" the family shouted in unison, for the first and last time.

After the lap of honour, we rushed down to the seafront where I marvelled at adults joining arms, having a knees-up and random strangers in cars hooting. My father bought four Union Jack flags from an opportunist salesman on the pier. I held his hand waving our flags. I briefly revelled in the belief that my father would love football after all, and that England would be world champions for decades to come.

8

MEMBER OF THE TRIBE

(1971)

I survived the last three days of term without running into
the Bish again. My nose was sore but there was no
permanent damage. I reflected on the incidents, particularly
wondering, *why me?* Why not Ink Bat or any of the other
oiks? I reflected on his comment that he was going to punch
me in my 'great big Jewish nose'. My nose didn't seem so
big, I'd never been teased about it before. Did he pick on me
because of my religion? Was this an anti-Semitic attack? If it
was, I felt sickened. A punch on the nose for a teenager in
1970's England was not uncommon, you took it on the chin
(or nose) and moved on. I couldn't. The pain of the punch
was excruciating and lasted for hours but the pain of being
racially abused lasts a lifetime.

I considered revenge, maybe Smithy could blow him up
or something. I hadn't told Jimmy about Ink Bat's betrayal
because I didn't want anything to disrupt my Weeley plans.
Ink Bat could be dealt with in good time, certainly
excommunication from the Third Tree Club at the very least.

The bully Bishop? Strangely enough this was his last act of violence at my school because he never returned after the summer break. His wealthy parents moved him to a private school. Maybe there was a God after all. I wouldn't see him again for four years, by which time I'd developed the concept of revenge and murder.

* * *

My father was a complicated, angry man, probably with good reason. He was born into a poor East End Jewish family. His parents, who both died when he was in his teens, were Russian immigrants with poor English skills and limited job opportunities. They were hungry poor. They relied on handouts from my father's uncle, Mory (Morris), who was the patriarch of the family. Legend has it, he was the nearest the East End came to a Jewish mafia don. Religion didn't play a great part in his house. Survival got in the way of the paraphernalia of religious practices. Him and his three brothers were invited to Uncle Mory's for Passover but that was about it. They were all bar mitzvahed, but my father refused to talk about it. Uncle Mory got my father who had had very little education an apprenticeship in a steelworks. He was there until he volunteered for the Navy on his eighteenth birthday in 1941. He returned to the factory after the Second World War, whilst there he met my mum, who worked in the canteen. And that's where his problems with his religion started.

Mum was from an Irish catholic family, which was of no consequence until they got engaged and approached Uncle Mory, who offered to pay for the wedding if my mum converted. He also offered them a rent free flat for a year. Normally, conversion would be a long painful (particularly for a male) affair, but Uncle Mory obviously had a Rabbi on his payroll and the paperwork was sorted in a matter of days.

Towards the end of the rent-free year Mum fell pregnant with Mark and Uncle Mory made my father an offer he couldn't refuse. He'd help my father purchase a small maisonette on the understanding Mark, and any future sons, were circumcised and bar mitzvahed! The first stipulation, although I'm sure was very painful, I knew nothing about. The second was a crushing humiliation for me.

My father's two remaining brothers (Uncle Joe died in the war) both married into the faith and my three male cousins all had big sparkling affairs and all read long passages in Hebrew. Mine was an embarrassment. I read a few lines phonetically and, even then, messed up. I'd had no upbringing in the religion and suddenly I was in a synagogue, surrounded by relatives and disappointed parents. It was a day of utter humiliation which scars me to this day. But my father had honoured his promise to Uncle Mory, it was the last time he would set foot in a synagogue. Whilst he spent the rest of his life avoiding his religion, every now and again I would be reminded of my roots, and not in a good way.

9

THE ROAD TO WONDERLAND

THE SUMMER HOLIDAYS did not start well for the Third
Tree Club. On the first day of seven long weeks of freedom,
we received a visit from Micky O'Neill. Micky was the
youngest of eleven siblings, all were to be avoided, even the
four sisters were hard as nails. Micky and his three closest
brothers hung out by the football changing rooms on the
other side of the park, but he decided to come and flex his
family muscle in our little patch.

Just as we'd sorted the three aside teams, he came up
and grabbed Perry in a headlock. "I want sixpence from each
of you in rent or else," he ordered as he tightened his grip.

Smithy tried to negotiate, but we were about to learn
about protection rackets. I was surprised when Jimmy was
first to cough up, but we later discovered that he was
keeping a low profile since he gave Micky O'Neill's sister a
love bite. We were told there would be a weekly rent due
and if we didn't comply he'd bring his brothers, we were
snookered.

We held a crisis meeting. I made a list of options, we decided to ignore them all and just pay up, hoping he might forget us. Smithy liked option three, but eventually decided blowing Micky up would be counterproductive. He'd have to blow up the entire family, which wasn't even on my list.

Jimmy then got spotted at the cinema snogging Julie O'Neill, Micky's younger sister. This wasn't going to help the situation. He was to spend most of the summer trying to avoid her brothers.

I thought it best to throw myself into the plotting and planning required to achieve our goal of attending the Weeley festival. I reminded our scout leader, Skipper Ron, about doing my camping badge on the August bank holiday weekend. My biggest challenge was keeping Ink Bat on side. His membership to the Third Tree Club was contingent on him lying to Skipper Ron that he was doing the camping badge with me, and then to make sure the secret was kept in house.

"What happens if your mum or dad calls my parents?" he asked.

"Why would they?" I mused.

"They might want to know if my parents had heard anything."

It was a fair point and I set about composing a list of possible scenarios. My ace card was my number one. I'd tell my parents that Ink Bat's mum and dad were going away for the weekend and would drop us off on the way and pick us up on Monday morning on their way back. This, of course, covered for the extra night, as the badge only demanded two nights. I spent a lot of time going through my plans with Jimmy, but he was preoccupied with trying to continue his dishonourable intentions with Julie O'Neill, whilst avoiding her brood of psychopathic brothers.

* * *

All my efforts had to be put on the back burner for two weeks as I joined my parents on our first holiday abroad.

Majorca in mid-August was near a hundred degrees, which did nothing for my father's mood. Apart from being our first foreign excursion it was our first holiday without Mark. I wasn't sure if this was down to recent friction or just that when you reach your twenties you do your own thing. Anyway, the entire holiday was spent seeking shade. There was a terrible friction between my parents. We went to a bull fight, my mum wanted to leave early, she was disgusted. My father stubbornly insisted we stay to the bloody end, but this was just a side show. I didn't understand then, but it was my brother who was the source of their endless rows.

We returned a week before D-day. I revised my lists and went into logistics overdrive. Jimmy seemed very relaxed about the whole thing, leaving everything to me. "I'll be at the station midday, don't worry about it," he confirmed.

My parents seemed completely side-tracked by their continuing angst with Mark, which made my life easier.

I collected the tent and associated paraphernalia from Skipper Ron. He asked me to remind him when we were going and who was taking us. I gave him the story about Ink Bat's parents and to my relief he said he was also away for the weekend, otherwise he would have paid us a visit. He asked if I had a camera to take some photos to confirm we had pitched the tent correctly and that was it, I left the HQ. I didn't realise it would be for the last time.

* * *

It was typical of my father that after showing no interest at all he decided to give me the third degree just before I was about to leave. He saw the tent and rucksack in the hallway. "Are your mate's parents picking you up from here?" he asked.

"No, Dad, I'm going to walk to his house."

"Do you want a lift, son?"

"No thanks, I'm a bit early," I replied.

"When you back?"

"Monday, Dad."

"That's a bloody long time in a tent. Where is it you're camping?" he asked.

"Mum's got all the details."

"Well, behave yourself." That was it, he turned and left for work.

I was free!

* * *

The half mile walk to the station seemed to take an age due to the weight of the tent, equipment and my personal stuff. There was no sign of Jimmy, even though I was a few minutes late. I sat on a bench hoping there were no last-minute issues with his mum. I stared at the red telephone box in the corner of the station and wondered if I should phone him. I looked at my watch and decided to wait ten minutes.

Twelve minutes later, just after I'd lugged the gear to the telephone box, Jimmy came into view carrying a small hold-all and blowing into his asthma puffer. There'd been a last-minute crisis, his mum said she wanted to speak to my parents to confirm all was kosher. Fortunately, there was no answer and she shrugged and told him to behave himself.

Jimmy was disappointed that we had to pay our tube fare as there was a ticket man at the entrance. He was determined we'd not have a repeat performance at Liverpool Street, so we slipped past the authorities and snuck onto the train. It was packed with rucksack-carrying fellow festival goers. The difference was, most of them were in their late teens and, I assume, hadn't had to lie to their parents.

We sat at a table opposite a couple of lads who were knocking back bottles of Newcastle brown ale.

"How old are you two?" one asked.

"Sixteen," Jimmy lied.

"Twelve, more like," the hairy inquisitor laughed. "You won't get into the arena kiddies, you've got to be eighteen!"

I looked at Jimmy, he didn't seem bothered. "Really?" I replied concerned.

"That's bollocks!" Jimmy exclaimed.

"You obviously haven't read the small print kiddies."

With that Jimmy elbowed me and nodded up the carriage where the ticket inspector had entered. We grabbed our gear and headed up the train as far as we could, finally seeking sanctuary in a compartment where four older hippy girls were tucking into sandwiches. They found our presence and age very amusing. We told them our story, which impressed them, particularly that we'd bunked onto the train. They told us we could hide under their gear if and when the ticket man got this far.

I dug out the original advert to see if there was anything about age restrictions, whilst Jimmy kept a look out for the 'Gestapo'. After a few minutes he shouted, "Quick, he's coming! Hide!"

The girls smothered us with an assortment of rucksacks and tents and tried to look as nonchalant as possible as the inspector entered the compartment.

When he'd gone, we were uncovered and profusely thanked them.

"You can put our tents up for us as a thank you," one of them suggested, but I wasn't sure how to put our own tent up and I knew Jimmy was totally useless on practical matters. I spent the rest of the journey worrying about erecting tents and getting into the arena.

* * *

We followed the crowd that streamed out the tiny station towards an open field full of tents. There were no stewards, absolutely no organisation at all, and people just plotted up wherever they could find a space. We found a space big enough for ours and the girls' tents and spent a good two hours struggling to put them up. Just as we finished, a posse of Hells Angels parked their bikes near us and started approaching the new arrivals. "It's a pound each boys," a hairy leather-clad monster of a man said as he put his head into our tent.

"What for?" Jimmy asked.

"Rent," the monster snapped.

"What rent?" I enquired politely.

"To use the campsite boys, should be two quid each but you can have half price given your age."

"It says on the advert, camping is free," Jimmy protested.

"It's free if you camp miles away, but this field will be a pound each. If you don't like it, pack up and fuck off," the monster growled.

We'd saved a pound each on the train, so it wasn't the end of the world, we reluctantly parted with the cash.

"If you want full insurance cover for the duration of the festival it will only cost you fifty pence," the monster added.

"What?" we replied in unison.

"For fifty pence each, I can guarantee your tent and contents will be completely protected for the entire festival. There's a lot of wronguns about."

"No thanks, mate, we'll be fine," Jimmy replied confidently.

We sat outside the tent eating cheese and cress sandwiches our mums had made us. The girls from the train offered us our first ever taste of wine. Within a few minutes the world looked a bit blurry. It was still three hours before the arena was to open. I thought about the age business, I hoped this wouldn't be a wasted journey.

The monster returned from collecting his rent. We were sitting on a ground sheet finishing our picnic with the girls a few feet from our tent. He stopped and glared at us and then started loosening the guy ropes on our tent and kicking out the pegs. We yelled our protests, I felt giddy from the mixture of alcohol and the heat.

"You should have paid the insurance," he growled, as our tent started to collapse.

Jimmy stood up and started to run towards the Hells Angel, which I thought was a seriously bad move. Jimmy laid into the monster who stood there laughing, he picked my mate up and threw him to the ground. I think this was the first time I'd actually thought I'd like to kill someone, though that might have been my bus stop attacker from a few weeks earlier. I was about to go to his aid when there was a commotion in the near distance.

The rest of the Angels were gathered around their bikes. Suddenly World War Three erupted as a group of skinheads attacked the Angels with baseball bats, knives and axes. We stood frozen to the spot as the protagonists tried to kill each other.

We scattered, as the Angels that were able to, made their getaway on their bikes. I was rapidly sobering up as I saw the monster coming towards us trying to keep control of his bike. He was being chased by at least four attackers. Just as he was adjacent to us, his bike stalled, and he came flying over the top. Our group ran to a cluster of trees, as he was overwhelmed by his pursuers. I can still recall the screams as he was beaten senseless. I saw one of attackers hack at his head with a machete! A siren could be heard in the distance as the protagonists scarpered.

A few people went to the monster's aid, as he lay lifeless in a pool of blood. *'I hope the fucker's dead,'* I thought.

Eventually, the police and an ambulance arrived. Rumour had it a turf war had broken out all over the area between the Hells Angels and the caterers, The Pie Men, as they were nicknamed, over who was in charge of security.

When the fracas had come to an abrupt halt, I went to look for Jimmy, who I'd lost sight of after his mad assault on the monster. I spent half an hour looking around but with no success, so I decided to make my way to the arena entrance, so we could get down the front when it opened. I thought I'd probably find Jimmy there, but there was still no sign of him. The entrance was staffed by a few old boys from the local round table who were completely overwhelmed by the size of the crowd and the violent chaos that was all around them. They had planned for around five thousand people to attend but there were now rumours that over one-hundred thousand were on their way!

The crowd was now a baying mob, we found a man in a yellow, fluorescent jacket with '*Weeley Roundtable*' written on the back with a felt tip pen. "When are you going to open the gates, mate?" I yelled.

"In half an hour. How old are you?" he replied.

My heart sank. "Sixteen," I lied.

"You've got to be eighteen," the jobsworth confirmed.

"There's nothing on the advert that says that, mate!" I argued.

"I think you'll find there is, show me the advert and if I'm wrong, I'll let you in."

"It's in my rucksack back at the tent, there's a riot going on, please let me in," I pleaded.

"You'd better go and get it and proof of your age."

I slinked back up the hill to the camping field. Suddenly, thousands of campers were running towards me and then a terrible acrid smell filled the air, followed by flames. I ran towards where we had pitched our tent, the whole area was a smouldering furnace. I saw the girls in tears, trying to salvage what possessions they could. I stood looking at where the scout tent had previously stood.

I asked the girls if they'd seen Jimmy. One of them said he'd been led away by a St. John Ambulance man, covered in blood after the Hells Angel had thrown him to the ground.

As I made my way to the first aid tent where I hoped I'd find my mate, I thought about the hairy monster and his insurance policy. I relived the machete lodging in his skull and wondered whether he was actually dead. I then realised I'd need to explain to Skipper Ron what had happened to his tent. He would no doubt involve my father. *Oh shit.*

10

TONY BECK

(1968-1970)

THERE WAS SOMETHING mysterious about Tony Beck.
He wasn't one of the lads (I wasn't either), but he wasn't one
of the nerds (I don't think I was). He was cool alright (I
wasn't). A clever sod who didn't make any enemies, kept
himself to himself, aloof certainly. In the two years he was
in my form he hardly ever engaged with me. He captained
both our football and cricket team, he was a superb
sportsman. He was never a bully and was never bullied.
Even the class psycho, Evans, kept his distance from him. I
never saw him out of school, but I walked past his spooky
old house on Basset Street virtually every day. A house that a
few years later would become infamous.

Tony Beck, top scholar, sportsman, a cool kid with a
one hundred-percent attendance record was absent the
Monday after October half term. At first, we presumed it
must be a severe bout of flu. However, by Thursday,
rumours ranged from chicken pox to him being killed in a
car crash. On Friday, one of the class nerds who lived near

him confirmed that his mother had seen a giant removal van outside Beck's spooky house during half term. The driver had said the family were moving to somewhere in Scotland. I recalled Beck once telling someone he was a Celtic supporter because his dad was Scottish, so I presumed there was some kind of family reason for the hasty move.

The next Monday, Evans came up with one of his crazy ideas. When the teacher calls the register, we were to take it in turns to shout "Here, sir!" when Beck's name was read out. By the Thursday it was my turn. "Beck!" Wilson, my form teacher, bellowed.

I hesitated.

"Beck!" he repeated.

I saw Evans glaring at me. "Here," I grunted.

"Here what?" Wilson shouted, without looking up from the register.

"Here, sir," I confirmed.

Beck was still a pupil and he became a legend when on Friday morning his name was on the year nine school football team sheet that was pinned to the sports notice board. On the Saturday morning we told the PE teacher Beck had twisted his ankle, and Gilly the sub was duly drafted into the team. In the following weeks, we conspired to get Beck into the chess team, the boxing team and even class prefect.

Eventually we were rumbled, but his name became part of the school vocabulary. 'Telling a Beck' meant you were fibbing.

A few years later, their spooky old house in Basset Street turned up on the news, when the current occupiers fled, claiming the house was haunted. It may well have been the reason the Becks left without notifying the school.

Anyway, I personally, and no one I knew, ever saw or heard from Tony Beck again, until Jimmy ranted about the record player. I told Trudie the story and, like me, she reckoned Jimmy's story was a symptom of his health worries. She suggested I ask Heena if he really was in touch with Tony Beck, but I didn't really want to know the truth. I never mentioned it until Jimmy brought him up on the way to football.

* * *

Fester wasn't a close friend, he was a casual acquaintance. Our only connection was that we supported the same football team. I'd seen him at the gym, he had a reputation, which his large shaven head gave extra credence too.

One evening in the gym changing room there was a lively conversation about football, in which I was defending the manager and his tactics, when Fester came over and put his massive hand on my shoulder. "A fellow blue," he grunted, before turning around to show me a massive tattoo on his back which read '*CHELSEA HEADHUNTERS*'.

Now and again I'd run into him locally. There'd only be one topic of conversation and if he was drinking, he'd ramble on about his hooligan exploits back in the day. I was in a cafe with Jimmy a few years back when he came in for take-away and they ended up in a long conversation about their mutual shenanigans. Fester was particularly impressed with Jimmy's *Daily Mirror* story.

The year after the Weeley debacle, Jimmy was uncontrollable. Like me, he was a compulsive truant, his poor mum never knew what he was up to. He'd fallen into bad company at football and smuggled himself onto a football special train to a midweek game at Stoke City. There had been a lot of crowd trouble, which had spilt onto the pitch. The next day, under the headline, '*SOCCER NIGHT OF SHAME*', on the back page of the *Mirror,* was a photo of Jimmy punching a policeman. Jimmy had phoned me early that morning asking me to rally the troops and buy all the *Daily Mirrors* from Bradley's newsagent, so that when his mum went in there on the way to work, her normal newspaper of choice would be sold out.

Fester had recently got divorced for the third time and had three jobs to finance the cost of his misdeeds. He claimed he'd never give up his season tickets, but found he had to sell them on for some games because of work and financial necessity. He'd offered them to me because he explained he could only sell them on to people who knew the ground and could be trusted to behave. He told me he treasured his tickets more than his kids!

For the first twenty minutes or so of the journey Jimmy was relatively quiet. I was reading the *Evening Standard* when he piped up.

"Heena bought me a new record player, Sid."

"That's great, mate, you got your vinyl down from the loft?"

"Not yet, it's still in the box. My daughter is coming out of rehab at the weekend and will come and collect the kids. Then I'll get organised."

"Where's she taking the kids, Jimmy?"

"To her stepsister during the week then to us at weekends."

"All four of them, Jimmy?" I queried.

"Yes, mate," he confirmed, seemingly unperturbed.

"Heena is a saint," I offered.

"Yep, you know Heena. Anyway, I'll sort the record player out once they've all fucked off."

The woman beside us glanced at him as he swore, I gave her an apologetic look, but he got louder.

"At least this record player will work, not like the fucking heap of shit that cunt Tony Beck gave me!"

"Watch your language, Jimmy," I pleaded.

"Oops, sorry mate," he whispered, realising his error. "Sorry everyone," he apologised to all. "I'm not too well, I'm going blind. Tell them about my condition, Sid."

I embarrassingly turned to the staring fellow passengers. "He's got a condition," I confirmed. "He's a bit down at the moment, sorry everyone."

"I do get a bit overexcited," Jimmy repeated.

After we changed from overground to a tube, I asked Jimmy how and when he'd reacquainted with Tony Beck. "Don't talk to me about that wanker," he snarled.

I waited a minute before asking, "When did he return from Scotland?"

"Fuck knows," he swore loudly.

I dropped the conversation and returned to the paper. I was convinced Jimmy's anger at his illness was affecting him mentally.

* * *

This was Jimmy's first visit to Stamford Bridge for many years. Since Heena returned from her spiritual walkabout, he'd confined himself to Barracks. Suddenly faced with his diagnosis and the fact he could no longer work or drive, he might as well enjoy himself while he could. We spent time in the club shop and then I took some selfies of us next to the statue of our boyhood hero Peter Osgood, the king of Stamford Bridge. We made our way to the automatic turnstile, I realised this was a first for Jimmy. I waited till we were right there and handed him the credit card style ticket. He looked confused.

"Just hold it up to the machine and wait for the green light," I instructed him.

A steward ushered him to an adjacent turnstile because of the growing crowd. I went through my entrance and waited for him to join me. A couple of minutes passed, and fans were streaming in, but there was no sign of Jimmy. I started to get worried and shouted to the steward who'd moved him. "Excuse me, I've lost my mate! He's a vulnerable adult!" It felt strange calling him that.

"His ticket didn't work. I've sent him to the ticket office," he replied.

I was struck with sense of complete panic. I pleaded with him to let me out of the ground, but he said only a supervisor could let me out. I ran around the packed concourse until I found a supervisor and explained the situation as best I could. I tried phoning Jimmy but as usual it went straight to voicemail. The supervisor escorted me through an exit and pointed me in the direction of the ticket office. There were four windows and a queue of at least four people in each. I looked round frantically but there was no sign of Jimmy. Eventually I got to the window and explained the situation.

"What was the name on the ticket sir," a woman behind the glass screen asked.

I almost replied 'Fester', but I knew his real name was Martin Jenkins.

The woman asked her colleagues and a male colleague of hers came to the window.

"I've confiscated the ticket, mate," he confirmed.

I honestly felt ill now. "Why?" I asked, "They were passed on to me and my mate by Martin Jenkins legitimately."

"That maybe so sir, but I need the address of the ticket holder before I can release the ticket sir."

"I don't know his address, I'm sorry." I was desperate.

Then he put his hand through the gap under the glass and took my ticket. "I'll have to take your ticket as well sir, I'll return them once you give me the ticket holder's address."

I could hear the crowd cheer a goal, my chest felt tight with stress. I felt worse than during my bankruptcy. I'd lost Jimmy and all I could think of was Fester's statement that the season tickets meant more to him than his kids. I calmed myself and scrolled through my contacts under F, looking for Fester. I called him, the phone rang for an age. Suddenly I heard his gruff gangster voice. "Sid, you okay, mate? Why aren't you at the game? Two nil en' it."

"Really sorry, mate, they are doing random checks on tickets. They won't let us in 'till I give them your full address."

"Fucking jobsworths," he grunted. "I'll text you my address immediately, mate, just make sure I have my tickets back on Monday, mate."

I stood staring at the phone thinking about Fester's history of violence. I thought about telling Heena I'd lost Jimmy. My phoned pinged, there was the address. I showed it to the ticket man and retrieved the tickets. I heard a collective groan from the crowd. 2-1? I was tempted to go and take my seat, but I had to find my mate.

I put myself in his head, *where would I wait?* The station, possibly. I ran out into the deserted Fulham Road and headed towards Fulham Broadway. I suddenly noticed the restaurant bar on my left. What once was our pub *The Britannia* was now a swanky eatery, which became a soulless pop-up bar on match days. I entered through the front door, barely acknowledging the bouncer. An hour earlier there would have been no room to spit, now there were barely a handful of punters. I saw Jimmy standing in what would have been our old spot, squinting at the screen showing the latest scores.

"Jimmy," I tapped him on the shoulder.

"Don't tell Heena," he said, holding up his pint glass. "Not meant to be drinking cause of the pills I'm on," he confessed.

"You okay, Jimmy?"

"They took the ticket off me, the cunts. I got confused, maybe I should have been more diplomatic."

"It's okay, mate, we could make the second half."

Jimmy's eyes looked vacant and lost for a second. "We had some good times in here, Sid, remember Spurs 1982?"

"Yes, I do, mate, you and all the top boys running up to Sloane Square for an ambush and then having an asthma attack because you left your puffer on the bar!"

We reminisced for a few minutes, then I led him back to the ground. By the time we were in our seats it was ten minutes into the second half, and it was now 2-2.

Jimmy looked tense and agitated, totally lost in the game. "I can't see the other end, you have to commentate," he requested.

Two minutes into injury time, Chelsea scored a lucky winning goal. Jimmy went crazy, he was still hugging me when the ref blew up for full time.

"That was the best game I've ever nearly seen," he blurted, kissing me on the cheek.

I guessed his over exaggerated description of an average league game was an acceptance of his problems, but after the ticket fiasco I was happy he was happy. I took a selfie of us with the pitch behind us then decided to get him home safely. It was the last time he'd visit his beloved Chelsea.

11

VINYL

(2013)

I RELATED THE story of the season tickets to Smithy, who I'd once introduced to Fester.

"Blimey, Sid, I wouldn't want to upset that nutter."

"I don't think I'll be taking Jimmy again, it looks like it's you and me in future," I confirmed.

I also related the Tony Beck story and the ranting in general. Smithy was planning to take Jimmy fishing in the hope it would calm him down.

I didn't see Jimmy for a couple of weeks until Heena called me. "Jimmy wants to talk to you, Sid," she said.

"Sid, it's Jimmy. Just checking the dates for Glastonbury."

"They're not on sale yet, mate. I've registered us but it's a lottery as to getting them," I explained.

"Yes, but what date is it? Need to put it on the calendar."

"Have you got a calendar for next year then, Jimmy?"

"What you on about, Sid?" He sounded agitated.

"Do you want to meet at Jack's café, ten tomorrow, for breakfast?" I asked, trying to change the subject.

"I'm not eating out anymore, Sid, come round for coffee."

I was about to have chat with Heena, but he cut me off.

* * *

I could tell Jimmy was struggling with making the coffee so I tactfully intervened. We sat in the conservatory, I noticed Jimmy was wearing an even thicker pair of sunglasses.

"Heena bought me a new record player," he said after a while.

"Yeah, you told me, Jimmy. I'd like to see your vinyl collection."

"Well, the thing is, I haven't actually worked out how it works yet. It's complicated."

"In what way complicated, mate? Has Heena had a look?"

"Don't like to bother her, perhaps you could have a look, Sid?"

"No problem, mate. I'll have a look in a minute. But I don't want to listen to that King Crimson shit." We both laughed.

There were a few moments pause in our conversation, I was discovering that I would have to take the lead. "Listen, Jimmy, Glastonbury tickets are difficult to get and it's a huge place, it may be better to go to the Isle of Wight, or a small festival like Latitude."

"We ain't going to poncey Latitude, fuck that, Sid!" he shouted. "We've got to go to Glastonbury, Sid. We've got do it before it's too late."

I assured him I'd try, whilst thinking about how my girls said it was far too bloated now and how it took hours to get from stage to stage.

* * *

Jimmy's house was a lot calmer in midweek without the invasion force. After coffee he led me up to his 'cell', the spare box room. I asked why he wasn't back in the main bedroom. He explained that the medication caused him to snore. I had my doubts.

I removed the record player, which Jimmy had crudely placed back in its box, it looked like a sewing machine. There was a cellophane bag with a couple of leads in it. "What's the problem then, Jimmy?" I asked.

"Well, where the fuck do those leads go?" he replied, with a hint of exasperation.

I took the lead that had the plug on it, put one end into the back of the box and the plug into the wall socket, turned the 'on' knob and hey presto.

"Fucking hell, Sid, you're a genius!"

I thought about asking if he'd tried this with the other record player but decided better of it.

"We can't christen it with fucking Crimson, mate," I exclaimed.

Jimmy agreed, and we adjourned to the hallway, after he explained his vinyl collection was in the loft.

"How do we get up there, Sid?" he queried, staring at the loft hatch like it was some mystical portal to another dimension.

"Should be a loft ladder," I said. I looked for some kind of implement to open the hatch but couldn't find it. Jimmy was no help at all, telling me Heena had probably hidden it.

"Shit, looks like fucking Crimson then," he moaned.

"Sod that, Jimmy, I'll get that hatch open, wait here." I returned with a kitchen chair and a flat head screwdriver, which did the trick. I pulled myself up and fumbled for the light switch. The loft was full of absolute junk. "Where about do you keep your records?" I called down.

"Fuck knows! I ain't been up there for years, it's Heena's domain!" Jimmy replied.

I navigated across the boarded area, avoiding the boxes stuffed full of Heena's spiritual shit and assorted suitcases and rucksacks. Eventually I came across a collection of boxes containing Jimmy's record collection. There wasn't any alphabetical system, just the albums randomly shoved into the cardboard boxes.

"Any luck, Sid?" I heard Jimmy shout.

"Yep, found them. Any requests, mate?"

"Mott the Hoople, going to have to christen the beast with a bit of Mott."

"Any particular one?" I hollered.

"I've got them all, bring 'em all down."

"Okay, mate, it might take a while to find them!" I started to rifle through the boxes, trying to organise them into some sort of order. Eventually I had all but one Mott album in a pile. I went through all the albums again looking for the missing one. I eventually hung out the loft and handed Jimmy a carrier bag with seven out of eight albums in it.

"Which one's missing?" he asked, counting the albums as I clambered down from the loft.

"Wildlife, not their best," I confirmed, as he spread the albums out on the living room floor.

Jimmy crouched down putting his face close to each one. "Fuck it," he exclaimed.

"Maybe it's somewhere else in the loft, it's pretty chaotic up there. I can have another look for it," I offered.

"No someone borrowed it, I can't for the life of me remember who." Jimmy looked so lost sitting amongst his Mott albums. I wasn't sure what was worse, his failing eyesight or the depression it was causing.

"Let's go out, Jimmy," I offered.

"Out? Where?"

"Soho!"

"Soho, Sid, what the fuck for?"

"Get you some vinyl, mate, we're going to my favourite record shop. They may even have your missing Mott album."

"But Heena hasn't left me any money, Sid," he protested.

"Debit, credit card?" I suggested.

"Heena's confiscated them, consultant's suggestion apparently."

"No worries, I'll sort everything out with Heena later. Come on, we'll leave her a note. Soho here we come!"

* * *

I led Jimmy down the stairs into the basement of the Sister Ray record store in Berwick Street. Jimmy was the most excited I'd seen him since his diagnosis. He looked around the racks of records in wonder, explaining that he could make out the vivid colours. I suggested we start with A and work our way round, but he was already leafing through the Ska/Two Tone section muttering to himself, he briefly had his sparkle back.

"Fucking Jesus, Sid, The Bodysnatchers, remember them?" He asked, holding up the album.

"Rock Steady, weren't it, what was the name of the singer, Jimmy?"

"Rhoda Dakar," he recalled immediately.

I smiled at my oldest mate. A fifty-six-year-old man who couldn't read his credit card number but could make out the definition of an album and name a female singer from a niche late-Ska band from his past.

After two hours he was up to the J section. I noticed an employee staring at us. I engaged him before he asked us if we were actually going to buy something. As I explained the situation, from Jimmy's condition to the record player and the missing Mott album, he was totally sympathetic. "We don't close till eight tonight, take as much time as you need."

We were interrupted by Jimmy shouting, "Fucking Jesus H Christ, Sid! Look at this!"

Displayed on the walls above the racks were the sleeves of the shop's most valuable albums. There it was above the J&K section, King Crimson's *In the Wake of Poseidon*, with the very same textured sleeve as Jimmy's copy. To our amazement there was a sticker on it with the price, £200. We told to the assistant that Jimmy owned the same album. He explained the features that made this edition of the album so valuable. We reckoned Jimmy's was exactly the same.

"Was the actual vinyl in good condition?" he asked.

"Mint, it's hardly ever been played." I confirmed.

"Because its fucking shit," Jimmy added.

"Well if you bring it in, we'll make sure it fits all the other criteria and make you an offer."

I told Jimmy to choose four albums, we'd share them. Another hour passed and he'd picked out Joni Mitchell's *Court and Spark*. "Good call," I ventured. We both had *Blue* but not this classic. We found a couple of Mott albums but not *Wildlife*. Various albums were chosen and then put back. More time passed before he picked out Sparks' *Kimono My House*. I didn't tell him I had that one. He was beside himself as he sang out loud, "This town ain't big enough for the both of us!"

I could hear his mobile ringing in his pocket. "I think your phone's ringing, Jimmy."

He looked panicked as he fumbled for it, I realised he was far more at ease with the distant past than the present. It was Heena, he answered in yeses and no's, before handing me the phone.

"Is Jimmy okay, Sid?" she asked.

"All good." I went on to explain the situation about the loft, she said she'd dig out the pole from the garden shed.

But then she had some bad news. "Don't tell Jimmy, but Molly has been arrested for dealing."

"Shit." I told her I'd keep a lid on the situation, Jimmy was too busy studying Neil Young albums. He added a Greatest Hits double album to our collection, then turned his attention to the Who.

"Who's next," he exclaimed.

"You've got that one, Jimmy, it was in the first box, defo," I confirmed.

"What shall I go for, Sid?"

I looked around, time was going on. "How about something more up to date?" I suggested.

"I heard Arcade Fire on the radio, they make a decent noise," Jimmy sounded positive.

We returned to the A-C section and added *Reflector* to our three other purchases. I made for the stairs up to the payment counter, but Jimmy stopped me. "Punk A to L!" he bellowed, "Fucking Jesus, Sid, look at this lot!" He dementedly started to go through pile. "Love a bit of Clash, got *London Calling* and *Combat Rock*, love 'em!"

"Remember Victoria Park?" I reminded him but got no response. There was equal excitement over the Damned, Sham, Stranglers, Skids, Pistols and Siouxsie. He spent a lot of time on the Ss! I suggested we finish our mission by a quick look through the punk/new wave singles.

Whist he concluded our search, I phoned Trudie to tell her all was good. She was delighted to hear Jimmy was having such a good time.

"Fuck me, the Lurkers. Where'd we see them, Sid?"

"Greyhound, the Kensington, Dublin Castle, one of them probably," I reminisced. "Come on, mate, we'd better pay for these and make tracks for home."

I beckoned him to the till. He had a last look around the basement making sure he hadn't missed anything.

"Holy fucking Jesus!" he screamed. The other punters all turned and stared. "Jesus fucking Christ, I don't fucking believe it!"

I felt a wave of embarrassment as my mate swore for England.

He was glaring at a small section of 'punk' singles on special offer, straining to get a close-up view. Jimmy held up the sleeve to within an inch of his eye. "It's fucking 'Where's Captain Kirk' isn't it Sid?"

"Sure is mate, it was by Spizz Energi"

"Remember we saw him supporting Siouxsie and the Banshees somewhere or other"

"I do indeed Jimmy, we were in Birmingham ,Villa away I think"

"That's the one, Sid. I've got to have this, shall I put Joni or Neil Young back?"

"I think the budget would stretch to an extra single," I offered.

We got to the payment area at the top of the stairs, the assistant who had helped us introduced us to the manager. "Hey guys, my colleague told me you were looking for Mott The Hoople's *Wildlife* album. I'm going to the world's biggest record fair in Utrecht in a couple of months, it will be like looking for a needle in a haystack but if you give me a contact number, I'll certainly give it a go," the manager said.

"Blimey, mate, top man. Thank you, mate!" Jimmy offered his hand, which the manager shook, whilst he gave me a knowing nod.

"Cheers pal," I said, thanking him as I paid for the records. I was waiting for our purchases to be bagged up when Jimmy suddenly started shouting incoherently. I could make out the series of expletives, and then surprisingly the name of an old friend of ours. The other customers were staring, I put my hand on Jimmy's shoulder and tried to calm him down.

"Cunt," Jimmy cursed in a whisper.

"I thought I heard you mention poor old Perry?" I queried.

"I did, it was Perry, the cunt." Jimmy was red with rage.

"Perry, what about Perry?"

"He's the cunt who borrowed my Mott Album."

"Perry?" I was mystified.

"Fucking Perry," Jimmy confirmed.

"Well, in that case Jimmy, it's a good thing our friend here is going to look for a replacement cause Perry won't be returning it anytime soon, mate."

"Why's that then, Sid?"

"Because Perry's dead, mate," I said, baffled.

"I don't think so, Sid."

"Yes, he died four years ago, Jimmy. The poor fucker fell off a train," I explained.

"He couldn't have done, Sid, I saw him a few months ago begging near Waterloo station."

"I don't think so, Jimmy," I tried to reassure him.

"Well it certainly looked like him, I walked on by, but I should have asked the cunt for my album back."

I assumed Jimmy's failing eyesight had confused him. I was sure Perry was dead, he was on my kill list, after all.

12

THE TENANT

I WAS RELIEVED to get Jimmy home safe and sound. We christened his turntable with *Where's Captain Kirk*. He was happy, I was exhausted. On reflection, the trips to football and Soho were a bit too much. I'd stay local in the future if I could, but of course there was the small matter of Glastonbury!

I brought Trudie up to speed. She told me I was a good mate to Jimmy, but what else could I be.

I tried to convince myself that Jimmy was mistaken in thinking he saw Perry. I can't deny I sometimes imagined he was lurking in the shadows, watching me, waiting to pounce. Sometimes when I came home late from a gig, I'd run the last few meters, paranoid that he was following me. But it was irrational, he was dead. He must be. The threats had stopped, the continuous demands for money, they just stopped.

We were close in our early teens but when his mum ran off with her boss, leaving Perry's dad to care for his five children. Perry became a liability. He was bitter, probably with good reason. It was odd that he was jealous of my seemingly stable home, whilst I was envious of Jimmy's circumstances. Things came to a head when his dad took to the bottle and was sacked from his job as a tube driver. Perry came round to my house and some money went missing from my mum's purse. We gave him the benefit of the doubt but soon after the same thing happened again, and my father confronted him. After that we both made sure our paths didn't cross. His dad decided a fresh start was needed and moved the family to the new town of Harlow.

I didn't see him again 'till the late nineties, when he walked into my shop. I was going through yet another disastrous trading period and had decided to turn the upstairs showroom into a studio flat to bring in some much-needed guaranteed income. I leased the building from a faceless landlord, there was nothing in the lease agreement that said I couldn't sub-let, but my decisions at the time were based on a combination of desperation and wishful thinking. I didn't want to get involved with costly solicitors' fees. I placed an ad on the property page of the local paper, which brought a surprising amount of interest. I'd showed four prospective tenants around, all seemed bona fide with decent references, then one afternoon Perry appeared from the past. I recognised him immediately, despite his long hair and bushy moustache. He looked like someone out of The Grateful Dead.

"Sid," he mumbled in total surprise.

"Perry," I acknowledged.

Over coffee we exchanged back stories. He had settled in Peterborough but had recently divorced and had decided to move back to the old manor, as his brother had set up a courier company and desperately needed drivers. I remembered his oldest brother, he was my postman for a while. Had a bit of a reputation in the less salubrious local pubs. I felt like life had dealt Perry an unlucky hand and thought he deserved a break. He paid the deposit and for a few months the rent was paid in cash on the nose, he was the model tenant.

I hardly ever saw him but one Friday evening he came up to me in the pub and asked what my poison was. I noticed he had a black eye. He explained that he'd had a major disagreement with his brother because he went to his mother's funeral. His brother had never forgiven her since she walked out on them. Perry had tried to keep some kind of contact. Over far too many drinks he told me that his mum left because his dad beat her, and his eldest brother was a chip off the old block. I questioned him about his divorce. He claimed they drifted apart because he was scared to have children. Almost as an aside, he mentioned that his brother had fired him and that he'd signed on and arranged for me to receive my rent directly from the DHSS.

The months rolled by and the cheques would arrive like clockwork, but his drinking got worse and, on more than one occasion, I had to knock on his door because he was either playing Metal music too loud or he'd be shouting, despite there being no-one else there.

It wasn't long before he was borrowing money from me, a fiver here, a tenner there. He'd pop into my shop once a week, I could see he was now on strong skunk and on a downward spiral. I had to confront him on a couple of occasions, he'd come in when I wasn't there and made Trish, my secretary, uncomfortable.

However, I genuinely felt sorry for him, I felt a duty of care for him. I recalled what a good mate he'd been before his family break up. I was supposed to check the flat every six months, but I completely buried my head, not wanting to see the state of the place. Besides, I was still getting the cheques, so I was mostly happy. He was like a toothache that came and went.

Tara and Leo were now both at Uni, business was shit and Trudie had discovered online shopping. I wasn't in the best place to help anybody else, either emotionally or financially.

One wet Friday afternoon, Perry came in, he stunk of garlic and weed. He ranted about how he'd got himself banned from his local Wetherspoons, describing how he'd racially abused a bar person who'd refused to serve him. "The fucking black bitch!" he shouted.

I was shocked, I tried to calm him down, but he got more and more agitated.

He then crossed a red line. "Where's Trish today?" he asked.

"Day off, Perry, why?"

"She's a lovely woman, Sid, I bet you've given her one."

"For fucks sake, Perry!" I snapped. "She's my secretary."

"Well I'd give her a good seeing to if I was her boss."

"Perry, don't you come in here without me being here," I warned him. "Here's a tenner, now fuck off."

He grabbed me by my shirt, his eyes were wild. "I need fifty quid, Sid." He was literally foaming at the mouth. I thought he was going assault me. "Give me fifty quid and I won't trouble you again," he said as he released his grip.

"And you'll keep away from Trish."

"I promise."

I gave him the cash and he left. I didn't see him for a couple of months.

I went away one weekend to the Cotswolds with Trudie. When I returned on the Monday, there was a note from Trish telling me she could no longer work for me. I feared the worst. I called her, she was naturally cagey until I asked, "Has this something to do with my tenant?"

"Yes," she whispered.

"Did he touch-"

"No, no, Sid," she interrupted. "He kept asking for money and he…" she hesitated, "He made an inappropriate suggestion."

I went around the back to the entrance of the flat, I noticed the drains were blocked with leaves and the ground was dirty and treacherous. I wondered about the state of the flat, it was good four years since I'd been inside. The bell certainly wasn't working, I banged on the door as loudly as possible. I could hear the dull thud of a deep bass, I waited two minutes and banged on the door again. Nothing. I took the door key out of my pocket, I hadn't used it for years. I tried to turn it in the lock, but it wouldn't work. It was definitely the correct key as it had a key ring with '*Flat*' written on it. It then dawned on me that Perry had changed the lock. I banged on the door even harder. I tried phoning him. I put my ear to the door but there was too much noise from nearby roadworks.

I phoned Smithy to put him in the picture and asked if he could recommend a locksmith, being in the letting business I guessed he'd have a contact. "I'll text you my locksmith, Eric. He's old school, just mention my name."

I returned to my shop, an hour later Eric the locksmith appeared. He looked a handful and explained that he'd get the door open for fifty quid, but it would cost extra if he entered the premises with me. I paid him the fifty, he had the door open in seconds. I asked him to wait outside until I confirmed I didn't need any further assistance.

The smell, or should I say stink, hit me as I climbed the stairs. I noticed the walls had been painted a dark blue colour and as the stair light wasn't working it was difficult to see where I was treading. I got to the top and shouted, just in case Perry was asleep. Nothing. I gingerly opened the lounge door, the first thing I noticed was that the TV was on. I turned the light on, I couldn't believe the state of the place. It reminded me of the film *Seven*, when Brad Pitt and Morgan Freeman entered the serial killer's apartment. The floor was covered in old bills and newspapers, the carpet, what I could see of it, was completely threadbare.

"You okay, mate?" I heard the locksmith shout from the entrance.

"Just hang on a sec, Eric!" I returned to the landing and opened the kitchen door, I wanted to throw up, there were rotting vegetables and god knows what on the work surfaces. The bin was overflowing and I could see movement, which turned out on closer inspection to be maggots.

I gingerly opened the bedroom door and turned the light on. The duvet was discarded on the floor, the sheet was filthy, as was the adjacent wall beside the bed. I thought I might vomit. Lastly, I braced myself to enter the bathroom. I tried the handle, but it wouldn't open, it could only be bolted shut from the inside.

"Perry!" I yelled, as I banged on the door. I put my ear to the door, I could make out a faint whimpering sound. "Eric!" I shouted, "Could you come up please?"

"It will cost you another fifty quid!" he yelled.

"No problem!" I replied, with a hint of desperation.

He ran up the stairs, stopping on the landing to survey the state of the place. "Nice," he whispered sarcastically.

I pointed at the bathroom door, intimating it was bolted from the inside. He stepped back removing his black Harrington and ran at the door. It didn't budge as he hurled his massive frame at it. I tried shouting one last time.

"Perry, open the fucking door, mate, we need to have a chat!"

The locksmith motioned for me to stand aside, he aimed a size eleven boot at the area the bolt would be, before taking another run at the door with his full weight behind his shoulder. I could hear a light splintering sound. "One more heave should do it," he grunted. He took a couple of steps back and tensed his right shoulder. Just as he hurled himself for a last attempt at the door, it sprang open and a startled naked woman stood dripping wet, opened mouthed, as were we.

"Who the fuck are you?!" she screamed, removing her earphones, before reaching for a towel to wrap around herself. She was a big girl and it didn't do much covering up.

"Good luck, mate," Eric said, turning to me, holding out his hand for his payment. I duly sorted it out and he left me to it.

"I'm the landlord, where's Perry?" I quizzed her.

"If you're the landlord, you want to sort that bath out, it's a health hazard," She said, nodding towards the tub. I didn't want to verify her complaint, I'd seen enough.

"Where's Perry?" I repeated.

"He's gone shooting with my husband," she confirmed.

The mention of Perry 'shooting' made me shudder. "Shooting?" I queried, hoping I'd misheard her, she did have a thick Brummie accent.

"Yes, they've gone to a farm somewhere, they'll be back this evening."

"And you're visiting then?" I was curious.

"Yes, we live in Wolverhampton. The farm is in Surrey, so we're staying over."

"Where'd you know Perry from?" I asked.

"Caravan club."

"Caravan club? Perry doesn't have a caravan."

"It's a long story, you'd better ask Perry."

"Well tell him Sid wants a word, urgently." I noticed the towel slipping a bit so made a hasty retreat, feeling very stressed.

Two days later Perry came into my shop, I smelt him before I saw him. He looked like he hadn't slept for days, the thought of him with a gun greatly concerned me. I told him that his behaviour regarding my secretary was totally unacceptable. He didn't apologise, he was clearly stoned and was incoherent. I should have told him to get out the flat there and then, but he was an old mate, so I gave him a final warning and told him not to come in my shop again.

I didn't see him for a few months. I buried my head as usual, hoping things would get better. They didn't.

* * *

Business was shit, I daren't tell Trudie, who continued shopping on an industrial scale, but I decided not to renew the lease. My landlords wrote to me explaining that I had to give six months' notice and that they would need to inspect the property in three months' time. Subject to the terms and conditions I could be liable for costs to repairs. This last point worried me. I put a letter through Perry's door explaining the situation.

I expected a reaction, but it was three weeks before I heard from him and that was only because I ran into him in the pub.

"I thought you were banned, Perry," I said. I was surprised to see him sidle up to the bar.

"New landlord, Sid, I'm on probation."

I noticed he looked a little more human than previously, his long locks were freshly washed, his clothes were clean-ish.

"Can you lend us a tenner, mate?" he asked casually. I thought it best to keep him on-side.

"Sure, Perry, and let me get you a drink." I was surprised when he clinked glasses with me once our pints had arrived.

"Cheers, Sid."

I was concerned how upbeat he was. For a moment I considered burying my head as usual, but then thought better of it. "You got my letter then?" I asked.

"Letter?" he repeated.

My heart sank. What if he thought it was junk mail whilst in one of his stupors? "About me giving up the lease," I said.

"Oh, that letter. Yes, mate, yeah, no problem," he smiled. I now wondered if he realised he had to get out.

"The shops not sustainable, mate, and the landlords want to turn the whole building into their offices," I lied.

"I'm sorry to hear that, Sid. What you going to do about work?"

His contrition surprised me. "Work off my phone, Perry, work from home, what you going to do, mate?"

"I'm sorted, mate. Tina, who you met in the flat, her and her husband Tony are going to put me up in their caravan."

I felt like I'd won the lottery, I'd lost countless hours worrying about Perry's reaction. I'd pencilled him on my kill list. Carbon monoxide poisoning was my first idea, then I thought a fire would solve all my problems. "Yes, she mentioned the caravan club and the shooting. I hope you haven't been keeping any unlicensed weapons in the flat, Perry?" I chanced.

"No, mate, I keep it in Tony's caravan," he replied, not confirming if it was licensed or not.

"So, how'd you get involved in a caravan club, mate?"

Perry took a gulp of his beer. "Not exactly a caravan club, more of a swingers club," he answered casually.

"A what?"

"They're swingers, I met them at my cousin's funeral a couple of years ago. They invited me to join them at a caravan park in Skegness."

"Which was a swingers club?" I interrupted.

"Not exactly, Sid, I had no idea. I thought they were just a nice couple who knew my cousin, who was a bit of a lad to say the least. Anyway, I got the train to Grantham and they picked me up from there. I'd had a few sherbets whilst waiting, and Tina had been on the turps, we were both half cut. Tony suggested Tina and I rest in the caravan whilst he drove to Skeggy. But I didn't get any rest, mate. She was still seducing me when we got to the caravan site. There were four couples all parked up together, they were at it all week and I was in and out of all four of them. I slept for a week afterwards."

I thought he was inventing the whole story, but then again, I'd seen Tina naked in the flat. If they were happy to put him up, good luck to them.

"She calls me her 'Viking'," he continued. "Tony is facing a knee replacement and she wants me to drive them about, and obviously give her a good seeing to."

"Sounds like a good deal," I concluded, and rubbed out his name on my kill list.

* * *

I was concerned the managing agents would crucify me with their repairs bill. There was no way I could let them inspect the property whilst Perry was living there, so I told them he was ill and it would be best if they came after he vacated, with a couple of weeks leeway to allow me to redecorate. I gave Perry a leaving date and buried my head for the next few months, until he put his head into the shop a week before D-day.

"Can I have a word, Sid?!" he shouted to me, as I busied myself in my office. I didn't want him coming in, but it was cold and wet outside, so I beckoned him in. He looked terrible and he stunk of booze and weed.

"Looking forward to moving in with the nympho?" I jested.

"I'm sorry, Sid, we had a fall out. I was in Norfolk with them last weekend and during my stay Tina only goes and tells her other half she is in love with me and wants him to fuck off when I move in. Well, he got upset and things got out of hand," he explained.

"Out of hand," I responded, with a feeling of dread.

"He came for me with his gun, I managed to grab it before he fucking shot me, but as we struggled the gun went off and a bullet went through the caravan roof! He started to reload another cartridge and I legged it."

"So where are you going to move to next week?" I probed.

"Well, the thing is, Sid, I was talking to the 'Judge' down the pub and he told me I could take a court order out against the landlords, which would probably mean I could stay another year before they get me out. It wouldn't cause you any grief.'"

I felt faint, my chest was tight. I thought I was getting a migraine. The tell-tale signs of double vision and a tingling in my mouth were sensations I'd not suffered for years. I mentally put him back on the kill list.

And then, I just said it. It came to me in moment of sheer divine intervention. It was a pure spur of the moment comment. As good a ruse as the Scout camp alibi that got me to the Weeley festival. It was my finest lie, save for the gem I told my headmaster after breaking the school truancy record. "I'm sorry, Perry, you have to vacate by next

Saturday as agreed. You do know who's bought the premises, don't you?"

"No, Sid," he looked confused, "I thought you were just handing it back to the managing agents. Anyway, whoever bought it will have to get a court order to get me out, I've got nowhere to go."

"Terry O'Neill." I could feel the colour come back to my cheeks as I pulled the lunatics name out of thin air. "With his brother Barry, you know, the mad one with the metal plate in his skull. They are into property development now. Apparently, they've bought it. So, I don't know about you, Perry, but I'm going to make sure I'm out well before Saturday."

"Fuck that! The O'Neills? I'm off." Perry staggered out the shop, reflecting on my brilliant misinformation.

I was hoping 'I'm off' meant that he'd be off for good.

13

A SECRET CIRCUMCISION

(1974)

BEING A SEVENTEEN-year-old boy in 1974 wasn't easy. Especially if you were painfully shy like me. All my mates were confident, larger than life characters. I lived in their shadow. There was nothing to do in the week, we all lived for the weekend. Well, actually, just Friday and Saturday, absolutely nothing happened on a Sunday, particularly in winter. Saturday was football and hopefully a discotheque. On Sundays, there was nothing to do except hang around. Our choice of location was the local franchise of the absurd restaurant chain 'The Golden Egg'. Basically, the menu consisted of hundreds of egg-based dishes, both sweet and savoury. Having normally enjoyed a massive Sunday roast with our families, we tended to stick to the dessert menu, waffles, pancakes etc., as we spent the dark wet boring Sunday afternoons hanging out.

On this particular Sunday, Jimmy, Smithy, Perry (for a change) and I were at our favourite table talking football and girls. Girls were now a good seventy-five percent of our conversation, though sadly I had little to contribute on the subject. By this time, Jimmy and Smithy were having regular rendezvous with the Crane twins. They claimed they were interchangeable. My young mind boggled.

The reason I recall this particular Sunday was because, unusually, a couple of the O'Neill brothers came in. We were alerted to the situation by Jimmy going bright red and swearing under his breath. "Shit, it's Terry O'Neill and his brother Barry. Fuck. I might have to hide in the loo," he said frantically.

I assumed there was still historic tension regarding Jimmy's dalliance with their sister. I had my back to them but caught Terry's eye as I turned briefly to see them sitting a few tables away.

"Shit, he's coming over," Jimmy muttered.

We pretended to be busy with our waffles.

"Ain't seen you for a while, Cyclops," Terry O'Neill addressed Jimmy, before surprisingly turning to me.

"You're Levinson?" he asked.

I nodded in confirmation.

"You're sort of a Jew boy ain't yer?" he worryingly stated.

I wasn't sure about the 'sort of' bit. Maybe he had seen me eating a bacon butty somewhere, but in hindsight, it wasn't a totally inaccurate description.

"Sort of," I mumbled in confirmation.

"Well I want a word with you outside." He nodded towards the door.

"Outside," I repeated hesitantly, wondering if Terry O'Neill had joined the national front and I just happened to be an unlucky 'sort of' Jew in the wrong place at the wrong time.

As I followed him towards the door, I looked back at my mates. I knew Jimmy was flushed with relief that he hadn't been asked outside. I knew he'd be smarting that O'Neill called him Cyclops.

It was freezing outside, there was the threat of snow in the air and I'd left my coat on the back of my chair.

"Fucking freezing en it," O'Neill muttered in a matey way, which took me by surprise as I was expecting a bout of racial abuse, possibly some kind of physical violence. "I want to ask you something Levinson, something personal." He spoke in hushed tones. "But let me warn you, if I ever hear you've told anyone about this conversation, I'll fucking kill you, you understand?"

"No problem, Terry," I assured him.

"You were circumcised then, Levinson?" he whispered in my ear.

"Yeah, I was, Terry."

"Did it hurt?"

"Sorry, Tel?" I wasn't sure I'd heard him correctly.

"Did it hurt?" he repeated.

"Did what hurt?"

"The circumcision, did it hurt?" he asked, clearly getting frustrated.

"I was only a few days old, Tel."

"But did it hurt?" He was close to yelling.

"Not at all, Tel, fairly painless if I recall." I lied just to placate him.

"That's good," he said, calming down, his voice returning to a whisper. "The thing is, I've had some problems with my foreskin, and I'm being circumcised on Tuesday."

"You won't feel a thing, Terry, honest." I wasn't sure if this were true, but I wanted to end the conversation sharpish.

"Well don't forget, Levinson, not a fucking word."

"Your secret is safe with me, Tel."

O'Neill grabbed my collar. "I'm sorry I'm going to have to hit you, Levinson, so that your mates think I've picked on you because you're a Jew boy. I won't hit you too hard, just enough to give you a nosebleed."

I thought of Bishop at the bus stop and prepared for the worse. Suddenly though, I had one of those moments of inspiration. "You don't need to hit me, Terry, I've got a better idea. I'll tell the boys you want to ask Sharon Cohen out and you were asking me, as a 'sort of a Jew boy' for my advice on how to go about it," I suggested.

"Sharon Cohen, fucking hell, those tits. Wow, if only…" O'Neill seemed to be miles away.

"Yes, Tel, if only," I agreed, realising that even I, a 'sort of a Jew', would stand no chance with the well-developed local 'It' girl.

"It's a brilliant idea, Levinson." He gave me a playful tap on the arm. This was encouraging, I thought.

"Do you think, just for arguments sake, she'd actually go out with me?"

This wasn't what I was expecting. I, and every boy I knew, had dreamt of a dalliance with Sharon Cohen. Ever since I discovered the joys of masturbation, she'd on many occasions been the object of my imagination. She lived just around the corner from me, we went to the same primary school, but I'd never uttered a single word to her and vice versa. Now she was going out with Clifford Fox, a proper Jew boy, his dad was minted. He was the first boy I knew to have a car, a brand-new red Cortina . He was in a different league, and so was she.

"What you reckon, Levinson? What are my chances?"

I wanted to tell him he had more chance of becoming Prime Minister, but I was freezing and my waffles were getting cold. "Why not, Tel, no harm in asking. Particularly as you will be, you know, sort of Kosher."

"That's right pal, I could tell her I've become a Jew boy, show her the evidence."

"Good idea, Tel, I'd let the scars go down a bit first though," I quipped, immediately regretting making the flippant remark.

"Scars?!" O'Neill barked.

"I mean swelling, just a bit of swelling."

"Yeah, okay, Levinson, cheers pal. So, you tell your mates what we've just discussed, Sharon Cohen, okay?"

"Sure thing, Tel, and good luck."

"Good luck with what?"

"Sharon! Sharon Cohen!" And that was it. I wasn't punched, and I wasn't exactly racially abused, win-win really. The boys were perplexed as I returned to the table and repeated the Sharon Cohen story.

"There's more chance of Chelsea winning the league!" Jimmy laughed.

As we made our way out, half an hour later, the O'Neills were tucking into egg burgers and chips. "See you, Levinson!" Terry shouted.

This was now a win-win-win, as I could see the boys were mightily impressed with my new friendship.

"Oi, Cyclops!" my new pal addressed my oldest pal. "Don't think we've forgotten you messing about with our sis, don't let us see you in here again."

That was it. We never set foot in the Golden Egg again.

14

THE EX TENANT FROM HELL, IN HELL

(2009)

AND JUST LIKE that, he was gone! I'd spent the night before D-day in a sleepless stupor, my mind churning over the scenarios if Perry didn't vacate. Bankruptcy and murder occupied the majority of my dark thoughts. As it turned out, my brilliant idea of mentioning the O'Neills had done the trick.

I arrived with a couple of lads who worked for me to find a pile of discarded furniture in the courtyard outside the back door, which he'd been left open. It was snowing heavily, and the flat was freezing and unsurprisingly in a state of disrepair. The bad weather worked in my favour, as the surveyor from the managing agents phoned me to say he'd be delayed because of the traffic problems, which gave us time to at least clear all the rubbish into my van.

But once the flat was empty it looked awful. If only I'd carried out my plan to set fire to the place, including Perry and my shop downstairs, all my problems would be over, I thought to myself.

* * *

Although the mention of the O'Neills was a spontaneous moment of genius, the roots of the thought had been planted a year earlier when Terry O'Neill came into my shop. I recognised him immediately, it took him a couple of minutes to recognise me.

"Levinson, you're Levinson! I remember you!" he exclaimed.

"Yep, that's me, I'm Sid Levinson. Terry, isn't it?" I shook his hand, wondering if he remembered our last conversation back in our teenage years.

"Sid Levinson, the Jew boy," he smiled.

He obviously had an equally accurate recollection of our conversation outside the Golden Egg all those years ago. Back then I was a cripplingly shy boy totally confused about who I was and where I was heading. Now I knew exactly who I was and, apart from Perry, I was scared of no man. I was a killer for fuck sake.

"Yes, that's right, Terry, I'm still a Jew boy," I replied coldly.

"Well I could have been one as well if Sharon Cohen had accepted my generous offer of a wimpy and a fuck in the back of my 'Cortina'," O'Neill laughed.

"If you'd asked for my advice in courting a nice Jewish girl, I'd probably have come up with a more subtle plan of action," I suggested.

"Yeah, I know, I was a bit forward, but I thought the 'Cortina' must have been tempting enough. Fussy cow," he laughed. "Anyway, Sid, you lied to me. The circumcision fucking hurt, mate."

I was now Sid, and mate, blimey we were grown-ups now! "Didn't want to give you sleepless nights, mate, besides I've never told a soul."

"I know that, Sid, I'm not here to kill you. I popped by because my brother Barry and me are doing a development and we urgently need a couple of bespoke fireplaces."

"That's a relief, Terry, you're in the right place, mate."

"I wonder what happened to Sharon Cohen, Sid? She was a classy sort for sure."

"Probably married a nice wealthy Jewish boy, so that would rule both of us out. How's all the rest of your family?" I asked.

"Lost four brothers and my sister to the big C, mate."

"Jeez, sorry to hear that, mate."

"Yeah, I haven't forgotten your mate Jimmy fucking about with Julie. Is Cyclops still about?"

"Haven't seen him in years," I lied.

I ended up doing a lot work with the O'Neills and, despite their reputation, got on really well with them. Plus, it was that reputation that finally got rid of Perry.

* * *

The meeting with the surveyor didn't go well. He pointed out in great detail that, according to the lease, the property had to be returned in the same order as when taken over and that I was facing a hefty bill for dilapidations. This tempered my relief at Perry going, but that was to be short lived.

I'd just sat down to dinner and was explaining to Trudie that Perry had finally gone. She asked where to, I felt a bit guilty telling her I didn't know, and I didn't care. Suddenly my phone buzzed, it was Perry, my heart sank.

"Hi, Perry, how you doing?" I tried to sound sincere.

"Fucking freezing, Sid, I need something to eat and some blankets, it's blowing a fucking blizzard out here."

"Where are you, Perry?"

"In the town hall multi-story, it's freezing."

"What are you doing there, Perry?"

"I was supposed to move in with a mate, but I've been let down, I'll get sorted in the morning, but I could do with some fish and chips and a couple of blankets."

"I'm on my way, Perry, I'll call you when I'm there," I replied. I looked at Trudie, I knew what she was thinking. We could see the snow swirling outside in the freezing gloom. "I'll get him into a hotel or something," I muttered, as I searched for some blankets.

I found him shivering by the pay and display machine on the second floor. He devoured the fish and chips as if he hadn't eaten for a week, maybe he hadn't. He looked and smelt awful, there was no way I could take him to a hotel. "Where're you going to go, Perry? You can't stay here, you'll freeze to death."

He covered himself up in the blankets. "I'll be off in the morning, Sid, I'm going to live with Tina in her caravan, sorted."

"What about her other half with the gun?" I probed.

"Fuck him, we will sort him out good and proper."

I wasn't sure what he meant by that comment and was slightly concerned he wouldn't survive the night. That's not strictly true, I not sure I'd be bothered if he didn't!

* * *

I didn't hear anything for the next couple of weeks from Perry, but I certainly did from the surveyor. The parasite was demanding £28,000 in dilapidations! After losing a night's sleep, I took my accountants advice and sent a cheque for £3000 and a letter that this was the best I could do, otherwise I would have to declare myself bankrupt and that, if they banked the cheque, we would assume they had accepted my offer. I received a swift reply stating that they would accept my offer providing we carried out a list of repairs, a new bath, cooker, new carpet and redecoration throughout. I put my boys to work on the flat immediately, and on reflection, I got away quite lightly considering the state Perry left the place in.

Three weeks after last seeing Perry in the car park, I received a call. He told me himself and Tina were in Sleaford, hiding from her other half. I was relieved he was far away from me, and seemingly out of my life.

However, a few weeks later I was awoken by him calling at five in the morning.

"Sid, it's me, Perry. Listen, I'm on a train to Kings Cross, I need fifty quid urgently. I promise it will be the last time I trouble you. I'll meet you in the Parcel Yard at eight."

Shit, he was back in London, and despite his promise, he was back in my life. He was top of my kill list.

I waited in the Parcel Yard 'till nine, there was no sign of Perry. My phoned buzzed, it was him. He was groaning and muttering incoherently, I couldn't make out was he was saying.

"Slow down, Perry, where are you?"

"I've broken my legs, Sid, I've called an ambulance, I can't breathe."

"What's happen, Perry? Where are you?"

"He was on the train, the fucker was going to kill me."

"Who's going to kill you, mate?"

"Tina's other half. I jumped off the train, I've broken my legs, my chest hurts, Sid."

"Where the fuck are you, Perry?"

I could hear an ambulance siren in the background. "I'm near Peterborough, the ambulance-" The phone went dead.

That's the last I heard from him, I presumed he died of his injuries. Now Jimmy was claiming he'd seen Perry begging at Waterloo. I hoped desperately he was mistaken.

15

WONDERLAND

(1971)

I MADE MY way to the first aid tent, it was like a war zone. The tent was completely full and there were dozens of casualties lying on the grass outside waiting for attention. There were only a couple of St Johns medics, they looked completely panic stricken. A couple of ambulances arrived but I couldn't find Jimmy anywhere.

I rushed back to where our tent and belongings were, thinking Jimmy might do the same, they were now just smouldering ash. The air was full of smoke and sporadic sirens. I waited anxiously for an hour before deciding to head to the arena, hoping I'd be allowed in.

I was delighted to see a huge chunk of the fence had been ripped apart, with everyone passing through unchecked. It was now basically a free event but the chance of finding Jimmy amongst an ever-growing crowd was remote. I wandered around looking for him in vain until it started to get dark.

A man on the stage announced the first act, Hackensack, would be on dead on midnight. I decided to find a spot as close to the stage as possible. My immediate neighbours were a mixture of lads in their late teens and young hippy couples.

"You on your own, pal?" A lad with a thick Brummie accent asked me.

I told him and his two mates my story, which they found fascinating, and I received a lot of sympathy. One of the hippy couples gave me some shortbread biscuits, which I was very grateful for. Just before midnight, I reluctantly had my first puff of marijuana, courtesy of one of the Brummie boys. My first taste of alcohol and drugs on the same day!

The MC returned just before midnight, he seemed stoned out of his mind as he declared that the 'Old Bill' estimated there were over a hundred thousand at the festival. The Clacton round table that put on the event had made provisions for around five thousand, but the line-up, plus the late cancellation of the Isle of Wight festival, had swelled the numbers beyond everyone's expectations.

I don't recall anything about Hackensack, or most of the acts that followed through the small hours, except for the crowd (those who were conscious) chanting along with The Edgar Broughton Band, "Out demons out!". This went on for at least ten minutes. I recall Edgar, with his mass of black hair, rousing the audience. Our paths were to cross a few more times over the next forty years.

I must have dozed off after his stirring performance. I was awoken around eight in the morning by the exciting riffs of young new band called Status Quo. I was desperate to go to the loo, so I asked my neighbours to save my spot and made my way gingerly to the festival village.

The toilets were basically a long trench to piss in, with a small canvas covered section at each end for a dump. I queued for ages at the 'section' with *Geezers* painted in large letters on the side.

On entering through a flap, I saw the distressing sight of two rows of holes in the ground with, if you were lucky, a roll of toilet paper on the small space beside them. Every half hour, an orange vested assistant would come pour a mixture of water and chemicals down the holes and *maybe* replenish the paper. I squatted between two stoned hippies, the smell and sounds stayed with me for years. Someone before me had pissed on my loo paper.

Despite this unsavoury experience I was starving, so I joined another queue for a bacon bap. By the time I got to the front they'd run out of bacon, so breakfast was a stale buttered roll washed down with mouthful of warm water from a communal water fountain. It would be hard for today's millennials to imagine a festival before bottled water and iPhones.

I kept my eye out for Jimmy as I made my way back to the small space that was my home for the next forty-eight hours. My first puff of weed had only seemed to send me to sleep, so I resisted further offers as Mungo Jerry got the crowd going with their recent hit *In the Summertime*. By now the schedule was seriously behind and I could see the roadies panicking between acts.

Stone the Crows came on some three hours after their allotted time of three o'clock, with Maggie Bell's rasping voice and Les Harvey's blues guitar riff the highlight so far. Poor Les was to tragically die a few months later when he was electrocuted on stage! I was getting concerned about what time the Saturday night headliners, prog rock legends King Crimson, would come on, and even more worried about Mott the Hoople, who were the reason for all the skulduggery and effort to get here in the first place. They were due on nine and midnight respectively.

The MC staggered on at ten and announced that because King Crimson were playing in Germany tomorrow night, the running order, which was now at least five hours (four bands) behind, would have to be juggled. Robert Fripp and his band came on minutes later to rapturous applause. A couple of songs in, I was passed a joint, which this time I accepted. Looking back, getting high was the only way to appreciate King Crimson.

Midnight came and went, no sign of Mott and no info on any times. I dozed off during Chris Farlow's *Colosseum*, missing Barclay James Harvest and Al Stewart's sets completely. I woke with a stir just before 6am. *'Shit'*, I thought, *'I've missed Mott!'*. I hadn't felt so deflated since the Antonio Rattín business during the World Cup some five years earlier.

The stage was being readied for the next band, everyone around me was asleep. An MC I'd not seen before came on and banged the microphone. "Testing, testing, three, four, testing. Ladies and gentlemen, wakey, wakey. It's my pleasure to welcome on stage, better late than never, one of this country's best live bands, all the way from Hereford, I give you Mott the Hoople!"

And there they were! I got as close as I could, stumbling over several sleeping bags, whispering my apologies but wishing I could wake the whole arena from its collective coma. I would guess only about ten percent of the crowd were awake as Ian Hunter approached the microphone, a mass of blonde curly locks and the obligatory shades. "Good morning Weeley, how you all doing? Wakey wakey! Should have been on six hours ago but shit happens!"

I stood transfixed as he tuned up his exotic Maltese cross guitar, the sun rose behind the stage. A few people stirred as the boys blasted through their half hour set, two minutes of which involved them throwing bananas into the crowd. Probably not their most memorable performance. Like my first sexual experience, it was all over far too quickly, but I've never forgotten either!

I hoped Jimmy was somewhere close by and, like me, thought all the plotting and planning was worth it. I made my way to the village for my morning constitutional. The first aid tent was less hectic than the previous day, so I went in and enquired after Jimmy. Because they'd been inundated with casualties, they didn't have time to keep records. They directed me to the information tent where there was a giant message board. I spent a good hour looking for a note from

Jimmy but no joy, so I left one myself: '*Jimmy. Meet you here four o'clock this afternoon. Sid*'.

After enjoying Lindisfarne, Groundhogs and the incredible Rory Gallagher, I returned to the info tent but there was still no sign of Jimmy. Maybe I'd see him at the train station the next day.

That hot Sunday afternoon, the crowd was full of anticipation for the looming performance of The Faces, and particularly their singer Rod Stewart. I knew nothing about them but pretended to my neighbours that I was excited, who all seemed to be big fans. They came on just as the sun was setting, Rod Stewart splendiferous in a pink satin suit and his soon to be famous feathered hairstyle. I may have come to see Mott, but Rod and the Faces set at Weeley was written into my top ten life changing gigs. I was mesmerised by the tunes, the look and Ronnie Wood's guitar. They finished with Rod telling the ecstatic crowd, "This is our new single!", and the world heard Maggie May for the first time.

They were followed by the main headliners T. Rex. I felt sorry for Marc Bolan, who was loudly booed by the crowd who regarded him as a sell-out for commercialising Tyrannosaurus Rex. I loved T.Rex and still do. Besides, Jimmy and I used to sing about Chelsea on the 'Shed' end to the tune of *Hot Love*. The music continued right through to 9.39am on the bank holiday Monday morning, when it decided to rain.

I slept through the night only waking when the band Stray let off some cheap looking fireworks, a precursor to the spectacular displays you now get after the headline acts on the Pyramid stage at Glastonbury.

I'd had enough and joined the exodus to the train station looking out for Jimmy, but there was no sign of him. There was a queue of thousands, and I managed to get on the third train to Liverpool Street. I sat looking out at the passing Essex countryside, no Jimmy, no rucksack and no tent. I was returning to a world of shit.

16

GROUNDED FOR LIFE

MY MOTHER SMELT me before she saw me. Four days in a field, shitting in a (communal) hole in the ground and no shower. "Good God, Sid, you stink! I can smell you from here!" she hollered from the kitchen.

"I'm going straight up to have a bath. Where's Dad? Where's Mark?" I asked.

Mum hesitated for a moment. "Out," was her unusual one-word reply, she was normally very exact on where anyone was.

I lay in the bath relieved and surprised that I hadn't been confronted on arrival. I expected them to pounce on me, asking where I'd been, where was the tent, my stuff, why had I lied? The bath water turned a horrible brown colour as I tried to wash away the festival. I emptied it, refilled it and lay there thinking about Jimmy and whether we'd be rumbled. Suddenly my mum was knocking on the bathroom door. "You've been in there ages, Sid, your father's home, we need to talk to you," she confirmed, sounding worryingly stressed.

"Okay, Mum, I'll be out shortly!" I yelled and started to rehearse the list of alibis I'd thought through on the train journey home. Unfortunately, I didn't have a pen and paper to prepare a proper list, but I'd considered two situations. If they just wanted to know what happened to the tent and my gear, then simple, we were robbed by some bigger lads. If it was the worst-case scenario and Ink Bat had dropped me in it, or Jimmy's mum had spoken to my parents, then I'd tell them we were attacked by bigger lads and hitched a lift to escape and ended up at Weeley. I realised this wouldn't really work and hoped I'd come up with an inspirational lie from somewhere.

My parents were sitting next to each other on the sofa in the living room. This was very unusual as my father always sat in 'his' armchair. He gestured for me to sit in 'his' chair, a worrying first. He looked more stressed than usual, if that were possible, and my mum looked terrible. She had obviously been crying, she looked like she hadn't slept for days. This was not good. Fucking Ink Bat had obviously dropped me in it. Or maybe something terrible had happened to Jimmy.

I swallowed hard and started to speak, "Our tent was-"

"Your brother has gone," my father stated with a slight crack of emotion in his voice, interrupting me before I could start my excuses.

"Mark, where's he gone?" I asked, taken aback.

"We don't know," he confirmed, and with that my mother burst in uncontrollable tears. I sat there totally confused as my father handed my mum his hanky before continuing. "We don't know, Sid, he's left home."

"Left home…when? Why?" I stuttered. My mum got up and fled the room, wailing like a banshee.

My father leaned forward, cleared his throat, before whispering, "I threw him out on Saturday."

I was dumbstruck.

"I had to throw him out," he repeated.

"Why, Dad?" I mumbled, now quite concerned.

"We found a letter, your brother is..." He could hardly speak and started to cough.

"A letter, Dad?" I queried.

After a pause he looked at the bay window and spoke in a matter-of-fact voice. "Your brother is a queer, Sid, I had to throw him out." With the revelation hanging in the air, he got up and went to the kitchen to console my still wailing mother.

I sat on the sofa trying to compute what I'd just heard. There had been a lot of friction between them of late, which I'd quite enjoyed, particularly as it meant I was under the radar. I just about knew what 'queer' meant, as it was thrown about in the school playground like confetti. The word 'gay' hadn't come into the English language as yet. I wasn't certain why Mark had to be thrown out, but I wasn't too bothered on two counts. First, this couldn't have happened at a better time and secondly, I'd get his much bigger bedroom. I ran upstairs to see if he'd left his stereo but alas, where ever he'd gone he'd taken it with him.

I wasn't fond of Mark, I just found him annoying, maybe it was the age gap of six years. Like my father, he had no interest in sport, but he did introduce me to proper music. It began to dawn on me that after all my worrying, it was my brother that had been grounded for life!

I sat on his bed contemplating life as an only child when I suddenly thought of Jimmy. *Shit, I'd better phone and make sure he's ok.* I crept into my parents' bedroom and phoned Jimmy from their extension but there was no answer.

I spent the rest of the afternoon moving my stuff into Mark's room without a trace of guilt. I was interrupted just before tea-time by a knock on the door and my dad yelling up to me. "Sid, it's your mate for you!"

"Jimmy!" I blurted out and ran down the stairs. To my horror Ink Bat was standing there with that stupid smirk on his face. "What the fuck do you want?" I moaned, disappointed that it wasn't my best mate.

"You're still alive then," he stated is his usual sarcastic manor.

"What do you want?" I ushered him into the front garden out of earshot of my parents.

"You heard about Jimmy?" he asked.

"No, I lost him in a fucking riot on Friday, I haven't seen or heard from him since."

"He's in Colchester hospital," he stated.

"What?" I croaked.

"Rumour is he's badly injured, lost an eye apparently," Ink Bat confirmed.

I stood there in a state of panic.

"See you at school next week!" Ink Bat shouted, as he disappeared on his bike.

17

CYCLOPS

RETURNING TO SCHOOL after the long summer holidays was always the worst day of the year. There was the homework that you had seven weeks to do, but hadn't bothered, then there was the new form teacher, who was always more sadistic than the previous one. The playground was awash with two rumours: First, our form had Mr. Foster, aka the Grim Reaper. This was terrible news, a year of purgatory beckoned. Secondly, and more worrying, were the rumours about Jimmy. Some talked of a fractured skull and brain damage, Ink Bat claimed he was blind! This was turning into the worst morning ever.

Despite seven weeks of tittle-tattle to catch up with, the classroom fell silent as the Grim Reaper, Mr Foster, entered. Years later, I likened him to the Raptor from *Jurassic Park* as they shared the same facial features and aggression. He prowled round the class glaring at us with total disdain. Suddenly, he stopped by the class psychopath Evans and gestured for him to swap seats with a boy at the front, by his desk. He made a frightening hissing sound as he breathed out. We later discovered this was due to a piece of shrapnel that had pierced his lung during the Second World War.

He moved slowly around the nervous pupils, giving us the thousand-yard stare, but stopped just behind Evans, where he cuffed the back of his shaven head really hard.

"Argggh sir, I ain't done nothing sir!" Gary Evans yelped.

"That's not for what you've done, Evans, that's for what you might be thinking of doing!" the Grim Reaper bellowed.

This was going to be a very long year.

* * *

Just as we settled down to geography, in our second lesson of the day, Mr. Groves, aka Peanut, was interrupted by Mrs. Jepson, aka Big Tits Jepson. She whispered in his ear as he was telling us about rainfall in El Salvador, which was really useful to a class of herberts who were lucky if they'd ever travelled further than Margate.

"Levinson," Peanut exclaimed, looking for me among the bored faces.

"Sir," I said and raised my hand in total shock at this intervention.

"Could you step outside with Mrs. Jepson please?" He nodded to the door.

I followed her down the corridor to the welfare office, without a word being uttered. She opened the door and there sitting at her desk was Jimmy and his mum. Jimmy was wearing an eye patch!

"I'll leave you to it, Mrs. Faulkner."

Jimmy's mum gestured to me to sit in an adjacent chair. I couldn't bring myself to look at Jimmy's bruised and battered face. "Jimmy's told me everything, Sid, about where you went, he's blind in his right eye," she confirmed matter-of-factly.

I didn't know what to say or where to look.

"You will have to make a statement to the police, there will probably be a court case."

I felt like I might vomit there and then. "How long will you be blind in that eye, Jimmy?" I mumbled.

"Forever, Sid, he's lost it," his mum confirmed.

I was in shock, I looked at poor Jimmy. "What happened, Jimmy? I saw the Hells Angel throw you to the ground and then all hell broke loose. I saw him getting attacked then I spent the weekend looking for you," I ranted.

"He's dead, the fucker's dead," Jimmy spoke for the first time.

"Language, Jimmy," his mum intervened.

"Dead," I reflected. "I saw him…a bloke hit him with a machete!" I cried, realising I'd witnessed a murder.

"The cunt deserved it." Jimmy sounded like Jimmy again.

"Jimmy!" his mum yelled.

"The bastard threw me onto a tent peg, ruptured my eye socket."

We sat in silence for a few minutes. "What will happen now, Alice?" I mumbled.

"We're not sure, Sid, the police will be in touch. I suppose, we haven't mentioned your name as yet, but you are a witness. We've been advised by Uncle Peter to sue the Weeley council or the Roundtable, but it won't bring Jimmy's eye back."

"Will I have to tell my parents?" I asked guiltily.

"That's up to you, Sid, but maybe you've told enough fibs already. They will want to know what happened to Jimmy won't they. What's the worst that can happen apart from being grounded for a while."

I liked the way she described my deception as a 'fib'. I thought about my father going ape shit and then realised I'd have to come up with a good story (fib) at Scouts the next night regarding the tent and equipment.

"Ink Bat will drop you in it anyway," Jimmy interrupted.

"Anyway, Sid, we popped in to see the headmaster and explain what happened, so thought we'd take the opportunity to see you. I know I can't lock him up, so I've explained that if he wants to go to football or concerts, whatever, just tell me where and I won't stop him," Jimmy's mum said.

This was an amazing response, one my parents would never have agreed to.

As I grew older, I realised that Alice was just a fantastic person and I adopted her approach when my own kids started to stretch their wings.

* * *

I buried my head of course. I never said a thing about what happened, except that Jimmy had had an accident. To be honest, I could have told them an alien stole his eyeball and they would have just nodded, they were so consumed in the business with my brother.

I didn't go to Scouts on Friday, I told my parents I didn't feel well and got away with it. In hindsight, this was a big mistake. There was a knock on the door the next afternoon, my mum was having a lie down, my father was doing some paperwork. He was always doing paperwork or cleaning his car.

"Get that, Sid!" he yelled from the dining room that doubled as his home office.

I opened the door and to my horror there stood my Scout leader 'Skipper' Ron.

"Good afternoon, Sid, I've come to collect the tent and equipment," he said, polite but firm.

I could feel my face burning up. "Didn't Ink...I mean Michael tell you what happened?" I stammered.

"Michael told me you took the tent etcetera to a music festival. I need to speak to your parents, Sid, do they know about all this?" He gave me an icy stare.

I felt dizzy and for a moment thought the game was up and I'd just have to man up and tell the truth, but I'd grown up over the Weeley weekend, there and then I played my ace card. "No, they don't, Skipper, I haven't told them anything about anything." This ambiguous statement stopped him dead in his tracks.

"I'm sorry?" He frowned, questioning exactly what I meant.

"I haven't told my dad about, you know, anything."

At that moment my father came to the door. "Skipper Ron, what a nice surprise! Come in."

My father shook his hand.

"It's okay, Mr. Levinson, I was just making sure Sid was okay after his camping adventures. I'll be on my way, see you next Friday, Sid."

And he was gone.

* * *

Two weeks later and my parents were still none the wiser about my weekend away. The whole campaign of deception to see Mott the Hoople had been worthwhile, save for Jimmy's life changing injury, of course. To be honest if I'd confessed, they'd have probably just shrugged. They were still full of grief over my 'queer' brother, whom I didn't miss at all.

I'd invested the last of my pocket money on Mott's second album, *Mad Shadows,* and the Melody Maker, which sadly didn't mention them in their review of the Weeley festival. There was however a lot of coverage about the trouble, with a sub headline of '*Hells Angel Murdered at Last Ever Non-Stop Music Festival*'. I wondered how the police enquiries were getting on. The government had acted immediately after the event and proposed a law stating that there had to be a curfew between midnight and midday at future festivals.

I was completely hooked, despite the discomfort, and saw an ad for a charity concert at the Oval cricket ground in a couple of Saturday's time. There was an incredible line up, including The Who, The Faces and Mott the Hoople! It was to run 11am- 9.30pm, so I'd see Mott at a civilised time. I had to go, but Jimmy was still recovering, and I had no money left. I asked Smithy and Perry, but they were skint as well. It was a pricey £1.25 a ticket. I knew I had to go though, so I started a very small list. *1) What to tell my parents 2) Money.*

Number one was easy, I'd tell my parents I was spending the day at Jimmy's, helping him catch up on homework. The money bit was more complicated, and I felt terribly guilty taking the odd sixpence out of the holiday jar.

In the meantime, Jimmy returned to school and faced some unmerciful teasing. Terry O'Neill had grabbed him by the collar on the playground to say, "Oi, Cyclops! Make sure you keep away from my sister or I'll sort you out once and for all."

Ink Bat was now excommunicated from the Third Tree Club, after squealing on us to Skipper Ron.

I managed to steal enough sixpence pieces to get to the Oval. It remains right up there as one of the best days of my life. The Who were out of this world, Keith Moon was resplendent in cricket whites and pads. *Maggie May* was high in the charts and Rod oozed confidence. Mott were only on for half an hour but were magnificent. I decided I had to get to one of their own gigs as quickly as possible.

I got into a bit of bother with my father when I rolled in at 11pm. It turns out my mum phoned Jimmy's house at teatime. Alice realised I was up to no good and covered for me, explaining she'd give me tea and may let me sleep over. God bless her. I told my father I wanted to come home because I missed Mark, which was total bollocks.

18

THE DARK AGES

(1972)

I DON'T REMEMBER my fifteenth birthday. I'm sure my mum would have made a cake, but I recall everything changing for my peers and me around this time. Our bodies were full of raging hormones and testosterone. Girls replaced footy and music as our obsession and the real world of work was on the near horizon. I was uncertain about everything, particularly girls.

Whilst my body developed at a rate of knots so did my shyness. Jimmy, on the other hand, discovered that his newly fitted glass eye was like a magnet to the ladies, word was out that he'd lost his virginity on a half term trip to Walton-on-the-Naze! Over the year, Smithy and Perry would both become real men, I wouldn't. These were my dark ages and they seemed to last forever. Jimmy would accompany me to football now and again, but the gang had been truly corrupted by the fairer sex. Looking back, going to a single sex school did me no favours and maybe the Mark issue had an effect on my self-confidence.

My world took a further knock when Jimmy got into the local shithole school on medical grounds, rather than the shithole two buses away. This was a huge setback to me and the start of a very difficult time. I was supposed to be taking schoolwork more seriously, O-level exams were only a year away, but a combination of apathy on my part and my parent's energy elsewhere sent me on a downward spiral.

Jimmy and Smithy now had girlfriends, Perry had discovered marijuana and Ink Bat was persona non grata. I had no real friends at school at this time, so I lived in my own world, a world of sport and music, though what I really wanted was a girlfriend.

At the end of February half term, I'd not done a jot of the coursework I was meant to complete for my mocks. I decided to throw a sickie, which normally wouldn't work but since my brother left, I could get away with a lot more. I feigned a raging headache for a couple of days and then a sore throat.

I listened to music all day on my parents new stereo in the living room. Mainly Led Zep *III* and The Faces *Every Picture Tells a Story,* both of which I bought with the HMV vouchers I'd got from Christmas. It wasn't worth going back to school for Thursday and Friday, so I convinced my parents I'd get stuck into my coursework, which was obviously not going to happen. I got my mum to write the obligatory 'Reason for Absence' letter and recovered sufficiently to get to Chelsea with Jimmy on what was his first day out since the Weeley incident.

Monday came, and I sat on the bus to school staring at the teeming rain and thought, '*Fuck it, I'm taking the day off*'.

I took the whole week off, forging a note explaining I had tonsillitis , even though I'd had them out as a baby. I'd get up, get my uniform on, go for a walk and then return after my parents left for work. After a time, I got bored, so I started to go up west, see a movie, look round record shops. This truancy went on for five weeks!

I knew the game was up when I got home from one of my jaunts. My parents were sitting together on the sofa, exactly as they did when they told me Mark had gone. I half listened to them carrying on about my future, "What if you don't get any O-levels? What have you been doing all day every day?"

I just sat there trying to think what I could possibly say to the headmaster to lessen the inevitable caning I'd get in the morning.

I lay in bed plotting and planning, I started to make a list of possible reasons. I started with the truth. *I just hate school.* I realised that this was not going to work, so started to come up with some fibs.

1) I was threatened by bullies.

This could work but I might crack when I was inevitably tortured for the names of the perpetrators.

2) I was bullied on the bus by boys from another school.

This could also work but may start a war if the headmaster contacts his counterpart from St John's. I lay there trying to reach deep into the depths of deviousness, deviousness that had got me to Weeley. Half an hour passed, I thought of everything from diseases to alien abduction. Then the moment of brilliance arrived. Racism!

3) Antisemitism from classmates, maybe a teacher.

I had a Welsh teacher that I had a bad feeling about, just something he'd said, his manner. It would be his word against mine. This was wrong on many levels, but it might just put the headmaster on the back foot.

* * *

My father drove me to school the next morning in total silence. What a disappointment his boys were to him. One a queer, the other a truant. He dropped me at the staff car park and made sure I went straight in for my 9.30am appointment with the devil.

I knocked on the headmaster's door for the first time since I arrived at this little corner of hell four years previously.

"Come!" he roared, sounding like he was having a bad morning.

I breathed in and opened the door to Satan's lair. He sat in a fine leather upholstered swivel chair, there were two more basic chairs opposite, I was offered neither.

"You must be Levinson?" he queried.

The 'Führer' now knew my name, was this a badge of honour or disgrace?

"Yes, sir," I replied.

He shuffled some papers and then looked at my very thin file. "So, you have lied to your parents and you have lied to us, haven't you, boy?" he said, whilst studying the lack of academic progress of the boy who stood before him.

"Yes, sir," I whispered.

"I don't like liars," he growled.

I noticed the cane resting against the radiator, it looked horribly flexible. At this moment I briefly thought of the film *Kes* and the infamous caning scene, when the innocent boy delivering a message gets six of the best. I wasn't innocent, of course.

"Why the lies, boy?" He stood up, blocking out all the early spring sunlight that had been illuminating me. He was massive, his hands enormous as they clutched the desk in front of him. He looked down at the file and then back at me. "Five weeks, Levinson. A litany of lies, why, boy?"

I thought of my list, I'd added a last-minute number 5 whilst in the car. Jimmy's accident, witnessing a murder, that would do it. In hindsight, it probably would have worked. Maybe a modern psychologist would have agreed it was the underlying reason for my absence and deceit, but at the last second, I thought of Ink Bat's betrayal. I couldn't bring Jimmy into this, and besides, the less said about the 'monster' Hells Angel the better. I'd not heard a word from the Essex constabulary. I was about to shrug and say, '*I don't know, sir*' and take my punishment, when one of those thoughts entered my head from nowhere.

My mouth had to work quickly as the headmaster reached for the cane, I didn't have time to analyse the thought, I either had to forget it or put it out there unfiltered. I did the latter, "I had some trouble, sir." I paused, this was mad, I should forget it and just shrug like a fifteen-year-old.

"Trouble?" he barked. "What kind of trouble?"

I answered but so quietly it was inaudible.

"Speak up boy, I can't hear you!" He was flexing the weapon and moving round the desk.

"Down below, sir, I had a pain, sir." I stopped him in his tracks. He put the cane on the desk and seemed lost for words.

There was a pause that seem to last forever before he continued. "What do you mean down below, boy?"

"I had a terrible pain down below in my testicles, sir." It was as if I'd been taken over by a superior being. The word 'testicles' seemed to be an even greater weapon than his cane. He looked stressed and confused.

"Pain...pain," he stuttered, "did you go to the doctor? Did you tell your parents?"

"No, sir, I was too embarrassed, too scared."

"And are you okay now, boy?"

"Yes, sir, the pain and swelling went about a week ago but because I'd been too embarrassed to tell anyone, I didn't know what to do."

He put the cane back by the radiator and sat down again. I suppose faced with a young lad talking about testicles, he decided to get me out of his life as quickly as possible. He scribbled what looked like a prescription, then addressed me. "Okay, Levinson, no more lies. I suggest you go to the doctor just in case, in the meantime I've written this memo to Mr. Banks. You're to show him your coursework every Friday lunchtime until you take your mocks."

And that was it, I was a free man. No cane. No punishment at all really. Yes, I'd have to knuckle down a bit, but I'd come out of things pretty much unscathed, yet again.

* * *

Unsurprisingly, my mocks were a disaster. The Grim Reaper unfortunately had the job of informing each of his form how they got on. "This isn't just a wakeup call, Levinson, it's a cold shower, boy. This is what happens when you decide not to bother coming to school."

I was pretty sure the headmaster would have kept the 'down below' details to himself. I went home practicing my apologies to my parents, I'd have two hours home alone before they returned home from work. I'd play some Sabbath and Purple to take my mind off the latest humiliation.

Summer was looming, I'd planned further one day concerts at the Oval, Hyde Park and the Crystal Palace bowl, wherever that was. A couple more months at school and I'd be able to enjoy my last long summer holiday, as I doubted I'd be welcome in the sixth form.

I threw my jacket over the bannister and my bag at the bottom of the stairs, got myself a glass of cream soda and entered the living room. I saw the records, three of them, before I saw him.

"Hope you like them, Sid," my brother said, reclining on the sofa.

"Wow! Atomic Rooster, Groundhogs, Pink Floyd." I didn't know whether to study these albums or my brother.

"Should keep you going," he said smiling.

"What are you doing here, Mark? Dad will..."

"I'm not stopping, just came to pick something up, still got my key. Also, I've got something else for you."

He threw an envelope onto the table. I opened it, there were two tickets inside. I studied them in fine detail.

"You and me, Sid, two weeks tonight. You'll need an alibi, sure you can sort it, we can meet outside WHSmith at Kings Cross station, six o'clock."

I nodded, still studying the ticket. Alice Cooper at Wembley Pool, plus support. "This is brilliant Mark. I saw him on the Old Grey Whistle Test, I read he bites the heads off live chickens!"

"Apparently, Sid, should be a great night. I've heard the support group are amazing, they're called Roxy Music."

"That's brilliant , Mark! Where are you living now?" I ventured.

"Limehouse, near the river. How's Dad?" he asked.

"Dad's Dad, always at work thank god." We both laughed, I wondered why he didn't ask about Mum. "Mum worries about you," I added.

"I know, Sid, I speak to her every day."

"Do you?" I was surprised.

"Yeah, she calls me from work. Don't tell Dad."

"Where you working then, Mark?"

"I'm working at Tate and Lyle, the sugar people, on the Thames. It's an office job, boring really."

He was gone a few minutes later. The 'queer' thing never came up and suddenly, for the first time I could remember, I liked him. Alice Cooper, School's Out. I couldn't wait.

19

STARMAN

THE CONCERT WAS beyond my wildest dreams. Roxy
Music were like nothing I'd seen or heard. I fell in love with
Eno, though a few years later I fell out of love with him.
Alice Cooper was everything he was hyped up to be, pure
heavy metal theatre. Balloons were burst over the audience,
containing thousands of maggots! However, my brother
hated it and left halfway through, meeting me outside
afterwards. I recall my dad calling Mark a drama queen, I
was beginning to understand why.

I'd told my parents I was going to football with Smithy
but the next day, Mum waited till my father went up for his
Thursday night bath (we had a rota) and whispered, "How
was Mark? Did you enjoy yourselves?"

"He told you then, Mum?"

"Yes," she smiled.

"It was brilliant, Mum!" I said enthusiastically.

"Well, hopefully he'll take you out again soon."

"I hope so, he said he'd take me somewhere in the
summer holidays."

My mum was obviously as delighted with this secret family interaction as I was.

But sadly, I wasn't to see my brother for another seven years.

* * *

I realised something was up as my mum was very quiet for the next couple of weeks. Then one Saturday, they had a blazing row up in their bedroom. It turned out that when Mark had let himself in the afternoon, he brought the records for me, he had rifled through my father's wardrobe. Knowing he kept a shoebox stuffed with cash, Mark had helped himself.

An air-mail letter arrived from America that morning from Mark. As soon as they'd read it my father had run upstairs, having realised how Mark had paid for the flight. It turned out, I wasn't the only devious one in the family.

When my mum composed herself, she told me my brother had got himself a job in California. "Your father has driven my boy to the other side of the world!" she yelled.

She sobbed for two days non-stop.

* * *

And then it happened, the second coming. The first Thursday in July, my last week before my last long summer break. I'd resigned myself to the fact that I'd not be going on to sixth form. I didn't really know what an abusive relationship was at this age, in fact, I didn't know what any kind of relationship was. But every Thursday, from the age of ten up to its dying embers in the late nineties, I sat and watched *Top of the Pops* religiously. And like an abusive relationship, you had to put up with a lot of shit, but now and again you'd see something wonderful, which would keep you coming back. This particular Thursday evening, I saw something so mind blowing, so jaw dropping, it literally changed my life and the lives of many others.

The spikey orange hair, the sexually ambiguous costume, the blue guitar. David Bowie, aka Ziggy Stardust, and his Spiders from Mars invaded my living room and my mind. The wink, the arm around the spandex-clad blonde guitar god Mick Ronson, was too much for my parents, who fled the room shaking their heads asking if this was a boy or a girl and mumbling various expletives.

This was the pre-video age. There were only two types of kids at school the next day, those who had seen *Top of the Pops* and those who hadn't. Half the class were in conversation about the three minutes that would change our world forever. Everyone was plotting and planning to get to their local record shop that weekend. When did the album come out? What else had they done? Wasn't that the same David Bowie who'd had a hit with 'Space Oddity' a few years earlier? Even the class psycho Gary Evans waxed lyrical about the Starman.

Since Jimmy had gone girl mad, I'd hardly seen him, so I had befriended a lad who sat behind me. For some strange reason he never had a nickname, John Lester was simply known as John Lester. He read the *Melody Maker* and liked Mott the Hoople, so he was alright by me. He'd not only seen *Top of the Pops*, he actually had information about concerts, influences and the like.

We met up numerous times during the summer and went to a few one-day concerts together. We got seriously lost trying to find the Crystal Palace bowl and slipped under a fence just in time to see Roxy Music take the stage. We also went to the Oval twice and marvelled at the likes of ELP and Frank Zappa, but most of our conversation centered around David Bowie and when we would actually see him. John got me into Lou Reed and the Velvet Underground, having read what an influence they were on our hero.

Sadly, Mott the Hoople had been side-lined, I'd heard rumours they were splitting up, but by now we had tickets for our first proper indoor gig and that's all I thought about. At the time I didn't know enough about Lou Reed to realise he was already a legendary figure. He was from New York and was friends with Andy Warhol. That was enough for this fifteen-year-old.

We were mesmerised by his appearance at the Sundown Edmonton, dressed all in black with a red guitar. The music was deafeningly loud. We realised indoor gigs were the way forward.

A few months later half the school had tickets to see Ziggy Stardust and the Spiders from Mars at Earl's Court. Everything else was unimportant, family, news, exams. Bowie was my all-consuming passion and my devotion was about to reach another level.

* * *

I'd pretty much given up on Chelsea, as the players I worshipped were transferred and the glamorous team that won the cup in 1970 started to disintegrate. Jimmy and Smithy rarely went, except if there was bound to be a lot of trouble. We rarely socialised around this period but saw each other every weekday evening, as we were all paper boys delivering the *Evening Standard,* ironically for the very same newsagent where Jimmy had honed his shoplifting skills! I earnt a pound for a round that took about two hours to complete.

For some reason, I had one extra paper on a filthy wet cold winter evening, so I took it home for my mum to do the crossword. Once completed, she handed the paper to me saying, "There's a bit about your David Bowie here."

I grabbed the paper and there was a small piece about the Starman giving Mott the Hoople one of his songs because he'd heard they were about to split up and he was a fan. I was dumbstruck. My hero was a fan of my heroes! What were the chances.

A few weeks later, Mott the Hoople appeared on *Top of the Pops* all glammed up performing '*All the Young Dudes*', a week later it entered the top ten. Along with Chelsea winning the FA cup, this was the most thrilling thing that had happened to me. Even now, it's right up there with the birth of my children and killing Roland, my first kill (sort of).

And then it happened! May 12th, 1973, we, eight of us from school, went to see him in the flesh. Right in the middle of our exams. I led the pack to Earls Court as I knew the area well due to my regular trips to Chelsea. We all dressed up, and to our amazement Gary 'Psycho' Evans turned up with a full 'Aladdin Sane' face.

We had seats, but the arena was complete pandemonium as the Spiders took to the stage, with thousands of kids rushing towards the front. And then he was there, under a spotlight, the second coming, a 'leper messiah'. I'd not known a moment so exquisite before or since. I'd seen Ziggy, whatever happened after that wouldn't matter.

What happened, is that I completely fucked up my exams. I was lost in my own world. If I left school without a job, so what? I'd seen the main man and, besides which, Mott the Hoople were now in the first division. They'd gone from being Millwall to becoming the Chelsea of bands. Not consistent enough to be Led Zep but on their day, just brilliant.

* * *

All this, of course, did nothing to help me in my exams. Looking back, it was probably a combination of my obsession with Bowie and Mott, along with being sent to a shithole (two buses away), plus the strange goings on at home. Consequently, at the age of sixteen, my parents resigned themselves to me leaving compulsory education and in early July I enjoyed my last day at school.

Mr. Foster, the Grim Reaper, was now assistant head. All the leavers had to go and have a one-to-one motivational lecture from him before we entered the big wide adult world of work. We sat on gym benches that were housed in the corridor outside his office, we were called in in alphabetical order.

"Levinson!" the Grim Reaper bellowed, beckoning me into his lair.

I couldn't recall him doing anything but bellow. I'd never heard him talk normally.

He pointed towards the chair opposite him and I was taken aback when he said in a whisper, "Let's have a look at this." He perused a sheet of A4 paper with my exam results on it, shaking his head as he trolled through the disappointing information. "Well, Levinson, you've completely wasted your time here and you'll no doubt go away and waste the rest of your life."

I sat and shrugged, waiting for the motivational follow-up, but it didn't come. The A to D leavers all conformed to the same template. I made a mental list: A review of the exam results (I'd just had that), a brief discussion about possible career paths and then a motivational concluding speech about having the ability to achieve anything with hard work. Lastly, a firm handshake and a 'Good luck boy'. I had to admit his summary of my results was harsh, but accurate.

I waited for him to continue with the career bit and looked forward to telling him I'd got a job in a carpet warehouse. I'd decided I wouldn't inform him my uncle got me the job. He looked at me for what seemed an age, his left cheek twitching almost uncontrollably.

"Your parents must be very disappointed in you, Levinson," he finally said.

I just shrugged again.

"Given you people normally excel at school."

The irony of this sentence didn't resonate with me at the time, I just wanted to get to the handshake and join my peers in a mass burning of our uniforms in the centre circle of the rugby pitch. I was to return to his words many times in the years that followed, even if he didn't.

"I've got a job, sir," I muttered, but he didn't seem to hear me. His face was bright red and his twitch getting rapidly worse.

"Just piss off, Levinson, just piss off to your dead-end job!" Mr. Foster was shouting again.

"Sir?" I mumbled in surprise.

"Unless you are telling me you're going to be a doctor or a lawyer or something worthwhile, just fuck off to Deadsville!" He was screaming now.

"Deadsville?" I repeated, wondering if this was a real place and when I was going to get the motivational speech… or was this it? I was confused and shocked by the swearing. "It's a carpet warehouse sir. My job."

He stared at me as if I'd insulted him, the veins in his shaven head looked like they might explode. "Daddy's," he snarled after a moment's pause.

"Sorry, sir?"

"I presume it's Daddy's carpet store."

"No, sir, I went for an interview sir," I lied.

"What did they ask you? Your name, boy?"

"No, it was hard, sir, they asked me difficult questions," I lied again.

"Difficult questions, to lug carpet around?" he quipped sarcastically.

"It's hard work sir," I insisted.

"Hard work, Levinson, what the hell do you know about hard work boy?!"

"It's hard on the shoulders sir," I replied.

At which he took his jacket off, flinging it at the coat hook on the back of the door. I turned and saw it miss and end up in a crumpled heap on the floor. "Hard on your poor shoulders," he confirmed in his narky way. "I'll show you some hard work on the shoulders," he continued, as he started to loosen and then remove his red tie.

None of this was on the mental list I made after we asked the A to D's what Foster had asked. He threw his tie on the floor and started to undo his shirt buttons. This was worrying, I started to plan my rush for the door. He unbuttoned his shirt before removing it completely and dropping it on top of his tie. I was about to leg it out of his office, down the corridor and into my post-compulsory education future, uncertain as it was, when I noticed his right shoulder.

"Yes, Levinson, quite a sight isn't it? Now you know why I always hit you imbeciles with my left hand."

There was a massive dent where his shoulder blade should be. It looked revolting.

"1942, Sicily, nineteen-years-old, hardly got ashore when the shell from a nine-millimetre canon got me. That was it, my war over before it began. I was one of the lucky ones." He was standing with his hands clasping the edge of his desk, he seemed quite controlled as he described the incident. I obviously regretted mentioning shoulders, but who was to know? He studied me for what seemed an eternity, he released his grip on the desk and made his way round towards me. I stood, expecting the final handshake.

The wound looked even more angry as he placed his lethal left hand on my shoulder. "So, Levinson, you take good care carrying those carpets won't you."

"Yes, sir," I stuttered, feeling like a complete idiot. He tightened his grip, his impossibly spindly fingers seemed to reach inside my skin.

"You're a spineless useless cretin, Levinson, you all are, to think we fought a fucking war for you useless, spineless idiots. Just piss off, Levinson!" He was shouting again, but he repeated his vice-like grip and I slunk towards the door without that good luck handshake.

I was about to exit when he continued. "There were fourteen of us got off that landing craft, all under twenty-one-years old. I was the lucky one, that shell saved my life." He turned and took a sip of water, he was sweating. "Three were gunned down within a few feet of me, the other nine made it to within a few feet of the German pill box only to get burnt alive by a flame thrower. Do you know what a flame thrower is Levinson?" he growled.

My hand was on the doorknob. "Yes, sir." I'd seen them in the movies.

"Sometimes when I'm calling the register, I imagine I have a flame thrower and wish I could change the cretinous blank expressions on your gormless faces and incinerate the lot of you little fuckers!"

He was now shouting so loud I was sure the L to Zs (Young was the last name on the register) waiting in the corridor could hear.

"Probably a sign I need to retire, but oh how I'd like to slaughter a class full of you ungrateful zombies before I do. Actually, you'd do, Levinson. I'd be doing you and the human race a favour if I just set fire to you. What fucking contribution are you likely to make to mankind?!"

He was now screaming at me. He started to move towards me, I can still recall his wild manic stare, his face now crimson, his bare torso. I started to turn the knob.

"I doubt your parents would be bothered and I'm sure the carpet industry would survive! Shall I, Levinson? Should I burn you alive, Levinson?" He grabbed me before I could make my escape, he slapped me round the head a couple of times before I heard a stifled cry. He collapsed at my feet clutching first his left arm and then his chest. His eyes stared up at me, he was trying to tell me something, I crouched down beside him. "Ambulance," he whispered. "Call an ambulance, Levinson. Please," he rasped.

I stood and stared at him as his life ebbed away, it seems ironic that the last thing he ever saw was my moronic expression. I managed to get the door open and shout for help, the headmaster looked confused as to why his dead assistant was semi-naked. I concocted a story that he just chased me around the office disrobing. It was a double whammy. Not only was the Grim Reaper dead, but now his legacy would be one of utter disgrace.

To this day he's known to all that survived that shithole (two buses away) as Foster the 'nonce'.

I'd now seen two dead bodies in a year, I wasn't at all bothered about either of them.

20

THE DEATH OF THE CARPET INDUSTRY AND FURTHER HUMILIATIONS

(1973)

MY CONTRIBUTION TO the carpet industry lasted all of three weeks. I turned up at the warehouse five minutes early on the last Friday of the month, excited about payday, having started three weeks earlier. My colleague Mitch, who started the same day, was sitting against the closed doors smoking a spliff.

"What's up, Mitch?" I asked.

"Check the padlock." He nodded towards the reception door, this was first time I'd seen it.

"That's new," I confirmed.

He casually got to his feet and beckoned me to follow him. We made our way round the back of the building where there was a grilled vent. Mitch pointed to it and I climbed onto a bricked-up window ledge and peered through. The warehouse was completely empty, even the fire extinguishers had gone.

"Fucking hell!" I exclaimed.

"I spoke to the security guy at the main gate of the industrial estate, he reckons two artic lorries came last night and emptied the place."

"But it's pay day," I moaned. "I didn't expect this to be a job for life but at least one pay packet would have been nice."

My uncle had got me the job because the owner of Exotic Carpets, Mad Mac, was his best mate. Mad Mac was called Mad Mac because his name was Mackenzie and he was mad. As mad as he was, he didn't seem the kind of man who would not pay our wages. We sat against the padlocked doors in the vain hope he'd turn up and tell us he had simply moved factory. After an hour we were about to head home, when a royal blue Rolls Royce pulled up.

The driver wound his window down and beckoned us over. "Mad Mac has done a midnight bunk," he confirmed. "I think the tax man was on his case. Anyway, he popped by my office last night and left these envelopes, presumably for you two."

We looked at the brown envelopes, our names were on them and inside was three weeks wages in cash.

"I suppose you two herberts want a new job, follow me."

We ran after the roller as it wound its way to the other side of the industrial estate. The car stopped in a reserved parking bay, there was a huge neon sign stretching along the two-story building, '*BRIMSTONE ENTERPRISES HOUSE*'.

The driver got out, he was a giant of a man, he gestured to us to follow him into the building.

"Good morning, Mr. Brimstone," the receptionist smiled. She was stunning.

He led us into a huge warehouse space containing rows of machines. "Space Invader machines, they're the future, every pub in the country will want one. I need a couple of fit young lads like you two to help with deliveries, same wages as Mad Mac paid you. You can start now."

The carpet industry was history, we now were helping to spread the invasion of the Space Invaders.

* * *

That bizarre last day at school wasn't actually my last. I had to go back two days later to meet the headmaster and the school secretary to go over the unsavoury demise of the Grim Reaper. I told them how Mr. Foster seemed agitated when I entered his office, he ranted incoherently about the war and how he wanted to burn us alive with a flame thrower. I then embellished the story by describing how he started to get undressed and chase me round the desk, before he collapsed.

The headmaster must have recalled our previous meeting regarding my truancy. He'd probably tried to forget the 'testicles' business and clearly was uneasy with where this was heading. "So poor Mr. Foster had a heart attack, I think we can leave it there," and that was the end of that.

One dead Hells Angel and a deputy head, and no repercussions.

* * *

The job was going well but I was distracted by Lisa the receptionist. I was the only one of my friends not to have a steady girlfriend. I was totally obsessed with Lisa, she was stunning. I decided to ask her out but every time the opportunity arose, I would burn up and start sweating profusely. I began to stutter my good mornings to her, I was a quivering wreck every time I saw her.

One morning I stood outside the reception window staring at her talking on the phone, rehearsing my chat up lines for the umpteenth time, when Mitch tapped me the shoulder. "You haven't got the bottle have you," he chided me.

"What you on about?" I snapped defensively.

"You fancy her like mad don't you, Sid, but you ain't got the bottle to ask her out."

"I'll ask her out on Monday." I shrugged, realising he was spot on.

"Take a couple of these, Sid, they'll give you Dutch courage." He held out two tiny blue pills in his hand. "Speed, Sid, they will sort out your nerves, I promise you."

After a few moment's deliberation, I swallowed the amphetamines and half an hour later, I had a date!

* * *

Lisa's mum answered the door. "Hi, you must be Sid, come on in," she said. Lisa's mum was as plain as her daughter was attractive. "Go into the sitting room, Lisa won't be long. Say hi to Roger, Lisa's dad."

I slinked into the living room. "Hi, I'm Sid," I mumbled to the man of the house, who was fiddling with the volume control on the TV.

"They must all be bleeding deaf in here!" he cursed, his voice had a familiar ring to it. He turned to acknowledge me, I recognised him immediately, shell-shocked. "Well, well, well," he sniggered. "Not sure how I feel about my staff fraternising."

"Mr. Brimstone," I mumbled in surprise.

"Yes boy, Lisa is my daughter. Wherever you're taking her, I want her home by ten thirty or you're out of a job lad."

"Ten thirty, yes sir," I mumbled, realising my plans for the evening might have to be changed.

"And where are you taking my Lisa lad?"

"I...I...I was thinking of going to the cinema, but I think the film might be too long," I stammered.

"Any later than ten thirty and your P45 will be on the door mat," my boss snarled.

I just wished I'd got a couple more 'blues' off Mitch. After a couple of awkward minutes that seemed like an hour, Lisa emerged , she looked absolutely stunning.

"I've told young Sid that I expect you home by ten thirty," her dad, my boss, confirmed.

"Yes, Daddy," she sighed, as if not bothered.

I certainly was bothered and worried. We left the house in silence and once on the pavement Lisa asked what film we were going to see. Since her father's ultimatum, I'd been mulling over the logistics. Given the film would end at around 10.15pm, unless I could hire a helicopter, we wouldn't get home until least 11pm, as the cinema was two buses away. I wasn't particularly bothered about the film, but I'd heard Jimmy and Smithy were taking their girlfriends and I really wanted them to see me out with Lisa. In a few months I'd hopefully pass my driving test and then the world would be my oyster.

"It will be fine, ignore what Daddy says," she casually answered to my concerns.

"I don't think we'd make the start of the film." I checked my watch.

"Let's go for a drink then," she suggested.

"Where?" I asked, worried I might not be served.

"We could go to the Star, it's only a fifteen-minute walk. Frank the landlord is a friend of my dad, I can get served no problem," she reassured me.

* * *

I gave Lisa the money and she returned to our table with a half a lager and lime for me and a Babycham for herself. We'd barely engaged in conversation when we were interrupted by a huge brutish bloke.

"Hiya Lisa, how you doing?"

"Hello Barry," she acknowledged him warmly, "This is Sid."

It turned out this thuggish looking fella was a milkman, her milkman. Lisa invited him to join us and I sat and listened to him talk for half an hour, whilst my supposed date constantly giggled. Eventually she excused herself and made her way to the ladies.

"What car you drive then, mate?" he asked after an awkward silence.

"I've only just turned seventeen, I'm having lessons, my uncle's going to give me his Hillman Imp California," I confirmed.

"I've got a nice new shiny red Ford Capri," he boasted. "How'd you get here?" he enquired.

"Bus," I answered with embarrassment.

He leaned forward so his face was almost in mine.

"Fuck off," he growled.

"What?" I croaked, stunned.

"Fuck off out of here or I'll lump you. I'll take Lisa home in my car, mate."

"I can't, I've got to get Lisa home by ten thirty or her dad will kill me" I muttered, realising this date was going horribly wrong.

"I fucked both her older sisters and I'm going to get the hat-trick mate, so do yourself a favour or I'm going to rearrange your face."

Fortunately, or maybe unfortunately, Lisa returned at this moment and the psychopathic milkman sat back casually in his chair.

"I was just telling young Sid that I'm happy to give you both a lift back to yours in my new car," he winked at Lisa.

"That's great, Barry, what colour is it?"

"It's a Capri, a red Ford Capri," he boasted.

"Wow, did you hear that, Sid? Barry's got a red Capri." Lisa was excited.

"I know," I sulked, and then sat and listened to Barry wax lyrical about his holiday on the Costa Brava for the remainder of the date.

Barry opened the passenger door and pushed me onto the back seat, whilst gently easing Lisa into the front passenger seat. I noticed his hand brush her leg every time he changed gear. We arrived outside her home, he got out and rushed round to open the passenger door. He gave her a peck on the cheek and then as an afterthought manoeuvred the seat forward so I could clamber out. By this time Lisa was at the front door, I sidled up beside her feeling like a complete idiot.

"Maybe we can go to the cinema next week," I stammered.

But before she could answer the mad milkman interrupted. "See you soon, Lisa, give my love to your sisters!"

And that was the end of my date with the boss's daughter, but not the end of my humiliation. I made my way to the bus stop thinking about the lies I would tell my mates. I would definitely tell them I felt her breasts at the very least. Suddenly, the red Capri pulled up beside me.

"Well that went well!" Barry shouted.

"Fuck off!" I shouted. I ran off down the street as he put his foot on the throttle. I got to the bus stop, but he was waiting for me.

It was a long lonely walk home.

21

LET THEM EAT CAKE
(1974)

A COUPLE OF weeks after my humiliating first date with Lisa, I was to discover it was also my humiliating *last* date with the beautiful boss' daughter. Smithy called me and said that him and Jimmy were taking girls to a disco at the local rugby club on Saturday night and suggested I bring Lisa. Of course, I'd told the boys a pack of lies about our date and made out we were virtually inseparable. "See you there!" I optimistically confirmed, and then sat staring at the phone trying to summon up the courage to phone Lisa.

I decided I'd ask her face-to-face at work in the morning, despite having agreed not to fraternise in the workplace. When I saw her in the reception, I went bright red and walked straight past, unable to even say good morning. I found Mitch in the warehouse and asked if he had any blues on him. He told me he'd get hold of a couple by lunchtime and when he did, I washed them down with my 7Up.

The afternoon went very quickly and at five I decided to make my move. The boys would be blown away when they saw my stunning girlfriend. I marched, with pill enhanced confidence, up to the reception desk. Unusually she wasn't there. I rang the bell and waited a few minutes, reckoning she was either running an errand or abluting. After five minutes or so I assumed that Lisa had left early for some reason and stepped outside.

And there it was, parked up just a few yards away, the red Capri! I could see through the rear window two heads locked together in a passionate kiss.

I slunk off in the opposite direction thinking about viable excuses I could offer the lads for not coming to the disco.

* * *

Naturally I changed jobs, rather than face the daily humiliation of avoiding the glamorous receptionist. The saga had a lasting effect on my confidence that not even amphetamines could help with. Like my mates I passed my driving test but as I approached my eighteenth birthday, unlike my peers, I was still a virgin. Of course, they didn't know that. They assumed my one-night stand at a friend from school's party was genuine. They didn't know that the momentous occasion was a fantasy. I'd told them that the deed took place in Tony Beck's house, with the fictitious ex-captain of the school team's fictitious sister. It took the heat off me, but it didn't help in finding a proper, a real, girlfriend.

At the same time, Mott the Hoople and Chelsea were both in steep decline, Bowie had met Eno and gone weird. I'd all but stopped going to gigs and football. I'd sat and watched England go out to Poland in a World Cup qualifier and convinced myself it was my fault because I'd lied about losing my virginity.

I rarely saw my mates who were busy dating. I invented a new pretend girlfriend as an excuse not to go to the lads regular Friday night pub meets. All this and a new dead-end job, which I hated. My humiliation was complete when I crashed my Hillman Imp, my eighteenth birthday present, into a lamppost whilst daydreaming. It was a write-off and whilst I was waiting for a tow truck to come and remove the wreck, a red Capri pulled up and I could see Barry and Lisa's smiling faces staring at me.

* * *

My eighteenth birthday came and went, I was living at home with my miserable parents. I was in a gig-less, sport-less, girlfriend-less rut. Suddenly, whist watching the *News at Ten*, my luck changed!

My cousin Trevor, three years older than me, was a loose cannon. Like my father, his dad, Uncle Martin, didn't follow sport but Trevor was sport mad. Uncle Fred, who took me to my first Chelsea game, had taken Trevor and me to many a match, cricket too. Unfortunately, my father fell out with his brother, Uncle Martin, in my early teens, so we didn't really see a lot of each other.

A few weeks back, we attended a family wedding and I was surprised to see my cousin sporting a skinhead haircut and wearing a two-tone suit. He'd always had ridiculously shocking red hair and from a distance it looked like he was wearing a swimming hat. As per usual, he was in my ribs about how much he hated my football team and that he was going to Rotterdam shortly to see Spurs play.

Two weeks later I was half watching the *News at Ten* when my attention was caught by mention of a riot at the Feyenoord verses Spurs game. There was footage of absolute bedlam in the stands and one particular incident was shown in slow motion. There was a fan wielding a large knife and a policeman being pushed down some steps. The film was a bit hazy, but the guy doing the pushing had a very familiar red swimming hat.

The next day I returned home from work and my mother told me I'd received an urgent phone call from a Mr.

Van Blot, she handed me a note with his number. Mystified, I called him, and he explained he was a lawyer in Rotterdam representing my cousin. He gave me confidential instructions detailing where I'd find a spare key for my aunt and uncle's house and where Trevor had hidden some cash, which I was to bring to the lawyer's office in Rotterdam.

I drove to their house the next morning, hoping they'd be at work. I found the spare key for the backdoor under a plant pot in the garden. I'd rang the doorbell to check no one was in but nonetheless shouted out loud as I entered, just to make sure. Following my cousin's instructions, I headed straight to his bedroom and to the bedside chest, where I removed the bottom drawer. There was a metal biscuit tin that just fitted in the space behind the plinth. I removed it and placed it on the bed, taking off the lid. It was chock full of cash, I emptied it and started to count it.

Suddenly, I heard the front door downstairs open and shut, someone was in the house. I crept onto the landing and nearly had a heart attack as a hoover roared into life in the downstairs hallway. It's was their cleaner. *'How long would she be there? Do I try and escape or hide?'* I pondered.

I stuffed the cash back in the tin and surveyed the room for possible hiding places. The wardrobe looked best, it's louvered doors good for airflow and spying. I guessed she'd only be an hour or two tops. I sat in the wardrobe surrounded by Crombie coats and all kinds of skinhead fashion and recounted the cash, just over two thousand pounds. There was a small bag of weed in there as well, I'd enjoyed the odd spliff, but speed was my drug of choice, and how I wished I had some on me.

After about twenty minutes, I thought I heard talking out on the landing. Suddenly the door opened, and the cleaner came into Trevor's bedroom. I peered through the louvres, hardly daring to breathe, and watched in amazement as she sat on the bed and took off her apron and then lifted her dress over her head. She laid back just in her underwear. I guessed she was in her late thirties, I noticed she had enormous breasts. I then heard a man's voice, "I'll be with you in a minute Suzy, take off your knickers."

I recognised the voice immediately but didn't want to believe it was him. Soon after she removed her knickers, I saw my Uncle Martin enter the room completely naked and jump onto my cousin's bed, where he started to fondle his cleaner's boobs. I felt sick and excited at the same time. Excited not in a sexual way, but at the thought of future bribery possibilities. The sight of Uncle Martin's fat hairy backside going up and down was absolutely revolting. Fortunately, I only had to endure a couple of minutes as he collapsed beside 'Mrs. Mop' completely spent.

After what seemed an eternity of grunting, he sat up and told her he had to get back to work and could she clean the oven before she left.

I had to hide for another hour before it was safe to let myself out.

* * *

I met Van Blot in a coffee shop near the central station. He looked too hippy to be a lawyer and he insisted I had to try my first 'cake' with my coffee.

I don't remember the taxi ride to the prison, I was totally away with the fairies. I must have completely lost consciousness at some point, as I found myself woken by an associate of Van Blot slapping my face.

"Where's the bail money? Where's the fucking money?"

I was sitting in the back seat with this massive guy sitting next to me. "Where is it?" Van Blot repeated from the front passenger seat.

"You will get it when my cousin is free!" I shouted, realising they had rifled through my backpack.

"That is not how this works, Sid Levinson," the so-called lawyer added calmly.

"No money, no cousin," the henchman growled.

"Okay," I casually concurred. I opened the door and attempted to get out onto the adjacent car park.

I was pulled back in roughly. "Don't be stupid, Levinson, you obviously have the money back at the hotel," the thug surmised, as Van Blot ordered the driver to head back to my hotel.

Suddenly there was an almighty smash as a brick hit the front windscreen.

"What the fuck!" Van Blot shouted, as we all instantly evacuated the car. I was grabbed and bundled into a taxi, which sped off before my previous captors realised what had happened.

"You alright, Sid?" Jimmy and Smithy enquired simultaneously.

"I told you that lawyer was bent!" Jimmy shouted.

"Fucking hell lads am I pleased you turned up. Where we headin'?"

"Round the block a couple of times then back to the prison to get your cousin," Smithy confirmed.

"How so?" I asked.

"Smithy has been busy, went to the British consulate and after a couple of phone calls and a thousand quid later, we've got this." Jimmy waved an official looking piece of paper at me.

"What's that?"

"Permission for your cousin's release," Smithy chipped in, patting a hold-all.

"Got nearly a grand left," he added.

"Should be twelve hundred," I insisted.

"We had to give Mehmet here two hundred quid." Jimmy tapped the Moroccan taxi driver on the shoulder who turned and winked.

"Remember, I've got to take at least five hundred out of that for fares and other expenses," I reminded them.

"Yes, Sid, and don't forget we only agreed to come because you promised us all the cake we could eat," Jimmy exclaimed.

"And you shall eat cake, I promise." I never told them how I reacted to just a couple of bites of the cake the charlatan lawyer gave me.

A few minutes later we returned to the prison car park and made our way to reception, where I handed over the receipt that the boys had obtained from the Consulate. We were told to wait in the car park, I thought of all the prison films I'd seen where the jailbird is released.

Half an hour later, cousin Trevor emerged carrying a hold-all. I opened the back-passenger door and he climbed in, barely acknowledging me with his usual serious deadpan expression. I introduced him to the lads and told him the story of how I was almost fleeced.

He mumbled his thanks and asked to be dropped off at the central train station. I could tell the lads were a little bit in awe of Trevor, it wasn't until Mehmet pulled up by the station that Jimmy piped up.

"What now, what about the remainder of the money?"

My cousin shrugged as he got out the car. "Cake, buy some cake," he suggested, before adding, "It's my 21st birthday party at my house Saturday week, you're all invited."

22

THE PROOF THAT GOD EXISTS

WE ATE A lot of cake. We got very high, Jimmy had sex
with two prostitutes, Smithy one, me none, but I lied to the
other two and told them I did. We blew most of the
remainder of Trevor's cash in the two days after he was
released. The remainder I gave to Mitch for a huge bag of
blues.

Saturday week came and the three musketeers, as we
now called ourselves, headed over to my uncle Martin's
house for our first proper party. My aunt and uncle had
disappeared to Broadstairs for the weekend and there was
well over a hundred guests filling the downstairs rooms.
Eventually we found cousin Trevor in the kitchen, he
seemed reasonably pleased to see us and introduced us to his
girlfriend Tracey who got us a cold beer each from the well-
stocked fridge. I washed down a couple of blues and we
decamped to the corner of the living room next to the DJ. A
group of slightly older girls danced round their handbags to
KC and the Sunshine Band.

My attention was drawn to a couple dancing in the middle, the girl was very petite, the guy was a huge lump. She was facing me, I immediately fancied her but there was something familiar about the guy, even if I couldn't see his face. As the song reached its climax the couple joined hands and did an improvised twirl. I saw his face fleetingly and recognised him immediately!

Trevor and Tracey were snogging in the kitchen, I coughed in an effort to interrupt them.

"What's up, Sid?!" my cousin yelled over the sound of Slade booming from the speakers.

"What's that cunt Grant Bishop doing here?" I screamed.

"He's in my class at college, how do you know him?" Trevor asked.

"Is he a friend of yours?" I quizzed him.

"No, I can't stand the wanker, but I invited the whole class."

I briefly told him the bus stop bullying story from four years previously. "And he was an anti-Semite," I added, recalling his threat to 'punch me in my great big Jewish nose'.

"Fuck that, I'm not having that," Trevor sneered.

I followed him into the living room. He grabbed Grant by his collar. "Oi! Grant! I believe you've met my cousin Sid before."

The bully looked at me and instantly recognised me. "Sid Levinson. Blimey, you are cousins, what a small world," he muttered, before Trevor headbutted him. Blood spurted everywhere as his nose splintered. His petite girlfriend screamed as Trevor dragged him through the stunned guests, out of the room and threw him out the front door. By this time Jimmy and Smithy were at my side.

"Go on then boys, give him a good kicking," my cousin gestured at Grant's prone body on the garden path.

I made some half-hearted kick at his legs, Jimmy gave him a real belter in his ribs.

"What you going to do when you see him next?" I queried.

"Hit him again if he rears up," Trevor confirmed.

We returned to the living room, the mad Bishop's date was still in shock. I explained to her the story even though the booze and pills were affecting my speech. She took great sympathy and suddenly we were kissing.

Half an hour later, after we'd crept upstairs to the bedroom where I'd spied Uncle Martin shagging the cleaner, I was no longer a virgin!

In the morning the boys and me sat on the train home in hungover silence. '*God exists*', I thought to myself in quiet satisfaction.

23

GLASTO?

(2014)

I TRIED MY very best to obtain Glastonbury tickets, but it proved impossible. I made a decision to buy tickets for the Isle of Wight instead, hoping Jimmy would be more than happy.

I took him to the 100 club to see a Clash tribute band. My plan was to casually mention the festival situation on the train journey, but within a couple of minutes he threw a spanner in the works. "You got the Glasto tickets sorted, Sid? There's only four months to go, I can't fucking wait, mate, we need to start preparing. I trust you've already made your lists."

I hadn't, I had other worries, which I kept to myself as Jimmy told me he'd asked his consultant to put off his op until after Glasto and that his depression and irrational behaviour, which he admitted he was aware of, was dissipated by the excitement of his trip to Glastonbury.

"Not a particularly strong line-up," I offered.

"Not even bothered, mate, couldn't give a shit. Five days in a field, music, beer, god knows what else." He was salivating.

"What else?" I queried.

"Fucking anything and everything that's going, mate," he confirmed worryingly.

"Has to be said, Jimmy, the Isle of Wight's got a cracking line-up," I chipped in, more in hope than any expectation.

"Fuck the Isle of Wight, Sid, we're going to Glasto!"

* * *

Jimmy's obsession with Glastonbury was not my only worry, in fact I'd made a list. Number one was my father's failing health. His dementia was worse, as was his physical condition. The doctor told me he was too old and frail for any aggressive treatment and that he was unlikely to see the summer.

I contacted Mark and warned him to be on standby to rush over from his home in LA. Obviously, I understood why my brother had made his life abroad and spent most of his adult life, to all intents and purposes, fatherless but ironically my father's dementia had brought them back together. My father quite simply forgot what happened between them and Mark, being a better man than me, embraced my father's new acceptance of him. All the same, I was left to sort out all the dramas and practicalities my father's demise presented.

Trudie, of course, went beyond what was expected of her. The news the doctor gave me was a relief to be honest and was linked to number two on my list, financial worries. Mark and I were paying for basically twenty-four-hour care for the old man and my business was on its knees. The glory days of fireplaces being the thing were over. In the back of my mind I was starting to rely on the fact that within a year there could be some inheritance coming my way. Wrong, I know, but I'd calculated that with the sale of their apartment, plus some savings, my half would get me out of impending troubles.

Of course, I also was worried about the worst-case scenario of my father snuffing it the day before the Isle of Wight festival or, even worse, during. Given Jimmy's excitement at the thought of five days in a field far away from Heena, albeit not at Glastonbury, he would be crushed if we couldn't go. This thought was a growing concern in my mind.

There was another darker thought that crept in all too regularly, Jimmy's possible sighting of Perry at Waterloo. I'd taken it for granted he'd died on that final phone call some five years ago. I started to imagine seeing Perry everywhere, particularly at night. If I was walking home from the station, I'd imagine him lurking around the house. I considered carrying a knife but thought better of it. I did, however, place several strategically around the house, under my bedside table, on top of the bathroom cabinet. I was secretly very paranoid.

* * *

Jimmy, to my surprise and concern, spent the entire gig in the mosh pit. I wasn't sure if he was bumping into people on purpose or by accident. At the end of the gig we made our way into the 100 Club's infamous toilet, where I stood beside Jimmy at the urinals, getting rid of at least three pints of lager. Jimmy shouldn't have been drinking on his medication but had matched me drink for drink.

A guy came in singing a garbled version of *White Riot* and stood the other side of Jimmy. After a few drunken grunts of relief, the guy looked at Jimmy's dark glasses and said, "Blimey, mate, the only people that wear shades inside are rock stars and wankers, which one are you?"

Before I could explain, Jimmy turned and shook the last drops of piss on the guy's leg. "Neither, mate," Jimmy casually remarked, removing his glasses to reveal his glass eye. "Eye cancer you cunt."

I knew what was coming but was powerless to stop him as Jimmy's right fist connected with the guy's jaw, knocking him clean out.

I led Jimmy out of the club as quickly as possible. Once out into the Oxford Street air, Jimmy blew on his red knuckles.

"Fucking hell, Sid, that's the first punch I've thrown since nineteen-eighty-five, Spurs away!"

I was rather concerned about how we'd survive five days at a festival.

24

WILDLIFE

THE PERRY THING was really getting to me. If he was still alive why hadn't he contacted me in the five years since the train incident? After all, he called me on average every other day in the months after he left my flat. If Jimmy was right and he had seen Perry begging at Waterloo, I could only come up with two reasons I hadn't heard from him. Maybe the accident resulted in a head injury causing memory loss, or he was biding his time, blaming me for his misfortune, waiting for the opportunity to punish me. The second option was unlikely, but if he was harbouring a grudge, what shape would punishment take?

I went up to the bedroom and removed the bottom drawer of my bedside chest, under which I kept small lockable box for personal items like my passport, will, and my kill list. I placed the A5 piece of note paper on the chest top, rubbed out the line that was scrawled through Perry's name and then re-wrote his name. It was the last name on the list, as an afterthought I added a question mark.

I perused the list, working backwards. Before Perry, was Ink Bat, another question mark. Then Heena, I decided to rub her name out. There was a time when all Jimmy had to say was the word, but she was now standing by him. Yes, she could be so fucking annoying, but that wasn't good enough reason to remain on my kill list. The next name was completely obscured by a thick black felt tip line. Roland Bartrop had to be killed, no doubt about that, and although I didn't actually know the fella, my future happiness depended on him being removed from mine and Trudie's life.

Erika, Erika was evil, Erika humiliated me. I plotted and planned for months a dozen different ways to kill her, but she lived so far away the logistics were too complicated. I let it go, regrettably.

Barry the milkman and Grant Bishop completed the kill list. I crossed Bishop off the list after his beating by Trevor at his twenty-first birthday bash. Barry, the thug milkman, with the red Capri was another story.

I was distracted by a text message: '*Hi mate, it's Zac from Sister Ray Records, I believe you were looking for Mott the Hoople's Wildlife for your mate. Well, I found a copy at the Utrecht record fair. Let me know when you want to pick it up. Regards, Zac.*'

This was good news indeed, I replied immediately and positively. I could break the news to Jimmy about us going to the Isle of Wight Festival, rather than Glastonbury, whilst presenting him with his missing Mott album.

* * *

I sat in a dark corner of a cavernous pub on the Charing Cross Road, studying the cover of the replacement album. My faith in human nature had been restored by Zac, who had discovered this needle in a haystack for me. I was expecting to have to pay a fortune for his endeavours but to my great surprise he told me he only wanted the twenty pounds he paid for it, as he could see we were proper Mott fans.

I decided I'd have to tell Jimmy about the festival situation ASAP. He was a complex character before his latest setback, I was certain his depression and the resulting behaviour were linked to his eye issues. I really wanted us to have the best weekend ever and I needed to plan it with a positive attitude. Perhaps the best plan would be to ask Heena if she could help soften the blow, but I doubted Heena would understand the situation. She was from a different culture and was wrapped up in her own world. I realised how lucky I was in my relationship with Trudie.

I thought about the kill list and particularly Roland Bartrop. Whilst Trudie and I had enjoyed a very successful marriage, our courtship had been a disaster. Not a day went past when I wondered, if Bartrop had lived, would Trudie and I and our kids have happened.

* * *

I phoned Heena knowing she'd be at work, she was surprised I'd called her.

"How do you think Jimmy's doing?" I asked.

"Well, his eyesight is definitely deteriorating, and his behaviour is…well let's just say he's hard to live with."

"I'm sure it is, Heena, you're a saint."

"Well, to be honest, the only thing that's keeping me going is the thought of you taking him to Glastonbury for five days. I'm going to enjoy every second of freedom, I promise you."

I paused and coughed before replying. "I'll be honest, Heena, I'm struggling to get Glasto tickets, no problem getting Isle of Wight tickets though! It's a much better line up," I said hopefully.

"Jimmy keeps telling me if you don't get Glastonbury tickets, he won't go anywhere else. For fuck sake, Sid, you can't let him down, he will be impossible."

I was about to come clean when the most stupid irrational idea in the history of the universe came into my head. "Okay, Heena, leave it to me. Good news by the way, tell Jimmy I've got his missing Mott album."

I sat with my head in my hands contemplating my ridiculous plan, I needed to make a list!

25

I DON'T LIKE MONDAYS

NOBODY LIKES MONDAYS and this particular Monday didn't start well. First, I received a letter from the Inland Revenue notifying me of a tax inspection the week before the Isle of Wight festival. Then, I took my father to his GP, who had bad news. Both my father's cancer and dementia had worsened, to such an extent that he felt there was nothing left to do but contact the hospice.

"How long do you reckon, Doctor?" I asked, whilst working out it was exactly two months until the festival.

"A month, two tops," he mumbled.

I was too busy doing the maths to ask the questions I should have. No sooner had I got him home, I had a rare call from Jimmy who explained that Heena had taken him back to Moorfields hospital as he'd had a bad weekend. They were insisting they needed to operate sooner rather than later and that he was being admitted in two weeks' time.

"How long is the recovery time, Jimmy?" I asked.

"About four weeks."

I was doing more mental arithmetic. "That's a bit tight," I suggested.

"Don't worry, Sid, I'll be at Glastonbury, even if I have to crawl there."

The mere mention of Glasto gave me a headache but I'd already started to think through my crazy plan, I'd even made a list.

* * *

Trudie knows me too well. I'd sat through dinner totally distracted, hardly saying a word. Sometimes I'm sure she'd like me to shut up for once, but it was obvious I wasn't enjoying some quiet time.

"You're not yourself, Sid, is it work?" She said, stroking my forearm.

I'd obviously mentioned my father and Jimmy's imminent operation, but I hadn't told her about the tax inspection and Jimmy's obsession with Glasto. I never ever talked about Perry, whom I was having nightmares about.

"Just tell Jimmy Glastonbury is sold out but you've got Isle of Wight tickets, it's a better line up anyway and they are showing the World Cup on the biggest screen in Europe. I read it in the papers yesterday," she said after I told her.

"I've tried, Trud, but he won't have it, he's totally obsessed with going to Glasto."

"So, what are you going to do? Besides , what with your father and Jimmy's op you might have to cancel anyway. I hope you're insured," she added.

"Yes, I paid extra given the circumstances, but I couldn't let Jimmy down, it's all he's got to look forward to." There was a brief silence before I gave Trudie a reassuring peck on the forehead. "I have a cunning plan," I quoted Baldrick.

"Which is?" She smirked.

"I'm going to pretend that the Isle of Wight is Glastonbury!"

"What? You are joking, Sid?"

"Well that's my plan b, if Jimmy's op is a huge success and he can see properly with his good eye he will be so

159

euphoric he won't mind where I take him. But if things don't go as hoped and he's in a bad way, I'm going to tell him the Isle of Wight is Glastonbury. Why not?"

"What about the ferry for starters?"

It was a sensible question. "Once on the ferry I'll tell him we have stopped at a service station."

"And what about when umpteen performers shout out 'Isle of Wight, make some noise', have you considered that, Sid?"

"It's a rock festival, not a rap concert," I replied unconvincingly.

"You really would give it a go wouldn't you, Sid, you're bonkers."

* * *

Trudie had never ever called me a liar but she knew my devious mind, I've lost count of the amount of times she asked me to come up with an excuse for her not to go to work or a social event. She didn't consider them to be lies, she found my fibs very creative. She considered me to be something of an artist. A master in the dark arts of making shit up. Trudie could never lie, her face would give it away in an instant. I'd bent the truth with Trudie many times since we met, particularly when the kids were small. Normally only to get to football or a gig, I'd never told her a serious lie, except the Roland business but that was more a case of misinformation than a lie.

I met Trudie at a party in 1980, I hadn't had a relationship that lasted more than three months since Erika, evil Erika, four years earlier. In hindsight, that couldn't be called a proper relationship. I was obsessed with Trudie the moment I set eyes on her. The problem was, the feeling was far from mutual. We were good mates and nothing more, she was happy with this situation, I wasn't. It took five months of plucking up the courage and a lot of speed before I managed to change the status of our relationship.

160

She was renting a flat with her friend Melissa who I ran into at the off-licence. She told me she was going to a party at her sister's house in South London, I asked her if Trudie was going. "Nope, she will be home alone. Why not pop round, keep her company?" she suggested.

So, I did. I popped round with a couple of Roxy Music albums, as I knew her idol was Bryan Ferry, plus a bottle of Blue Nun. I knew how to woo a girl. The problem was, I called round and she wasn't there. Her flatmate seemed sure she was staying in and I got the vibe she was keen for us to get together. Melissa had a boyfriend who was a policeman, I couldn't warm to him though. There was something about him, he was too cock sure, too full of himself

I sat beside their door and took a couple of blues with the last drop of 7Up. I looked up and noticed her bedroom window was open. A few moments later, I had a surge of amphetamine induced confidence and decided I would leg it up the drainpipe like a superhero. Speed took all my fear away, all my inhibitions. By this stage I was completely addicted and dependent on it to get me through any social discourse. I made it up to the window ledge and opened the window to its full extent. I didn't so much as climb through, I fell through, knocking over Trudie's triple mirror which sat on her dressing table. Fortunately, neither the mirror nor me were broken.

I felt like a burglar, putting the mirror back and closing the window. I exited the bedroom straight into their living room and made myself comfy on the sofa. I didn't want to give her a fright and started to get second thoughts. I went to put the Blue Nun in the fridge but thought a glass would be helpful. I sat on the sofa for the next hour demolishing the bottle.

It was now 10pm, I wasn't sure what to do. I made a corporate decision and returned to her bedroom where I stripped down to my underpants and climbed into her bed in a tactical effort to turn our friendship into something different! I must have dozed off for at least an hour or so and was woken by a door closing and muffled voices. I suddenly remembered I'd left the Roxy Music albums in the living room. The bedroom door was slightly open, I caught a glimpse of Trudie but couldn't see who she was with. I then heard a male voice.

"Who's the Roxy Music fan?" he said.

"I love them, why?" Trudie replied.

"There's a couple of their early albums here." I recognised his voice, it was Melissa's policeman boyfriend.

I saw Trudie pick them up off the coffee table. "Wow, *For Your Pleasure* and *Stranded,* what great albums. I guess they must be Melissa's." She guessed wrongly.

"I didn't think Mel was a fan," he shrugged.

"Anyway, Doug, thanks for the lift, it was very handy running into you in the Co-op, thanks mate. I'm going to turn in, I take it you're going to wait for Mel to get back?"

"Mel won't be back till the small hours, let's have a drink, Trud."

I peered harder and saw him put his hand on Trudie's shoulder, she moved uncomfortably away from him on the sofa. He then grabbed her with both hands on her forearms. "Come on, Trudie, let's have some fun."

I had déjà vu, I thought of Uncle Martin and the cleaner.

"Doug, I'm going to bed." Trudie tried to break free from his grip, but he leaned over her, blocking her escape.

"I'm going to fuck you, Trud, you might as well enjoy it. I've heard you screaming with delight when that posh git Roland comes around. Come on, let's go to bed." He pulled her up by her collar, ripping open her blouse. She tried to scream as he put his hand over her mouth and twisted her arm behind her back as he violently pushed towards her bedroom. I thought about hiding under the bed, but I just pulled her duvet over me.

"You're hurting me, Doug!" she yelled, trying to break free.

"Good, I'm going to fuck your brains out, you stupid bitch!"

He pushed her into the bedroom. I was paralysed with fear, she was crying and struggling as he pushed her onto the end of the bed and ripped her skirt off. "I'm going to fuck your-"

Before he could finish his sentence, I jumped up, scaring the living daylights out of both of them. "Fuck off you cunt!" I bellowed. "Or I'll call the cops, you fucking rapist!"

He was too stunned to fight me, he just legged it out the room and out the flat.

I was standing beside Trudie's bed in my dark blue boxer shorts looking and feeling very awkward. Trudie stood at the end of her bed, within touching distance of me, shaking. "Are you okay, Trud?" I asked, embarrassed.

"What are you doing here, in my bed?" she asked a perfectly sensible question.

I decided to tell the truth. "I ran into Melissa in the offy and she said you'd be on your own and I should pop round and keep you company."

Trudie wiped her tears and laughed. "Melissa told me to invite you round but, but…" She stopped there.

"But what?"

"Oh, I don't know, you were saying?"

"So, I came round with the Roxy albums and a bottle of wine but you weren't in, so I sat on the doorstep for half an hour and I was about to go, and I realised I'd forgotten my house keys. I saw your bedroom window, so I climbed up the drainpipe and let myself in." I was rambling, the booze, speed and events had all kicked in.

"So, you got undressed and got in my bed?"

"I…I waited but guessed you were out for the night and…"

"And what?" she snapped.

"And I decided to get into your bed because I don't want to be just your friend anymore." I went for broke.

"You don't want to be my friend anymore?" She was confused.

"No, I want to be more than your friend, Trudie." I left the hint hanging in the air as I bent down and went to put on my discarded jeans, but before I could pull them up Trudie moved towards me and grabbed my arm.

"You are more than a friend, Sid, you're my hero. Get back into bed, I'm going to have a shower and wash that bastard off me."

I lay there, my heart bursting out of my chest with anticipation, cogitating over the madness that I had just witnessed.

Ten minutes later Trudie returned wrapped in a towel, which she dropped to the floor and climbed in next to me. She wrapped herself around me and asked a good question. "It's been about 5 months, why didn't you just ask me out?"

"I don't know, I guess I was petrified of you saying no," I replied honestly.

"Well, go on then," she pinched me.

"Go on what?"

"Ask me out."

And before I could muster up the words she leaned forward and kissed me.

After a frantic hour or so she was fast asleep. I basked in the elation of the moment, of finally curing myself of the humiliation evil Erika caused me. The scars of which were still raw after four years. I was drifting off, thinking about where to take Trudie on our first proper date, when a dark thought entered my mind. Who was the 'posh git' Roland I'd heard Doug mention?

26

COURTING DISASTER

(1982)

DISASTER STRUCK THE night before my first proper date with Trudie. My ex colleague, friend and supplier of my confidence boosting, shyness-reducing amphetamines, Mitch, was stabbed to death in a feud with a rival on his estate.

I'd gone to our normal meeting place and after ten minutes his sister turned up in a terrible state and gave me the bad news. Notwithstanding losing a mate in such tragic circumstances, I would have to face what was to be a torturous courtship with Trudie without my usual crutch.

Then there was Roland. After barely two or three proper dates, Trudie sprung a fly in the ointment on me. She confessed she'd been seeing a married man on and off for six months and although she had all but ended the relationship, she was committed to a weekend in the Cotswolds with him that he'd arranged ages ago. All my pleading and begging was in vain and I found myself spending the next weekend with my old bedfellow, humiliation.

I was obsessed with Trudie but was aware of the fact that if she had strong feelings for me, she'd not have gone away with this Roland character. I didn't help myself by parking up near Trudie's flat on Sunday night when she was due home, technically this was 'stalking'. Eventually a snazzy sports car pulled up and I watched them retrieve her case from the boot. I shuddered as he disappeared with Trudie through her front door.

Looking at his flash motor reminded me of that thug milkman and his bloody Capri that enticed Lisa away from me. Lisa, Erika and now Trudie. This was the last straw, I couldn't take any more pain.

I sped off towards Camden in the hope of finding a new supplier, but eventually lost my nerve as I surveyed the dodgy figures lurking in the shadows on Camden high street.

* * *

So, I was faced with wooing Trudie away from my wealthy older rival, without the help of my preferred drug. For a few months I enjoyed dates to the theatre, cinema, fancy restaurants and Roland Bartrop's name was never mentioned. But he was like a black cloud lurking in the corner of a deep blue sky.

I phoned her one Thursday night to arrange to go and see Lou Reed at the Shepherd's Bush Empire on the Saturday night, but got no reply. I'd completely forgotten about gigging and football, my infatuation with Trudie was all-consuming. In normal circumstances I'd have already sorted tickets to see Lou Reed, for the sixth time, but after two days of not hearing from Trudie, I decided to go around to her place in the desperately naive hope that her phone was out of order. I'd then try and get tickets for us from a tout.

I saw Roland Bartrop's flash sports car the second I turned into her road. I parked up, head thumping, a sickness in my stomach. I sat there for three hours, I should have been plotting and planning, but I was so full of anger and heartache I couldn't think straight. My state of mind wasn't helped by seeing the front door open and the two of them laughing and giggling as they placed all manner of picnic paraphernalia in the boot. I watched them drive off and placed my hands on the steering wheel, lowering my head between them, and started to cry.

I was in this position for a good five minutes when suddenly there was a tap on the window, giving me the fright of my life. It was Melissa. I wiped my eyes and wound down the window.

"Hi, Sid, are you okay?"

"Fine," I lied. "I've just got here, is Trudie home?"

"No, Sid," she hesitated, "She's just gone out."

"With him?" I mumbled.

Melissa nodded sheepishly. "Why don't you come in? I've got a bottle of gin that needs emptying."

It was an offer I couldn't refuse.

I watched Melissa pour two ridiculously large gin and tonics before she joined me on the sofa. "So, how's our hero?" She wiped a remaining tear from my cheek.

"I'm okay, I take it you haven't heard from that wanker?' I realised I wasn't the only one suffering, recalling Melissa's so-called boyfriend attacking Trudie on this very sofa.

"Not a word. I told Trudie she has every right to press charges, what with you being a witness."

We discussed the incident for a while then she recharged our glasses. There was a silence before she brought up the inevitable. "You're upset about Trudie and Roland, aren't you, Sid?"

She hit a nerve. I swallowed hard before answering. "I guess I thought she was over him, I'm confused."

"She's very young, Sid. She's what, four years younger than you?"

"Yes, but she's seventeen years younger than him," I chided.

"I know, Sid, but Trudie's still only twenty, she's something of a free spirit, I'm the same."

"But, but what do you think I should do, Mel?"

"Bide your time, her relationship with Roland will fizzle out in time." I dwelt on her advice, she put her hand on mine. "You've probably met Trud two years too soon."

"How can I compete with his money, his sports car?"

"I don't think that's the attraction, he's as mean as fuck with his money. That's why's he's got it."

I shook my head in bewilderment. We demolished the gin and some beers before Melissa suggested getting a Chinese takeaway, which we demolished too. After, we shared a joint. We both concurred that Trudie wouldn't approve. The drink, food and hash conspired to send us both asleep curled up on the sofa.

In hindsight I can picture the situation, but at the time I wasn't thinking rationally. I assume Trudie returned to the flat with Roland and found her flatmate and best friend curled up on the sofa with her supposed boyfriend. This probably contributed to why I woke up to the sound of Trudie's loud screams of ecstasy emanating from her bedroom. Every rhythmic thud of the headboard was like a dagger in my heart. I couldn't take any more, I was a broken man.

I unfurled myself from Melissa's embrace and stood at Trudie's bedroom door, clasping the knob. I went to turn it but then resisted the temptation to open it and attack Roland. Instead, I screamed, "You fucking old cunt, Roland! Get back to your fucking wife and leave my girlfriend alone!" Again, in hindsight I childishly and stupidly interrupted them in the throes of passion.

A few seconds later the door opened and Trudie stood there in her towelling dressing gown. "For Christ's sake, Sid, just go!" she shouted.

I did go, but initially not far. I sat in my car in no fit state to drive. On reflection, I was having a complete breakdown. After a few moments I went to my boot, removed the rear wheel and took out the tyre iron. I got back in the driver's seat and waited for Roland to leave. I planned to smash his skull and to hell with everything.

I sat there a good two hours clasping the weapon. Suddenly, Roland emerged with Trudie still in her dressing gown, they kissed, and he ran down the steps and made for his car.

I started to climb out of mine, wrench in hand.

27

LIGHT MY FIRE

I HAD EVERY intention of killing Roland, literally bashing the brains out of a man I'd never actually met. Such was my total obsession with Trudie that I was willing to lose my liberty, even my life. If I couldn't have her, what was the point of carrying on in any normal way?

* * *

I'd also intended to kill Barry the milkman by creeping up on him as he delivered milk to Lisa's family home and smashing the back of his head with a hammer. I actually was waiting in the bushes at some ungodly hour, ready to pounce. The milk float pulled up and as he walked up the path, I went to make my move. Thank god I noticed this milkman was some six inches shorter than my intended target and I crawled back into the bushes.

I discovered a few days later that Barry had sold his Ford Capri and emigrated to Australia. Lisa had hooked up with a helicopter pilot, which neither Barry nor myself could ever compete with. She married him and had a baby, who was only three months old when Lisa's husband of barely two years got into difficulties whilst transporting a millionaire businessman in inclement weather. He crashed into tree in the Cotswolds and they both died instantly. I took no satisfaction on hearing this news. Lisa was a lovely girl, I realised I just wasn't her type.

I've seen her around town over the years and she has unsurprisingly aged very well. Last time we spoke in Waitrose, she'd just divorced husband number three. Maybe the thug milkman did me a favour.

* * *

And killed him I would have, but just as I was about to attack him Trudie shouted, "Hang on, Rolly, I left my purse in your car!" and started towards him. I held back and the moment passed.

I waited for Trudie to disappear back inside and then followed Roland's TVR at a discreet distance. Twenty minutes later I knew where he lived, his house was massive, it would be a lot to give up.

I spent the next day in a state of utter despair. I must have picked up the phone to call Trudie over a hundred times. Then I did a very stupid thing, I wrote a letter:

Dear Mrs. Bartrop,
I think you should know that your husband has a lover who is only twenty.

I didn't sign it, I wrote her name and address on the envelope, put a first-class stamp on it and walked around the corner to the nearest letter box. I stood there for over half an hour before posting the letter. I felt like I needed some speed, poor Mitch, poor me.

That evening I sat on my bed swigging whiskey and staring at a bottle of sleeping tablets, realising that I'd made a dreadful mistake and that my stupid childish letter would probably bring Trudie and Roland together. I lay back sobbing like a baby, before I mercifully dozed off and slept for ten hours straight.

When I woke up the bottle of tablets was still in my hand unopened. I looked at the *Aladdin Sane* album cover that I'd had framed. I'd not listened to DB for ages, I'd not seen Jimmy, Smithy or anyone for ages. I'd not been to a gig or football, I'd been completely lost in a futile quest to have a girlfriend. As I lay there staring at one of the most iconic images of the twentieth century, I made an inspired decision that was to both save and change my life.

I searched my address book for a scrawled international telephone number. I picked up the phone and dialled. The unfamiliar dialling tone dragged for an age but just before the answerphone interrupted, I heard a click and a faint voice.

"Hello, who's this?"

"Mark, it's Sid."

"Sid?"

"Sid, your brother," I confirmed.

"Hi Sid, are you ok?"

"I'm fine, Mark, how you doing?"

"Good, good, it's just that it's three in the morning over here."

"Oh shit, I forgot. How's LA, mate?" I enquired.

"LA is good but I'm leaving for San Francisco tomorrow, what's up in your world? Any good gigs lately?"

I hesitated before answering. "No, just been working. Listen, Mark, fancy a visitor?"

This time Mark hesitated. "You're not in trouble are you, Sid?"

He was probably wondering why on Earth I'd want to visit him. I hadn't seen him in the seven years since he left. We wrote to each other about twice a year and spoke now and again. Mum had visited a couple of years previously. Dad never mentioned his name.

"No, I just need a holiday, and I'm desperate to visit California."

"And I'll be only too pleased to show you around, do you need money? For the fare."

"No that's okay, I'll scrape that together, just need a sofa to sleep on."

"Well let me know when you're coming, Sid, and love to Mum."

I hung up and suddenly had a new sense of purpose. I searched for my *Best of the Doors* album, soon I was singing along to *L.A. Woman*.

* * *

Melissa called me to make sure I hadn't done anything stupid. I had, of course, but I don't think that was what was on her mind. She told me she'd explained to Trudie about the drink, spliffs etc. and that we were just looking out for each other as friends. She suggested I give it a few days and call her. She also mentioned she had a feeling something might have happened between Trudie and Roland. I thought of the letter and for a moment I felt elated but then realised I couldn't afford another humiliation, I had to get away.

I wasted no time in applying for a visa and started to plan and plot further travels around Mexico and then up north to Canada. Money was an issue, so I made a list of potential sources, starting with Mum. She was both delighted and concerned as I'd never shown any interest in my brother since he left home. She thought there might be something wrong, this was 1982 and AIDS was becoming a thing on the news. I cruelly and cynically played this to my advantage by leaving a small nugget of doubt in her mind.

"Mark is fine, Mum, apart from a cold he can't seem to shake off," I lied.

That was enough to secure my air fare from her. I drained my savings account but needed significant further funds if I was to fulfil all my travelling plans. Last on my list was Uncle Martin. I went to see him, and he was mightily surprised to see me, particularly since my father and him hadn't spoken for years. I kept in touch with my cousin

Trevor who had gone in with an uncle on his mother's side of the family who had a niche business making wellington boots. It was by royal appointment and Trevor had brought in some new ideas and was doing really well. My Uncle Martin's fireplace business on the other hand was really struggling and Trevor had suggested I might be interested joining him and trying to inject some new blood. I was going nowhere career-wise, just like my love life. The opportunity came at the wrong time for me, as I was deep into my travel plans, but I had a far more devious reason for visiting Uncle Martin.

It was a strange start to our meeting in his study, as he asked me to remind him why my father and him weren't speaking. I seemed to recall my father saying it was all to do with events leading up to my grandmother's passing, but I just shrugged and told him that I didn't think my father could remember the reason. I suggested they try and catch up, knowing my bone-headed father would have none of it.

We were interrupted briefly by Aunt Sophie, she gave me a surprised stare in grudging acknowledgment. She was always icy cold with everyone, totally aloof. "Hello Aunt Sophie," I said, smiling.

"Sid." She stated her feelings on my appearance in her home with a simple 'Sid' and she was gone. No offer of a cup of tea or a glass of water. It was her home, her mother's family were loaded. They were the wellington boots people.

I listened to Uncle Martin drone on about the fireplace trade for a good half hour. He had a monotone voice that could send a screaming baby to sleep. Suddenly, a vaguely familiar woman put her head round the door and then her whole self. I recognised the huge boobs! She apologised for the interruption and Uncle Martin asked her to make his study her last job.

"So basically, I need someone to try and sell our products to developers etcetera, Trevor recommended you, Sid. You'll start on the minimum wage, but I will pay you a generous ten percent commission."

I told him of my imminent travel plans and said I would be happy to take the job on my return, whenever that might be.

"I can't hold the job for you indefinitely," he moaned.

"Oh, I think you can uncle." I looked him in the eye.

"I'm sorry," he said, taken aback.

I'd had enough humiliation, it was time to man up and move forward. "Not only will you keep the job open for me, but I want six months' pay in advance," I ventured.

"What?" Uncle Martin mumbled, shocked as I played my ace card.

"I know about you and the cleaner." I nodded towards the door that she had just closed.

Uncle Martin went bright red and broke into an instant sweat. "What the hell are you on about?" he gasped.

"You've been fucking your cleaner for at least six years, I've seen you in action." I told him about me sneaking into the house six years previously to collect Trevor's bail money. He looked ill as I continued. "I'm going to go outside and wait for you to bring me either a cheque or tell me to sling my hook. You know what the consequences will be if it's the latter."

"Are you blackmailing me?" He went to shout but lowered his voice, realising he was fucked.

"Yes, that's absolutely correct, I'm blackmailing you." I left the house and sat on the front wall and waited.

28

LET THEM EAT CAKE, REUNITED

(2014)

EXACTLY ONE MONTH before we were due to go to the Isle of White festival, or should I say exactly one month before Jimmy thought he was off to Glastonbury, I received two bits of bad news. First, Heena left a message that Jimmy had gone into hospital that morning for an operation, which took me by surprise. Then I got a call from the warden at my father's place and it wasn't good news, he had caused chaos all night, constantly pulling all the panic cords in his flat.

Trudie and I organised a crisis meeting with the warden, his GP, carers and the local hospice. The conclusion was that he couldn't stay where he was, but he was unlikely to last more than two or three weeks. It was a dilemma, but I confess my thoughts were almost totally linked to mine and Jimmy's trip.

When I got home, I tried to call Heena but got no reply. Over dinner I reminded Trudie of the letter my mother left me when she died. My mother was no fool, she thanked me for my patience with my father and also for tolerating the situation with my brother. She asked that my father, when the time comes, didn't die alone and that she would like him to stay at home as long as possible. She knew he'd be lost without her, she wasn't meant to go first. We decided we'd try and keep him at his apartment as long as possible, Trudie contacted the Hospice at Home team accordingly.

* * *

On the bright side, my tax inspection was deferred for three months, after my accountant explained about my father's imminent demise. I decided to bury my head on the matter, although I started to realise the financial benefits that would eventually come my way after my father's death. I felt a little guilty having these mercenary thoughts, but only a little.

After a couple of days, I received a call from Heena explaining that Jimmy was home resting after some pretty intensive radiation treatment, which they hoped had dramatically shrunk the cancer cells. She was concerned that he was still hellbent on going to Glastonbury and asked if maybe I could talk him out of it. I decided to be sensible and told Heena about my father and my concerns about his rapidly failing health, but not that we weren't going to Glastonbury. I said I'd pop round the next afternoon to see him, Heena said she'd really appreciate it as she was going on a two-day course. I felt the least she could do was look after Jimmy while he was recuperating, besides it was one of her 'courses' that caused all the aggro in the first place.

I was surprised when Smithy answered Jimmy's door. I hadn't seen him in ages, since he'd move to Blackheath after his latest divorce. He led me into the living room where Jimmy lay prostrate on the sofa with an eye patch over his now not-so-good eye. There was a tupperware box on the table, Smithy noticed me curiously studying it.

"I've baked some cakes," Smithy stated, trying to suppress his mischievous grin.

"Are you sure that's a good idea?" I was concerned about Jimmy overdoing it.

"Put the kettle on, Sid, tea and cake, fucking marvellous," Jimmy laughed.

An hour later we were off our faces reminiscing about the trip to Holland to bail out cousin Trevor. "Smithy's going to do a fresh supply for us to take to Glastonbury!" Jimmy yelled.

"It's the least I can do lads, I only wish I could come with you, but I've got my nephew's fucking wedding that weekend," Smithy replied.

A feeling of guilt replaced my ganja cake dizziness as I realised Glastonbury was two weeks after the Isle of Wight, so Smithy could possibly have made it. "Come on, Smithy, let's make Jimmy some lunch." I nodded towards the kitchen.

"I'll have some more cake," Jimmy laughed.

"No, Sid's right, you need some proper nosh. I'll make you some fresh cakes for you to take to Glastonbury." Smithy made for the kitchen, following me.

Smithy started to search the fridge and cupboards for something for Jimmy's lunch. "I'll bake some double strength cakes for you and Jimmy mate, you two can roll around the 'healing field' till your hearts content."

"Smithy, I'm sorry, mate, but we're not going to Glastonbury." I owned up and then went on to explain the circumstances. "Worst of all, Smithy, the Isle of Wight is two weeks before Glasto, you could come."

"Too much on, mate, I'm off to Paris with my new girlfriend that weekend."

"Blimey, Smithy, you don't waste any time. I thought you were going to have a break after divorce number two," I teased him.

"Got to get back on the bike ASAP, Sid. Right, let's keep this simple, I'll do some beans on toast." It was a joint effort, Smithy looked at me like I was mad as I buttered the toast. "What happens when Anthony Kiedis shouts out 'How you all doing Isle of Wight'? Jimmy's going blind not deaf!"

"I know, I know, by the time the Red Hot Chilli Peppers come on stage hopefully Jimmy won't care where he is. Make sure those cakes are super strength," I jested.

We watched Jimmy struggle to eat his lunch, Smithy played an ace card. "So, you lucky bastards are going to see the Red Hot Chilli Peppers?"

"And the Kings of Leon," I added.

"I'm well jell," Smithy stated.

"The only negative is that Glasto won't be showing the World Cup games," I added, knowing that the Isle of Wight had the biggest screen in Europe to show it.

"They must show the England games?" Jimmy protested.

I decided to change the subject to something weighing on my mind. "Jimmy reckons he saw Perry around Waterloo not so long ago," I said.

"I thought he was long dead," Smithy confirmed.

"That's what I thought!" I snapped.

"I definitely fucking saw him," Jimmy interrupted. "He looked a right state," he continued.

I was now wishing I never brought it up.

* * *

Just three weeks to go and I was busy with my Isle of Wight list. I had four sections: 1) Travel 2) Equipment 3) Provisions 4) Jimmy.

I then had long sub-lists taking everything into account. My plans were clouded by my father's deteriorating health. Realistically, I needed him to die at least a week before the festival and even then, there could be complications. I decided if he was still lingering on in a week's time, I'd either have to cancel the whole idea of going to the festival or consider drastic action…

I feel slightly guilty admitting that mercenary thoughts were entering my head at this difficult time. His flat was pretty modest but would be easy to sell and he had substantial savings and pension pots. I was power of attorney, due to Mark living in LA. I'd been scrupulously honest and transparent with my brother over everything, but I felt slightly peeved that when the time came, everything would be split down the middle, when I'd had all the grief of sorting out care and all the dramas.

The inheritance would be the answer to all my problems. If he died a few months earlier, I could have splashed out on VIP Glasto tickets. But for now, it would have to be plan b. I sat and started to flesh out my festival list.

29

BAD TIMING

IT WAS TYPICAL of my father to stubbornly hang on and mess up everyone else's lives. My brother flew in three days after I called him to say that Dad was close to death. As great as it was to see Mark, I knew he'd be a complete drama queen. I tried to take Trudie's advice and not rise to the bait, but it didn't take long for him to wind me up with his comments.

He suggested that our father should be in the local hospice. I was immediately on the defensive, explaining that he was too weak to leave his bed, notwithstanding Mum's wishes that he, if possible, die at home. I was the one who had lived with his disease, the warnings etcetera, Mark swans over from sunny California and puts his oar in. Besides, I'd started to dwell on my plan b, there were only seven days until Jimmy and I were due to leave for the festival.

We sat in near silence eating dinner. For the first time in many years, Trudie, Leo, Tara and myself were joined by my brother. It was Tara's question that ignited a fresh list in my head. I'd been rehearsing my pending call to Jimmy, telling him the trip was off. "Do you think Grandad should have a Jewish funeral?" she asked.

"I'm not sure he can have one?" Trudie queried.

"That's right, I've never known him to go to synagogue in my life," Leo added.

"Of course he can," I snapped. "He's a paid-up member of the local liberal synagogue, been a member for years, something to do with his arrangement with Uncle Mory."

"Well you'd better contact the Rabbi then," Mark chipped in.

And I did contact Rabbi David the very next morning. He was a client of mine, a bit of a character to say the least. I'd told him about my father's attitude to the faith, he was very understanding.

I sat at my desk staring at my laptop screen, I'd googled suffocation. I started to flesh out my to do list. Suffocation was *1a*, calling the Rabbi was *5e*. I thought I might have to promote phoning home to *5b*.

I called his secretary, who explained he was talking to some soon to be newlyweds and that he'd call me back, which he did a few minutes later. We talked about the fireplace I installed and then I told him about my father's imminent demise. I then gave him a load of bullshit about how despite my father's lack of faith, the one thing he wanted when he died was to be buried as quickly as possible, i.e. the same day. Rabbi David accepted my story and told me he'd put the undertakers he favoured on notice and that I should call him whatever the hour when he dies. I completed the list and then put a few ticks on my Isle of Wight list: *torches, sleeping bags, pump, pillows*. Everything was falling into place in my mind.

I phoned Jimmy and he was surprisingly realistic. "How's your dad?" he asked.

"A matter of hours, mate."

"I understand that our trip's off, Sid," he stated solemnly.

"Not necessarily," I said, surprising him.

"But, Sid, he's your father, there's only a few days till Glasto starts, you can't be jumping about if he's only just died, can you? What about all the funeral arrangements?"

I thought about his point for a few seconds. "He's Jewish, Jimmy, everything's arranged. I've emailed you a list of what to take, Heena will read it to you. We are going, mate," I said with finality.

"But suppose he's not dead, Sid?"

"He will be, by Tuesday the latest. Get packing we are going to Glas-, the festival."

* * *

Trudie woke me on the Saturday morning to say the doctor had phoned to let me know my father wouldn't last the weekend. However, he was a stubborn old fighter, he really shouldn't have made it this far. Mark was on his way over, we'd agreed to watch over him in shifts. Mark had already wound me up with complaints about the carers, I knew he'd also be difficult around my plans for a quick funeral.

Trudie and I sat in silence eating our breakfast when she surprised me. "You're going to your festival whatever happens aren't you, Sid?"

"I can't let Jimmy down, can I?" I replied guiltily.

"Don't bring Jimmy into this, he'd understand. I know you too well Sid Levinson, once you've set your mind to something, there's no force on earth that can stop you."

She was dead right of course, nothing could have stopped me seeing Mott the Hoople at Weeley as a fourteen-year-old. The same as Roland Bartrop couldn't stop me in my pursuit of Trudie. Besides, I'd written my lists.

30

THE STORM BEFORE THE STORM

I TOOK OVER from Mark Sunday morning, he was convinced our father wouldn't last the night. I couldn't tell him I hoped he was right. After the Hospice at Home carer had come and washed him, I laid on my mum's old single bed, which was separated from the old fella by a bedside chest. I read for a while and then drifted off around midnight.

I woke with a start, I felt a hand on my throat. I fiddled for the bedside lamp switch and managed to turn it on. There was a wild eyed, long haired, toothless tramp sitting astride me strangling me with one hand and holding a hammer aloft in the other.

"I'm going to fucking kill you, you bastard," he snarled.

I shone the light in his face, it was my old friend and tenant Perry. Jimmy was right, he was still alive.

I screamed and begged forgiveness.

"You thought I was dead, didn't you, Sid?" He smiled as he prepared to bash my brains out.

I yelled so loud I woke myself from the nightmare. I was in a sweat, my father snored gently. The fucker wasn't going to die, and neither was Perry.

I put a message on my phone first thing Monday morning saying I was on holiday for two weeks and set about reviewing my lists, particularly the Isle of Wight festival and what to take. I got all my camping paraphernalia out of the loft and packed my rucksack. Trudie gave me a look as she returned from shopping. "Just a question, Sid, what if your dad is still alive Thursday morning?"

I just shrugged and told her I was replacing Mark at seven that evening.

I spent the day packing and sorting out my car. I was waiting, hoping Mark would call, but it got to 6.00pm and I'd heard nothing, so I retrieved my to-do list, placed it in my overnight bag and headed off to do hopefully my last shift.

"He's always been such a stubborn fucker," Mark observed, as we stood over my father, who, apart from the odd facial twitch, slept gently.

I regarded Mark's comment as something of an understatement given my father's attitude to him being gay way back when. I recalled my father exclaiming in those dark days after the Weeley fiasco, "Your brother's a fucking queer!" I'd been reflecting since Mum passed, how difficult the whole parent thing must have been for Mark. First the Jew thing and then him being thrown out. If I'd been Mark, I'd have thought 'Fuck Dad' and stayed in the Californian sunshine. But I'd learnt that Mark loved the drama around bereavement. It was like he was on the stage. The endless transatlantic calls to his buddies describing his days sitting by his father's 'death bed'. I recalled his eulogy at Mum's funeral, it was punctuated with faked near fainting and forced tears. He'd taken me aside on his recent arrival and told me that he was leaving the arrangements to me when the time came and asked if I'd thought of a eulogy for Dad. I'd certainly thought a lot about the arrangements for my father's funeral for my own selfish reasons, but I'd not given a moment's thought to what I'd say about the old cunt.

* * *

I waited a good half an hour after Mark had left, pulled the to-do list out of my pocket and placed it on the arm of the armchair I'd pulled up beside my dying father. I'd done the '*preparation*' and went to number two on the list, '*The night before*'. Like clockwork, the night carer arrived and busied herself for a couple of hours, cleaning my father's bits and administering the pills that had probably, along with his stubbornness, kept him alive.

She left dead on ten. I wasted no time reaching for the pillow in the top cupboard above his bed. I set the alarm on my phone for 6.00am and settled back in the chair, closing my eyes, wishing sleep would come instantly. But of course, it didn't. I wondered if Trudie suspected anything and whether Mark and me would ever see each other again after the funeral. Would I be bothered if I never saw him again? The age difference, his queerness…yes, I'd totally accepted the situation, but we had absolutely nothing in common except our mutual angst with our father, who one way or another would be history by the morning.

* * *

I reflected on the time when I couldn't wait to see him back in the early eighties. It was still painful to reflect on the Roland business, but because of his relationship with Trudie it forced me to visit Mark in California. I can still recall the strange sensation of consciously hugging my brother for the first time in my life in the arrivals hall at San Francisco airport. I hadn't seen him in eight years, the last time I was still basically a child. We were more equal now, we were both adults. I still recall the tour of San Francisco he gave me in his tiny compact car before arriving at a bohemian apartment in a very trendy part of town. Over dinner he told me he'd temporarily moved from his apartment in LA to look after a friend who was very ill in hospital. He didn't elaborate and I didn't push him, but there wasn't a good conclusion. After a few days, I left Mark for LA to take over from his cat sitter who was also unwell.

Looking back, this was the epicentre of the health catastrophe that decimated my brother's community. At the time, I was pretty oblivious to what was happening, I was having too much fun trying to forget about recent humiliations back home.

On my very first night, I got a bus to the strip and within minutes of entering a seedy bar some revellers heard my accent and adopted me for the night. After being dragged around various bars, I was shoved into a taxi and taken god knows where to a party. I was introduced to my first 'designer' drug and woke up with a young lady, who introduced herself as Mia. I hadn't recalled meeting her, everything was a complete blur.

"Did we?" I asked, opening an eye.

"No, Sid, but we can if you'd like to, I've never fucked an Englishman before."

I opened both eyes, she looked very young.

"How old are you?" I queried.

"Seventeen," she said smiling.

"And where are we?" I was curious.

"My house," she confirmed, playing with my manhood.

"You're very confident for a seventeen-year-old."

"That's because I started young," she replied mysteriously. She went on to explain that she was basically raped by her uncle when she was fourteen and had been his plaything ever since.

I should have been alarmed at this revelation but first I thought, '*This is LA, everyone is fucked up*'. Then I thought about Uncle Martin and the cleaner. Good old uncle Martin, I knew he'd come and join me outside on his front wall with his cheque book.

"Where are your parents, Mia?"

"They are away at the aforementioned uncle's for the weekend," she smiled.

I stayed there for a couple of days before finding my way back to my brother's apartment, where I found him waiting in a sombre mood. He didn't want to talk about his dying friend, he told me he had some work to do and I could join him. He had an interesting job, he was a 'mobile personal shopper' he told me. I didn't have a clue what he was on about, but I was about to find out.

We jumped in his compact car and headed to a salubrious suburb where we picked up a very sophisticated middle-aged lady called Carly. We then headed to Rodeo Drive. I noticed Mark got camper when he spoke to females, him and Carly clearly knew each other well as they mutually bitched about her recently outed husband number three.

"So apart from the fact Richard was absolutely fucking loaded, Carly, darling, I can't think of one redeeming feature," Mark chortled, as we swung into the last remaining parking bay.

I followed them to a swanky boutique, which had a sign on the door '*Strictly appointment only*'. Mark pressed the buzzer, a few seconds later he was warmly greeted by the owner Frankie, who I immediately realised was a cross-dresser. Carly was introduced first and then Mark said I was his slightly younger brother who he was training to be his assistant.

"Any interesting clients lately, Frankie?" Mark asked, and Frankie reeled off a list of names I'd never heard of, except for the last one.

"Oh, and we had Shirley MacLaine in yesterday, she drove me mad but at least I can pay my rent now bless her."

Bizarrely in the centre of the shop was a small circular bar. Mark introduced me to Wayne the barman who stood like a statue resplendent in a lime green suit and matching bow tie. "Fix my slightly younger bro up with a large G&T please Wayne, whilst I look after Carly," Mark requested.

I watched the bartender pour the largest amount of gin possible, leaving hardly any room for the tonic. "Wow, that's powerful," I stated, taking a sip.

"Well if I know Carly, you may be here quite some time sir, enjoy."

We made some small talk about the queen, Wayne was disappointed I'd never actually met her, before he ran through a list of famous Brits he'd had the pleasure of serving in the four years he'd been working in this shop.

"I had what's his name in here yesterday, the Eurythmics guy?"

"Dave Stewart," I clarified.

"That's the one, nice fella, likes a Tequila Sunrise."

"Who's the most famous Brit you've served then Wayne?"

"Too many to mention, Elton of course, he's a shopaholic and an alcoholic, so we love him here. Sean Connery's been in a few times, he likes a malt, not a Martini. But our number one client is," Wayne looked around the shop and then whispered, "David Bowie." He let the name linger.

"Wow, what was he like?"

"A gentleman, a true English gentleman."

"He's my music god," I confirmed.

"Yes, yes sir, that's exactly what he is. My hands were shaking when I made him a Margarita, but he was so polite, so lovely."

"I'm not sure he's actually English, Wayne, I think he came here from another planet."

Wayne laughed. "I like you, Sid, I like your brother, god save the queen!" He clinked glasses with me.

He was right about Carly, she was a good hour and a half shopping, by the time she was done I'd demolished three of Wayne's G&T's. I climbed into the back of my brother's compact car and closed my eyes, but the world started to spin so I kept them open. I could hardly see out the windows for all of Carly's shopping bags, I felt I might throw up at any moment and lose my brother one of his best clients. The thirty-minute drive to her home seemed like a lifetime. I don't recall saying goodbye, but I remember yelling at Mark to stop the car at the end of her road, where I was as sick as a dog on the kerbside.

I thought it would be the last time Mark invited me out with a client. However, the next day he went out cycling whilst I nursed my hangover. That evening he called me from the emergency room at the local hospital and told me he'd been knocked off his bike by a refuse truck and had broken his ankle. In an instant, I became his driver for the next three months.

I soon discovered my brother was a bit of a dark horse, as not only did he have his connections in the swanky boutiques of Beverley Hills, but he also supplied his clients' other services. He sent me over to Carly's with a bag of grass, it turned out he was a drug supplier to the rich and almost famous in and around LA.

Carly seemed very pleased to see me, probably because of what I was delivering. She asked after my brother and insisted I had a cold beer. She sat on the sofa next to me, I guessed her age at around forty-five. She was attractive for her age, Mark had warned me she had a reputation as something of a man eater with three ex-husbands on her CV.

"I love your brother, Sid, apart from being so knowledgeable with fashion, and so well connected, he's just such a fabulous human being. I'd make him hubby number four if he wasn't, you know…"

She hesitated, so I interrupted. "Gay."

"Exactly, Sid, he's told me about why he came to the states, it must have been so difficult."

"It's been difficult for all of us," I confirmed.

She disappeared into the kitchen for a few moments before returning with a freshly rolled spiff between her lips. She took a long puff before offering it to me. "I take it you indulge, Sid," she whispered.

"I'm more of speed man to be honest but hey, when in Rome." I felt an instant buzz as I inhaled, trying not to cough.

"Well I'm sure your brother can sort out whatever you require, Sid." She put her hand on mine and inhaled a long draw of her spliff. "Let's go and fuck," she whispered, pulling me up off the sofa.

I was beginning to enjoy California, first Mia and now Carly, some twenty years older than me. I was thinking of Trudie and Roland less and less by the day.

* * *

I'd dozed off for a couple of hours, I was woken by my father's strange breathing noises, the like of which I'd never heard before. I could only describe it as a death rattle. I looked at the pillow at my feet. I knew the old fella would put up one hell of a fight just to be awkward. I checked my list, *3d – 6:10am suffocation (allow 20 minutes?)*. That seemed excessive but I wasn't going to take any chances if my plan to be at the Isle of Wight festival in three days' time was to succeed. I thought about my family and friends' reaction if I actually went to the festival the day after my father passed.

The primal like noises he was making were overwhelming, I decided to pick up the pillow and made my way to the living room. I slinked back on my mum's old sofa and tried to block out my present problems by returning to the past.

31

CALIFORNIA DREAMING

(1983)

I SAT ON Mark's balcony sipping a tequila sunrise, having taken a couple of blues from a huge biscuit tin that Mark had recently acquired for me. I'd dropped off a couple of designer trouser suits and a small parcel to Carly that afternoon. We'd had our usual sex session, she even tipped me when I left. The humiliation and shyness around women that had blighted me for so long back home seemed a million miles and a lifetime ago.

I'd got myself a regular girlfriend, Jenny, a hippy chick who worked at a local bar. For the first time since the Lisa fiasco, way back during my brief flirtation with the carpet industry, I was happy to be chased rather than do the chasing.

Mark came and joined me, placing his broken foot on the small wrought iron table between us. He told me how grateful he was having me around to help him, he was slurring his words and looked wild eyed.

"You okay, Mark? I've not seen you so pissed and stoned bruv."

"Two bottles of Chardonnay and too much of this stuff." He pushed a small diamond encrusted snuff box towards me, which I opened. It was packed with white powder.

"Fucking hell, Mark, is this what I think it is?"

"I don't normally touch the stuff, but I've had a bad day," his voice croaked with emotion and he buried his head in his hands. "My friend died last night," he choked.

"The one in San Francisco?" I guessed. He just nodded. I knew it was AIDS, I knew the cat sitter probably had it. I was suddenly filled with terror, Mark sensed my fears.

"I'm fine, Sid, I've been very careful, but don't let Mum know about any of this."

We drank and chatted till the sun came up. I tried to keep his spirits up, I mentioned that my tourist visa would soon run out. Mark's reaction took me by surprise.

"Not a problem, marry Carly," he casually suggested.

"What?"

"Husband number two was a French friend of mine, he paid her two thousand dollars and got to consummate the marriage!"

"What if I just overstay, just carry on working for you cash in hand?"

"No problem until you leave, you'll be banned from returning."

"Seems less drastic than marrying," I confirmed, as I staggered towards the sofa and proceeded to sleep all day.

* * *

So that's what I did, I overstayed my visa by six months. I became an integral part of Mark's operation and spent many a happy hour sharing drugs and bodily fluids with Carly, Jenny and occasionally Mia. Not forgetting regular dips in the Pacific, warmed by the ever-present Californian sun. I was truly in paradise and couldn't see myself ever leaving, until I received a rare letter from Trudie.

It was almost two pages of tittle-tattle, she'd been to see the Damned and ran into Jimmy and his strange new girlfriend. The last sentence changed everything. *'I have to tell you that Roland is now divorced and has asked me to marry him. Not sure about the age gap to be honest but I'm rather flattered.'*

I made a list of the possible reasons for her giving me this information:

1) She was just being honest.

2) She was digging the knife in.

3) She was trying to shock me into rushing home.

4) A combination of all three.

I spent the next 24 hours ignoring paradise and mulling over the last sentence. Was I prepared to give up the climate, easy drugs, easy sex, easy cash? There was no contest, that old cunt Roland wasn't going to get the better of me!

Mark had gone up to San Francisco to a memorial for three of his closest friends he'd recently lost. I felt bad leaving a short note saying I was returning to freezing grey London. I knew there was no coming back.

Forty-eight hours later, I was on the Piccadilly line from Heathrow to North London, already plotting and planning my twin track strategy. On one hand, I had to woo Trudie away from any interest in Roland, on the other, I had to deter him from realising his plan to marry Trudie.

I made my mental lists. I was flushed with a new-found confidence after my sojourn in sunny California.

32

THE BIG WOO

MY MUM WAS pleased to see me and delighted to hear my glowing account of Mark's life. I obviously didn't furnish her with the more sordid details related to his career. My first call back home was to Uncle Martin, telling him I was back and keen to start my brilliant career in the fireplace industry, and that I'd need an advance on my wages. I then called Trudie's flatmate Melissa, who was delighted to hear from me. I'd embarrassed myself the last time we met but I knew she was a trusted ally and wasn't a fan of Roland at all. I told her a few details of my plan and how she could help, most importantly stealing Trudie's passport and a bag of clothes. I also asked if she knew anyone with a spare room, as I couldn't bear the thought of staying with my father. Lastly, I asked Melissa if she knew where I could get a small supply of speed.

She came through on all four requests. She met me at her brother Craig's flat, he worked nights as a tunneller on the underground and told me I could rent the spare room for a very fair weekly payment. She also mentioned Craig could get me whatever I needed on the drug front. Speed was what helped him work nights in atrocious conditions.

In a couple of days, I was sorted in my room and had a good supply of blues and beer ready for operation 'Big Woo'. My lists were written, I was ready to call her. The last time I'd spoken to her I was not in a good place but several months and a few Californian girls bedded, I felt my credibility was restored.

I'd downed a couple of blues and a couple of neat scotches, I felt good. As soon as she answered a newfound confidence took over, after all *she'd* written to me. Yes, I'd considered that it was, bearing in mind her last sentence regarding Roland's proposal, a further and possibly final humiliation. But, on reflection, I knew she was too nice a person to consider such a thing.

"Hi Trudie, it's Sid. I'm back!" I started.

"I heard, Sid! What you up to?" She sounded pleased to hear from me.

"I'm just tying things up here and then I'm moving to LA to help my brother with his business." It was sort of a lie, as I knew I'd probably been banned from entering the States for ten years due to my visa overstay, but I had considered trying to re-enter illegally.

We made some small talk for a few minutes before she asked, "So what exactly were you doing over there?"

"Why don't we meet for a drink and I'll tell you all about it, Trud?"

There was a pause.

"I don't want to hurt you anymore, Sid, you obviously got my letter."

"Well I'm sure you're not married yet, just a drink for old times' sake," I casually stated, when really, I wanted to plead with her.

"Just a drink," she whispered, as if someone else was with her.

I felt a pang of the old heartache. "How about I pick you up Friday when you finish work?"

"Okay, Sid, just a drink and a chat okay?"

"Deal," I lied. One half of my plan was moving in the right direction, the other half would have to wait.

* * *

I had two days to plan the 'Big Woo'. By the time Friday came, I had a rock-solid itinerary sorted. I didn't have time to meet Jimmy, I phoned him and told him I was back, and I'd be busy for a few days. I popped round to pick up a Ford Escort from Smithy, who was now buying and selling cars. I realised the light blue wreck of a car he lent me was not any match for Roland's silver machine, but it would hopefully serve its purpose.

Trudie opened the door to her flat, I'd forgotten how beautiful she was. She literally took my breath away. My return to grey wet miserable England from the sun-drenched paradise that was California was instantly vindicated. She pecked me on the cheek, and I led her down to the pathetic looking wheels Smithy had lent me.

"It's temporary," I stated embarrassingly.

"Where we going?" she quizzed me, as she struggled with her seat belt.

"A drink, maybe something nice to eat."

"Okay," she nodded.

"Leave it to me," I muttered, as we pulled away.

"You look very well, Sid, very tanned," she said smiling.

I drove a strange route towards the North Circular, I'd factored into my timing the Friday rush hour traffic.

"Where the hell are we going?" Trudie sounded concerned as we turned onto the congested A406. I waited until I was on the outside lane and got up a small head of steam before dropping the ultimatum that would decide my whole future.

"Look on the back seat, Trud, there's a holdall."

She loosened her seat belt and managed to reach back and pull it onto her lap.

"Have a look inside."

She took a peep inside, her passport was lying on top, she pulled it out and opened it up bewildered. "This is my passport, what the hell is going on, Sid?"

"Okay, this is the situation, Trudie." I paused whilst I negotiated the dreaded Hanger Lane gyratory system. "We're on our way to Heathrow, I've booked two nights in a swanky hotel in Paris. We can either carry on or I will turn back at the next junction, drop you home and I'll return to California via Paris." All of this was true except the California bit, but I did plan to travel some more if the 'Big Woo' didn't work. Besides, I would have to lay low for a while if I had to get rid of Roland!

"How did you get hold of my passport and clothes?" she queried after a brief pause for thought.

"Melissa," I replied, feeling I was dropping her in it.

"She bloody would, she's always telling me you're the one for me, she can't stand Roland."

"We are approaching the next junction, what's it to be, Paris or a U-turn?"

"Just how swanky is this hotel?" she asked.

"Very, four stars."

"Separate rooms?"

"No, but I promise I'll behave. Plus, I've booked a meal on a boat tomorrow night that cruises slowly down the Seine." I got to the junction.

"Okay, drive on, but definitely no funny business."

* * *

We arrived at the hotel just before midnight. We dumped our bags in our sumptuous room and headed for a late-night bar nearby that the concierge recommended. We demolished two bottles of champagne, tried to enjoy the house jazz band, despite both of us confessing we hated the genre, and laughing as we did Cleo Laine scatting impersonations. We were both extremely drunk when we returned to the hotel.

"Don't forget, Sid, no funny business," Trudie laughed, as she jumped on the bed naked.

By the time we actually got to sleep, it was getting light.

I woke with a start. "Shit it's midday, our cruise on the Seine leaves at one!"

We quickly showered together, got dressed, jumped in a taxi and made it just in time.

We sat at a table by a port hole and within minutes of our departure we were drinking champagne again. "Hair of the dog." I clinked glasses with Trudie.

"So, you said something about a drink and a chat," she teased me.

I made my move. "So, when you getting married, Trud?"

"Married?" She looked perplexed.

"To Roland," I confirmed.

"Oh yes, he asked me a few weeks ago when he was very drunk, I'm not sure if he meant it," she casually replied.

"I assumed from your letter it was a serious request."

"Oh," she said and simply shrugged.

I wondered if I'd given up paradise for nothing.

"Anyway, he's too old for me, Melissa calls him the 'pensioner'."

"So, you're not going to marry him then?" I pressed.

"Well, unless he makes me an offer I can't refuse, no. I'm too young to settle down anyway. Besides if I was serious about accepting, would I be here with you?"

This was encouraging. There was maybe no need to kill Roland after all.

"So, what about you, Sid? Have you got a tanned blonde Californian girl waiting for you?"

I told Trudie about Mia, Carly and Jenny. I felt I was gaining some pride back after my humiliations.

"Blimey, you rascal. You didn't miss me then."

"Well I tried to keep busy so I wouldn't miss you, but obviously I did."

She smiled and held my hand. "I did miss you, Sid, I'm sorry I drove you away."

"It wasn't you," I lied, "I wanted to help my brother."

The river cruise was a spectacular success, as was the rest of the weekend.

* * *

We were back on the dreaded North Circular heading home when I made my move.

"So, what now, Trudie?"

"What do you mean, what now?"

"What now for us, where we going next?"

"California seems very nice," she laughed.

"It's overrated," I said, knowing I wouldn't be taking her there anytime soon. "I was thinking more of a movie or a gig."

"Good idea," she agreed.

I turned the radio up, the song was new to me but I instantly recognised the singer's voice. "Sounds like Paul Weller," I commented, whilst turning the radio volume up a notch or two.

"It is Paul Weller," she confirmed, "and his Style Council."

"His what?" I was confused.

"You do know the Jam split a few months ago?"

"They what?!" I exclaimed, suddenly realising I'd been out the loop musically during my time in the States and before that, during my humiliating stalking period.

"Weller decided the Jam had gone as far as it could musically and has started a new band. I like them."

I listened to the rest their first single, *Speak Like a Child,* in silence. "Sounds like a soul record, it's not the Jam is it."

"It's not supposed to be," she chided me.

We drove back to Trudie's flat with me ranting about how the Jam would have surpassed the Stones if they'd stuck together.

Later on, in Trudie's bed, I sat up and continued expressing my disappointment. I should probably have been reflecting on the success of the 'Big Woo' but Trudie's casual revelation of the Jam splitting up had reminded me of what, on reflection, was the greatest year of my life. Well, almost.

* * *

I must have dozed off again, I looked at my phone it was 3.17am. The old man's 'death rattle' was now a primal scream. *Should I suffocate him now and be done with it?* No, best stick to the plan, to the timings on my list, I could do with a couple of hours sleep. I was facing a hectic few days.

33

NINETEEN SEVENTY-SEVEN
(1977)

THE MID-SEVENTIES were not the best. Bowie had dispensed with the Spiders and my love for him diminished with every album from *Diamond Dogs* onwards. He was now in Berlin with the self-described non-musician Brian Eno. He was lost to me, of course, I would fall in love with him again in the early eighties when he re-emerged for the *Serious Moonlight* tour with his bleached blonde hair and tan, with Nile Rodgers helping to give a fresh new sound.

Mott were history, bands like Led Zep, Pink Floyd and Sabbath were bloated versions of their former selves, making concept albums that said nothing about the world I was struggling to make my way in.

On the football front, England had failed to qualify for another World Cup and Chelsea were facing relegation, my heroes were all long gone.

My humiliating struggle to find a permanent girlfriend continued fresh from the Erika fiasco. I drifted in and out of a succession of dead-end jobs. I'd not seen a lot of Jimmy and Smithy, due to them having girlfriends and me losing my mind over Erika.

Just as 1976 drew to a close, Jimmy called me and told me he had split up with his girlfriend on Christmas Day due to the present he'd given her. The good news was he'd met some girls on the underground who'd invited him to their flat for a New Year's Eve party. That was the good news, the bad news was it was in Stockwell, which meant an expedition south of the river.

For the first time in at least two years the old gang were reunited. Jimmy, Smithy, plus an old friend of ours, Clive, and I made our way to what we called bandit country. We plotted up in a pub close to the address Jimmy had scrawled on the back of cigarette packet, it was possibly the worst pub I'd ever set foot in. Jimmy waxed lyrical about how attractive these girls were and told us that the party didn't start until eleven o'clock and would go on all night.

We had a couple of pints catching up on recent dramas, mostly focusing on Jimmy's split with his girlfriend of two years. She didn't appreciate the vibrator he'd bought her for Christmas, particularly the embarrassment of opening it in front of her family. We bought four cans of beer each from the off-license attached to the pub and followed Jimmy, who was carrying an A to Z map.

It was around 11.15pm when we found the block of flats, it was four stories high and of course the girls flat was on the top floor with no lift. Jimmy rang the bell, there was no answer but we could hear KC and the Sunshine Band booming from inside, so we guessed no one inside would hear the bell. Smithy stepped forward and banged on the door with his closed fist. A few seconds later, the door opened, and two huge bruisers stood staring at us.

"Who the fuck are you?" one of them snarled.

"The girls invited us," Jimmy answered.

"I don't think so matey," the other thug grunted.

"Elsa invited us," Jimmy pleaded.

"Oh Elsa, I see. Okay lads, in that case follow us."

Jimmy gave us a triumphant thumbs up as we followed them down the hallway into the kitchen, where two more heavies were smoking spliffs. We could see a load of girls dancing in the living room.

"Okay lads, put your booze on the table and fuck off before we fucking break your ugly faces," the nutter that first opened the door threatened, as one of the blokes grabbed Clive and held a pen knife to the side of his head. We dumped our cans on the table and legged it out the flat and down the steps.

There was only fifteen minutes left of 1976 and there we were on a pavement in deepest South London and it was starting to snow!

"You fucking idiot, Jimmy!" Clive cursed.

"What now," I pondered aloud.

"Fuck them, I'm going to get our beers back at least!" Jimmy yelled and ran like a mad thing back up the stairs. We stood there waiting for what seemed an age.

"Fuck it, we'd better see if Jimmy's ok," Smithy exclaimed, so we reluctantly started up the stairs again. We'd reached the second floor when we heard shouting and suddenly, we saw our mate rolling down the stairs with a couple of guys shouting that they'd kill him if he ever showed his face in these parts again. We picked him up and led him downstairs.

Jimmy had a black eye, fortunately his glass eye, a bloody nose and at least two teeth missing. He was clutching one can of cider.

We sat in the entrance trying to keep warm. We heard the church bells ringing out and toasted the arrival of 1977 with the one can of cider.

"Happy new year boys!" Clive threw the empty can against the door of a flat.

"Another let down, Jimmy, what now?" Smithy moaned.

Before Jimmy could answer, the door to number one opened and a middle-aged woman literally fell on the floor drunk as a skunk.

"Happy new year boys!" she squealed, as she tried to get up, but she was so pissed she just lay there laughing.

Clive and Smithy went to her assistance, helping her up, taking her inside her flat and laying her down on her sofa. Jimmy and I followed, the flat was in a terrible state. Empty Vodka bottles were strewn all over the place, the fridge door was open, the place stunk.

"Fucking hell, let's get out of here," Jimmy exclaimed.

"We can't just leave her lads, she could do herself some serious harm," Clive protested.

"Okay, let's tidy the place up for her, we've got nowhere else to go," Jimmy said finding some black sacks in the kitchen.

We spent a good hour cleaning up this poor woman's flat, after which we carried her from the sofa to her bed without her stirring. We decided to crash in the living room as there was no way of getting home.

We were woken up at 7.00am on New Year's Day morning by the woman screaming. "Who the fuck are you lot? What are you doing in my flat?!" She hadn't seemed to notice our sterling efforts in sprucing her home up.

"Have you taken liberties with me? I'm calling the police!" she bellowed.

We all legged it out of her flat and headed north towards the Thames. It was absolutely freezing, we were dressed for partying, not a blizzard, and we were starving. Smithy persuaded us to head towards Covent Garden, where his next-door neighbour had a cafe that opened every day of the year. Jimmy looked a terrible state with his black swollen eye and his split lip, it was minus two centigrade and we were in our party gear.

We arrived at Tony's Cafe but there was no sign of life.

"I'm getting the tube home, I'm fucking freezing and starving," Clive grumbled. I felt the same.

"Give Tony ten minutes, he's always boasting he's never not opened in the fifteen years he has owned the café," Smithy pleaded, but Clive shrugged and was off.

We waited a good fifteen minutes, reflecting on what a shit New Year's Eve we'd suffered, and were about to head home when Tony came shuffling through the snow with his wife.

"Tony, thank god you're here, we are cold and hungry." Smithy embraced his neighbour.

"What the hell have you lot been up to?" he asked, spotting Jimmy's wounds.

"Don't ask, Tone, just get us three full English breakfasts and three teas on the go, mate."

We warmed ourselves up sitting by the three-bar heater and sipped the hot tea like it was a drug. We discussed the night's incidents - football, girls and whatever happened to Ink Bat.

We wolfed our breakfasts down and Tony brought more teas. "On the house boys, you can't leave yet, there's a blizzard out there!"

We must have been in the cafe for at least two hours when a group of eight Punk Rockers entered the café, instantly taking it over. At least three of them had guitar cases, there were six fellas and two very loud girls. One of the musicians looked familiar, his mate sitting with his back to me seemed to be the centre of everyone else's attention. We didn't realise that a few years later he would be a bona fide music legend!

A few of them studied Jimmy's wounds. Tony came out to take their order, he embraced the leader of the pack and the familiar looking guy. "Tony, meet the band!" he bellowed.

"Blimey, Joe, there's a lot of you," Tony laughed.

"Our entourage," Joe boasted.

"We've got a gig round the corner in Neal Street tonight, I'll put you and Mrs. Alfano on the guest list if you like," he offered.

"Thanks, but no thanks, Joc, the missus and me prefer a bit of opera, not your bloody noise."

The three of us talked about whether we were fans of punk music. Smithy was certainly still into Pink Floyd and

King Crimson, two bands I'm sure our fellow diners would hate. Jimmy and I mentioned the last gig we saw together at the Greyhound, Fulham Road, Dr Feelgood, who many now cite as a forerunner to Punk. We also saw Be Bop Deluxe at the Hope and Anchor a few times.

"What became of your beloved Mott The Hoople?" Smithy asked.

"Mick Ralphs is on a stadium tour with Bad Company and Ian Hunter is doing well in the States," I confirmed, and at that moment I realised that's where I knew the young punk guitarist on the next table from. I stared at him and realised we'd definitely met a few years before.

"You got a problem, mate?" he snapped as he caught my stare.

"No pal, it's just that I just realised where I know you from, Mott The Hoople, you're Mick. We've met outside the London College of Print, you ran the fan club, you got me in without a ticket. Must have been about four years ago," I guessed.

"Yeah, I was there," he confirmed, and came and sat at the spare chair Clive should have been sitting in.

"Hi lads, I'm Mick. Fuck me, mate, looks like you had a fun night," he teased Jimmy.

"You should see the other fella," Smithy joked.

"So, you know me from following Mott?" he addressed me.

"Yes, mate, I recognise you from those days, you blagged me a ticket when they did that random gig at the print college at Elephant and Castle, I told you I'd run away from home to see the boys at the Weeley Festival."

"Fucking hell, I think I remember, didn't you get into a lot of trouble?" Mick recalled correctly.

"Yes indeed, Jimmy here lost his fucking eye on the first day, didn't even see them!"

"I didn't fucking see anyone," Jimmy interrupted.

Mick turned and shouted to the geezer who was the centre of attention. "Oi Joe, these lads were at Weeley to see Mott, this geezer lost his fucking eye there!"

"Top lads!" Joe acknowledged us with a thumbs up.

"What you up to today lads? Our band are opening a new venue in Neal Street tonight. If you want to hang around and help get our equipment in etcetera, you'll get free entry and all the booze you want."

We looked at each other for a millisecond before all shaking his hand.

"What's your band called Mick?" Jimmy asked.

"The Clash!" he answered, re-joining his mates.

* * *

We spent the day lugging equipment into what seemed an impossibly small venue. We were told the capacity was around a hundred, but when The Clash came on there was at least double that number. We didn't realise that this was the official opening of The Roxy. This gig and venue would go on to become the subject of films, documentaries, books and all sorts. We were there, guests of the band, but not one of us can remember a thing. Mick was true to his word and then some. Apart from all the beer we could drink, there was an endless supply of amphetamines. We were totally wasted. To this day we can't recall anything about that evening, we were there and that's all that matters. New Year's Eve might have been a disaster, but New Year's Day 1977 was a day the three of us would never forget.

We all went to Tony's funereal in Peterborough where he retired to when he sold the cafe. They played Sinatra's *My Way*, but I thought *London Calling* would have been more appropriate. We followed The Clash for a few weeks, the Roundhouse, the 100 Club, the Greyhound, we spent every Saturday afternoon watching Chelsea trying to get back in the top division and a punk gig in the evening. Just because of the name, we started following the group Chelsea, whose singer Gene October was a force of nature.

Watching football and gigs was a dangerous pastime in those days. Jimmy with his nickname Cyclops was a bit of a face on the terraces. One Saturday in March he got involved in fight with some Portsmouth hooligans and lost yet another tooth, then in the evening we were in the middle of a mass brawl at a Sham69 concert at the Roundhouse, causing the gig to be abandoned after just two songs.

Smithy went missing after April, falling hook line and sinker for Beverly. Jimmy and I were having the time of our lives though. Music, football, booze and drugs, that was it and no ties. Of course, I would have liked to have been tied, but as the previous year had been shit for music and football, plus the whole humiliating Erika business, a year off from what normally ended in abject failure was in hindsight a bit of a godsend. Jimmy and I were averaging a gig a week, sometimes two. The highlight of the year came about in mid-July, when we went to see Chelsea at the exotically named California Ballroom in Dunstable.

I was driving a bright yellow Austin 1100 at the time, which regularly stalled on the slightest hill and the reverse gear was very hit and miss. We spent a large percentage of the journey to Dunstable jump-starting the car. I decided to drop a couple of blues on arrival and planned to crash in the car after the gig. We got into the Bedfordshire town's hottest venue just as the first band, The Saints, from Australia, were finishing their set. We plotted up at the upstairs bar and were surrounded by hardcore punks. We got chatting to a couple of local girls who were there for the headliners, whoever they were. We were there for the next band on, Chelsea.

Jimmy whispered to me that there might be better options than sleeping in the 'custard jar', as we called my car. There was a fair crowd for Chelsea and within a few minutes the singer/frontman Gene October was covered in spit, which we had learnt was a sign of appreciation at punk gigs.

We joined in the 'pogoing' for the forty-minute set, before retreating back to the bar covered in sweat and god knows what. We approached the girls and Jimmy asked if they wanted to show us the delights of Dunstable. They declined as they wanted to see the headliners, so we decided to have one more drink before maybe heading home whilst I was still sober.

We were heading for the exit when the headliners came on, we heard the first familiar chords of the Batman theme and both stopped in our tracks, nodded to each other and legged it back to the ballroom. We pushed our way to the front, the crowd were going mental. The three band members were dressed in black suits, white shirts and black ties, they were covered in spit and sweat.

The only splash of colour were the red guitars, which were played at a frenzied pace. I clocked the simple band name on the base drum, The Jam. We were hooked for life. Here was a band whose songs were about the world we lived in. At the end of the gig we took a crude DIY flyer with a long list of their future gigs, we were already planning the next one.

We saw the girls outside who told us they lived with their parents, but we could come and meet them the following Saturday as their parents would be out. We arranged to meet by the church in the town centre.

What a night, spoilt only by the journey home as the car stalled and spluttered all the way home.

A week later we made the return journey to Dunstable to meet the girls. This time the custard jar behaved itself, thanks to Smithy, who serviced it for mates' rates during the week having just concluded his apprenticeship as a mechanic.

We were sat on the church wall having arrived twenty minutes early. We discussed The Jam, who we planned to see at the 100 Club the following week. Jimmy then brought me up to speed with regards to the latest developments in his search for his birth parents. Since he turned eighteen, he'd been proactive on this issue, particularly when between girlfriends. He'd had a meeting with a lady from social services who'd informed him of possible developments. I asked him if he'd discussed the matter with Alice, who I knew he would always consider his mum. He confessed he couldn't bring himself to talk to her about it, though he knew she wasn't stupid, she'd have realised he would naturally be curious about his past.

We sat there talking until half past eight. "How long we going to wait, Sid? Do you reckon we've been stood up?"

"Give it another ten minutes, you know what girls are like," I mumbled, having no real idea what girls are like at all. We discussed Chelsea's promotion back to the top division and their chances of staying there. A car pulled up on the other side of the road, two thuggish looking geezers got out and strolled over to where we were perched on the church wall.

"Are you Sid and Jimmy?" one of them asked politely.

We both nodded.

"Debbie and Sue can't make it," the other one said smiling, before punching us both in the face.

We both fell backwards into the small cemetery behind the wall. It took a few seconds for us to come to our senses.

"Fuck it, my nose!" I cried, wiping a stream of blood away with my hand before reaching for my hanky.

"I've lost another fucking tooth!" Jimmy confirmed, picking it up from the floor.

"It's fucking dangerous meeting girls with you, mate," I stated, thinking about the New Year's Eve fiasco.

We trudged back to the car and drove back home in silence until Jimmy declared, "I'm going to fucking return there and sort those wankers sometime!"

* * *

Two weeks later, the four of us went on our first 'lads' trip abroad to sunny Ibiza. It wasn't quite the twenty-four-hour party island it is now, but it was getting there, and we did our best to lay the groundwork for future generations of ravers.

Within an hour of arriving at our San Antonio apartment, we ran into a Chelsea hooligan who recognised Jimmy, his reputation on the terraces was worryingly well known since the incident at Stoke. We went for a drink with

Gareth and his mates and after a while he slipped into the conversation that he had a massive bag of blues in his hotel room.

We went back and ended up spending virtually all our pesetas on a week's supply, plus a bag of cocaine, which Jimmy decided we needed to try. Clive wasn't really into substances, he certainly didn't need a confidence boost, he was a really good-looking lad who had no problem with girls. Whereas Jimmy, Smithy and I were always desperate for a steady girlfriend, Clive would love them and leave them. Whilst we were getting completely off our heads, he was laying by the pool enjoying the blistering hot sun, whilst a Swedish beauty rubbed suntan lotion into his back.

On the third day, Jimmy, Smithy and I were booked on a round the island boat trip, we decided this would be a good opportunity to experience our first go at cocaine. Jimmy claimed to be an expert on weights and measures and divided the spoils appropriately. The boat was basically a disco on water.

I recall the three of us dancing like maniacs amongst a throng of German women and then the boat docking at a beautiful unspoilt beach where we were supposed to enjoy a giant communal paella. The last thing I remember is desperately seeking shade from the burning sun. And then, nothing. I remember nothing at all.

I woke up on a huge hotel lobby sofa, it was the next morning, I'd lost eighteen hours. I sat up trying to remember how I got there but my mind was a complete blank. A few young tourists passed me by on their way to the breakfast hall, some looked at me smiling knowingly. A fella then came out the lift wearing an England football shirt, he limped towards me and stopped, removing his sunglasses.

"You're still alive then, mate?" He laughed.

"I think so, where am I?"

"Santa Eulalia, mate," he confirmed.

"Is that near San Antonio?" I chanced.

"Other side of the island, mate," he chuckled.

"Shit, how the fuck did I end up here?"

"Well the first time I saw you, you climbed into the luggage hold under our coach claiming you needed some shade. You were clutching a carafe of Sangria, I was impressed. And then when we got back here, the driver opened the hatch and out you danced asking where the nearest bar was!"

"Jesus, how the fuck do I get back to St Antonio?"

"You could try the bus station or wait till tomorrow evening when we are being taken by coach there to a disco."

"Who's we?" I queried.

"We are on a Club 18-30 holiday. I'm Billy," he introduced himself.

I was starving, I needed food. I made my way to the hotel restaurant, a young lady in a smart uniform asked me my room number, which normally would have thrown me, but the cocktail of drink and drugs had given me a new-found confidence. "Two two seven," I stated, and to my astonishment she smiled and gestured for me to go in.

I attacked the buffet like there was no tomorrow, I couldn't recall ever feeling so hungry. Eggs, bacon, tomatoes, beans, bread and all those German cold meats were piled up on my plate. I found an empty table and got stuck in, washing the food down with a jug of fresh orange juice. Two young ladies approached me, giggling.

"You've stopped dancing then?" one of the them chortled.

"I'm sorry?"

"You've stopped throwing yourself about," the other one stated in a thick Geordie accent.

I explained that I had no memory of the night at all and I was in fact a refugee from St Antonio. They sat opposite and told me that I'd climbed out the luggage hold on their coach and followed the crowd to the pool side bar, which basically was a twenty-four hour open air disco, where I spent from four in the afternoon to four in the morning throwing myself around the dance floor! I shook my head in disbelief and explained my situation.

Mary and Jane took me under their wing and let me use their shower. I was wearing the same t-shirt, shorts and flip flops I'd been wearing since leaving St Antonio. I thought about finding a shop and buying at least a new t-shirt and pants, but I checked my pockets and they were empty. I reckon I could have only slept for two hours tops, someone must have taken my money.

I sat on Jane's bed and explained my situation.

"Well you'll have to stay in our room until the coach leaves for St Antonio tomorrow evening." She smiled and sat next to me touching my face. "Your poor forehead is peeling," she whispered.

"It must have been that bloody beach, all I remember is being desperate for shade."

She kissed me and ten minutes later we were laying naked on the bed getting our breath back. I closed my eyes and slept for fourteen hours straight!

When I awoke the room was empty and in total darkness. I could recall the mornings events, but my mind was still a blank from before then. I had no watch and there was no clock in the room, all I knew was I was wide awake. I put on my now smelly clothes and went out on the balcony and looked down on the hotel pool. There was a throbbing beat coming from two giant speakers and a throng of revellers dancing. I was tempted to go down and join the party but didn't want to risk being thrown out the hotel. I thought it best I wait as long as possible in the sanctuary of the girls' room before stowing away on the coach to San Antonio.

I sat for a good hour watching the party before I heard the room door open and a lot of laughter and merriment. I decided to sit on the balcony chair and feign sleep.

"Someone left the balcony door open," I heard Mary drunkenly exclaim, before closing it and locking it.

For the next two hours l was subjected to the sounds of passion emanating from the bedroom, particularly the spasmodic thud of the headboards smashing against the concrete wall. I suddenly developed a terrible thirst, realising I'd not had any refreshment since breakfast. I felt faint and nauseous, it was a struggle to get out of the chair. The world was spinning, I felt sweat dripping into my eyes. I thought I might lose consciousness, so I crawled to the balcony doors, it took all my strength to tap on the glass panel.

A minute later Jane opened the door and saw me prostrate at her feet.

"Fucking hell, Sid, we thought you'd gone out! Are you okay?"

I tried to speak but no words would come.

I then heard one of their guests call out, "Who the hell is that?"

"It's Sid, he's our tenant, quick, get some water, he's in a bad way."

"Tenant?" I heard a Geordie accent say.

"It's a long story, Phil. Quick, help me get him to a tap, I think he's dehydrated."

These were the days long before bottled water was a thing. The two fellas dragged me to the bathroom and held me up, so my mouth was against the sink tap. I drank and drank, probably not the cleanest water on earth but it saved my life. I didn't do much for the girls' party, as I alternated between drinking frenzies and violent vomiting. The combination of sun, booze and cocaine had conspired to completely fuck me up. To their credit, the girls, who happened to be student nurses, really looked after me and managed to smuggle me onto the coach to San Antonio.

I laid on the floor under the feet of the occupants of the back row, clutching a bottle of lemonade that the girls had given me. I was rehydrated but my head was throbbing, I just wanted to get back to the apartment, shower and put on some fresh clothes. When the coach pulled into San Antonio bus station it was 7.30pm, the rep announced that the group had a free couple of hours and then they should meet outside Club Galaxy 9.30pm. I told the girls I'd meet them in there, and I headed up the main drag towards my apartment.

Just before I reached it, I heard a shout from Bar Skanda, which we'd made our meeting point. "El Sid lives!" I heard Smithy roar.

I staggered over to the outside table where Smithy was sitting with Clive. They smelt me before I joined them.

"Fucking hell, Sid, the state of you." Clive held his nose.

"Where the fuck have you been? We were going to call the embassy and report you as missing," Smithy stated.

It was two and half days since they last saw me seeking shade on that beach. I gave them the edited headlights, stating that I wouldn't touch cocaine again.

"Where's Jimmy?" I asked.

"He's been nicked," Clive said casually.

"What?"

"The cocaine and sun got to Jimmy as well. About an hour after you went missing, Jimmy got a touch of sun stroke and basically went berserk," Smithy confirmed.

"Berserk?"

"Yes, he went totally berserk, he was laying on the sand, basically frying alive when some German bloke playing volleyball accidentally fell over him. Jimmy got up and kicked sand in his face and then ran around the beach kicking sand at everybody."

"And he was arrested?"

"No, the boat crew tried to calm him down, as did I, but he was like a rabid dog. So they tied him up and locked him in the engine room on the boat and then later, when we set sail again, he got loose and attacked the captain. The police were waiting for him in San Antonio and put him in a cell at the local police station."

"Has he been charged with anything?" I questioned.

"No," Clive replied. "I popped in there yesterday morning. They said when he cooled down, they'd release him. I guess he's still calming down."

"Two days in a cell is a lot of calming down," I stated.

"This is the first time in three days I've seen Clive." Smithy punched his mate on the shoulder.

"I've been busy." Clive gave a mischievous smile.

"Swedish?" I guessed.

"No, met Caroline in the lift just after you lot went on your lovely boat trip, we've been inseparable ever since. I tell you this is the real thing lads, I'm in love."

"On that note, I'm going to go and change. I suggest we meet at the Club Galaxy, ten-ish, trust me it's going to be wild," I predicted.

* * *

We managed to commandeer an alcove upstairs at Club Galaxy, where I introduced Smithy to Jane and Mary. I felt like a new man since freshening up.

Suddenly, Jimmy was standing with his arms outstretched beside us. "I'm free!" he bellowed.

We exchanged stories over a couple of beers, before Clive appeared dead on midnight with his 'inseparable' girlfriend of three days, Caroline. Normally we were insanely jealous of Clive's conquests, but we were in all honestly totally shocked at her appearance. She was wider than she was tall. A plain-ish face would be a kind description.

Clive put his arm around her and squeezed her tight before declaring, "Lads, I'd like to announce that Caroline and I are engaged to be married."

There was a mixture of laughter and expletives. Caroline flashed her engagement ring like a trophy.

"I suppose I'd better get some bubbly!" Smithy yelled.

The rest of us took the opportunity to hit the dance floor. Jimmy seemed very smitten with Mary and they disappeared shortly after.

The Jam, The Clash, the craziness in Ibiza, these were the best days of our lives. None of us would forget 1977.

34

THE WORLD'S MOST

DISSAPOINTING SERIAL KILLER

IT WAS NOW 4.47am, I was relieved to still have just over an hour before I killed my father. I stared at the ceiling and felt euphoric thinking about the best year of my life.

I thought about Clive and the little 'dumpling', as we called Caroline, whom he married within a year. Both were only twenty-one, but we learnt that her father owned seven hotels in the UK and Clive went from postman to head of procurement, Europe division, in an instant. Our Clive was no fool.

Having said that, he was now living in Florida with wife number four.

I suddenly realised my father had ceased making that awful death rattle. I put the light of my phone towards his face, wondering if the old bugger had snuffed it, and got the fright of my life.

His eyes were wide open, and he had a knowing smile on his face. I turned on the bedside lamp, his eyes flickered, he was definitely still breathing. He started to make a soft hissing sound.

I got out of my chair and knelt beside him, clutching the pillow wondering if I should end this now. He was trying to whisper something, he hadn't uttered anything coherent in weeks. I put the pillow down and put my ear to his dry sore lips. I couldn't make out what he was saying, which worried me as it might be important information about some secret stash of cash. I picked up his water bottle and squirted some into his mouth. He tried to clear his throat and managed to grip my index finger with his spindly bony hand.

"Antonio," he whispered quite clearly.

"Who's Antonio, Dad?" I whispered back.

"Antonio Rattín," he spat the words out.

"Antonio Rattín, what about him?" I replied, confused that my father would mention the Argentinian captain who was sent off in the '66 World Cup quarter final.

"I'm sorry, son, I should have come in and watched it with you." Tears now streamed down his gaunt face as he squeezed my finger. I recalled the crushing disappointment when he ignored my excitement and continued cleaning his car ready for the holiday to Devon. I wiped a tear from my cheek and for a second I felt a flicker of warmth for him.

"I'm still not sure why he was sent off, Dad," I mentioned, but his eyes had closed and he was gently snoring. I considered tearing up my list but then thought of Jimmy, who was no doubt thinking of Glastonbury.

* * *

My father was number eight on my kill list, Grant Bishop, Barry the milkman, Erika, Ink Bat and Heena were all still alive for various pragmatic reasons. I presumed Perry had died as a result of his injuries sustained in the train incident, but Jimmy cast a doubt, not that given his sight and mental condition he was in any way a reliable witness. Nonetheless he'd planted a seed of doubt that was causing me regular nightmares about Perry exacting revenge for his plight on me, giving me a permanent state of paranoia. That, of course, left Roland, whose name on my kill list had been permanently hidden by a thick black marker line since February 1984.

The 'Big Woo' had been a great success, but I knew Roland wouldn't accept the fact he'd lost out to the better man. I'd ticked off all five points on my 'Big Woo' list. Paris, river boat cruise from Camden to Little Venice (Inc. Sunday lunch), Grease the musical, David Bowie live at the Milton Keynes Bowl and the V&A museum. All helped to cement my relationship with Trudie, but there was always a black cloud lurking in the corner of the blue sky, waiting to rain on my parade.

I started a new list, collating information on Roland's routine, what time he went to work, train times etcetera, even his Saturday morning runs were timed and logged. One morning after she had gone to work, I had a sneaky look through her bedside chest drawers, I just couldn't help myself. I found four letters clipped together, all recent, all from Roland. They were full of poetry and prose, pleading with her to move to the coast with him.

I was interrupted by the doorbell, it was a delivery of a huge expensive bunch of flowers. I knew who they were from immediately. I placed them on the dining table and stared at the small envelope sellotaped to the wrapping paper. Obviously, after a few minutes' deliberation, I opened it.

My Trudie,

I can't imagine a life without you.

Please please please meet me you know where tomorrow midday.

Roley xxx

I stared at the message, my brain crackling with hate and confusion. When I looked up, I saw Melissa standing in front of me. I must have looked very sad and guilty.

"Bin them," she said, giving me a knowing wink. She will forever remain on my list of people I'd do anything for till my dying day.

* * *

I knew his Saturday routine wouldn't change, he'd leave his house 7am, check his watch and embark on his five-mile run, which would take around fifty minutes. The first half of the route would be along fairly busy streets, then he would go through a large wooded area, which I'd scouted and knew exactly where I'd strike. At the four mile point he'd cross the country lane that dissected the woods. I'd visited the spot four times at 7:30am and not seen a vehicle pass in the five-minute periods I'd waited.

I parked my innocuous Mitsubishi Colt in a small lay-by some fifty meters from the spot where he'd emerge in around ten minutes. I felt a mixture of nervousness and excitement. After the aborted killings of Bishop, Barry the milkman and Erika, at last my career as a serial killer could get going. I didn't have a desire to kill for pleasure, I saw myself as like a superhero, punishing those who bully and humiliate, those who deserved to die.

Grant Bishop got his just deserts at the hands of my cousin. I was within seconds of bludgeoning Barry the milkman to death and Erika, oh how I would have loved to kill Erika, but Cornwall was so far away. I suspect there's a litany of fellas she's ruined who wish I had, she was one evil woman.

I'd tried to blank the humiliation I'd suffered at the hands of Roland out of my mind but the sound of Trudie's screams of unbridled passion emanating from her bedroom haunted me. I'd forgive her anything and everything, but he had to die, he deserved to die, an older man taking advantage of a young girl. I thought about the madness he drove me to, writing that pathetic letter to his wife, sobbing like a baby in Melissa's arms. Fuck him.

My plan was simply to run him over, as he ran across the road checking his watch again. From where I was parked, I could see him approach the crossing some thirty meters into the wood. I'd worked out, allowing for the steep incline he'd have to negotiate, that with the engine running I'd impact with him at fifty miles an hour, killing him instantly. I'd then drive eight miles east to an empty house I'd recently installed a fireplace in and clean up any evidence on my vehicle.

In those pre-CCTV/DNA days, murder was so much easier.

There was roughly a couple of minutes left until he would come into view. I thought about the flowers, the note, then one of the letters I'd found in Trudie's bedside chest. The words echoed in my head.

"Be honest, Trudie, you'll never find a better lover than me, you said so yourself."

"Fuck him!" I shouted aloud, as I opened the car door and ran around to the boot, clutching a big ugly claw hammer, running into the woods and hiding behind an oak tree by the path Roland would imminently be pounding along.

I tried to control my breathing, which was heavy and laboured after my brief sprint from the car. A few seconds later, I heard his pounding feet in the near distance. I edged to the side of the tree, holding my weapon aloft.

He came towards me faster than I thought, looking fit and lean in his yellow vest and black shorts. I made my move as he drew level with me, I screamed as I tried to smash his skull with a single blow.

"You cunt!" I yelled, making sure he'd know, albeit briefly, that it was I that ended his life. But I slipped on the wet roots that surrounded the tree and succeeded in only catching the back of his knee with the hammer.

He gave a yelp of shock, rather than pain, and broke from an impressive jog and into a manic sprint up the incline. I got to my feet and gave chase, but I knew he'd get away and for a brief second I realised I was about to lose everything. My freedom, job, family and worst of all, Trudie. In that instant, had there been a cliff, I would have thrown myself off, but then I heard the scream and screech of brakes from the road.

I ran as quietly as I could to the opening before the road, crouching down, hammer in hand, behind a small bush. I stared in bewilderment at Roland's mangled lifeless body that was some twenty yards up the road, a trail of his blood was smeared from opposite me, where he'd run across the road in panic up to where he now lay. I saw the heavy goods truck stationary a further forty meters up the road.

A few seconds later, the door opened, and the driver got out and ran towards Roland's body, which reminded me of the wicked Roman governor that came a cropper in the chariot scene in *Ben Hur.*

I crouched down as he stopped a few feet from the body. He looked up and down the road. "Shit!" he yelled, before running back to his truck and driving off at speed. I hurriedly retraced my steps back to my car, returned the hammer back to my boot and drove swiftly back up the road, not seeing one car coming the other way in the two minutes it took me to return to the endless maze of suburban streets.

Roland was dead, I was free.

Yes, Trudie was very upset for a few months. She came home one day and told me the coroner concluded it was hit and run case, clearly involving a truck but it was unlikely the culprit would ever be caught. Of course, I was responsible for his death, in the four times I'd spied him run across the road he hesitated, looking both ways before sprinting over it. I never physically killed him though, so that was seven serial killings that I hadn't carried out.

Father would be my first and hopefully my last.

35

THE END

"MR. LEVINSON, MR. Levinson, wake up, wake up!"

I was woken by the carer, she was gently squeezing my arm.

"Mr. Levinson, wake up."

I came to from the deepest sleep I could recall. "What time is it?" I groaned in panic.

"Just gone seven," she confirmed.

Shit, seven, I was supposed to be up at six, I should have carried out at least ten items on my to do list by now. The carer's arrival was 4e! *4e - 7.00am Carer let's herself in and finds me asleep next to the deceased. She will wake me and inform of the sad news. I will ask for a few moments alone. She will probably go to kitchen and put on kettle.*

And she did all of 4e. Except I had slept through 3a to 4d.

"I'm sorry, Mr. Levinson, your father has passed," she whispered with a great professionalism.

I looked at my father, his eyes were wide open, as was his mouth, as if he died angry. I looked nervously down at the pillow, my supposed weapon of choice, it was unmoved from when I put it there. The old bugger had saved me at least twenty minutes of effort. He joined my list of near kills.

I burst into action, whilst the carer made me a cup of tea, studying the list.

5) *Phone calls*
   a) *7.20 - call doctors surgery to report death*
   b) *7.22 - call Mark*
   c) *7.24 - call Warden*
   d) *7.26 - call Rab*
   e) *7.30 - call funeral directors*
   f) *7.35 - call Leo and Tara*
   g) *7.40 - call Trudie (Maybe I should call her first?)*
   h) *7.50 - call Jimmy*

6) *Wait for doctor to come and certify death*

7) *Liaise with Mark*

8) *Liaise with Rab/funeral directors*

9) *Once funeral arranged wait for Mark/Trudie/kids to arrive and get them to contact all on separate 'guest' list*

10) *Confirm logistics with Jimmy re festival*

11) *Destroy (Burn?)*

I called and left a message on the doctor's surgery answerphone, explaining that my father had died. I called and woke Mark, who, after a manufactured silence, told me he was on his way.

The carer brought me tea and two slices of buttered toast. I thanked her for everything, giving her a twenty-pound note, which she embarrassingly accepted. Next was the warden, who told me she'd come up after she'd showered and put her face on. My next call was vital, if Jimmy and I were going to make it to the Isle of Wight in two days' time. I know I shouldn't have been thinking of that, but all my plotting and planning was for that very cause.

I went into my iPhone address book and pressed Rab.

"Hello," the Rab answered hesitantly, as if expecting a nuisance call.

"Good morning, Rabbi, it's Sid Levinson. I hope I haven't woken you."

"No, no, good morning, Sid, I'm guessing it's bad news."

"Yes, Rabbi, my father passed an hour ago, the thing is I told you of his cynicism regarding his religion, but his dying wish was to be buried as quickly as possible, just in case." I felt a flash of guilt lying to a man of God when in fact my dad's dying words related to the disgraced captain of the Argentinian football team. I thought about my crushing disappointment when he told the nine-year-old me that the car wouldn't clean itself. I never forgot it and it seems neither did he.

"Yes, just in case. Your father clearly believed in the 'dry bones' prophecy."

"I guess so, any chance of him being buried today?" I chanced my arm, feeling guilty.

"No, take a breath, Sid. It won't be today."

"Okay, but I feel I will have betrayed his wishes if he's not buried tomorrow."

"I'll call the undertakers on his private line now, you phone him at nine when he opens his office, we will liaise."

"Thanks so much, Rabbi," I said with all the sincerity I could muster.

I decided to call Trudie next.

"I'm on my way, Sid, Mark called me, you okay?" she shouted into her phone, as she turned on her car engine.

"I'm okay, Trud, I'll call the kids, see you soon."

I called Leo but it went to voicemail, so I left a short message telling him to call me. I then woke up Tara.

"Dad, what time is it?"

"Eight-ish," I informed her. I heard her yawn then she stirred.

"Shit, it's Grandad, isn't it?" she guessed.

"Sorry love, he passed a couple of hours ago."

"I'll come now"

"Okay love, try and get hold of Leo."

"Will do, Dad, see you soon."

"No rush," I reassured her.

"Oh Dad," she hesitated before continuing, "I take it the funeral won't be for a couple of weeks. Only I'm supposed to going on a girls trip to Ibiza on Thursday."

"It's probably going to be tomorrow." I felt a terrible pang of guilt.

"Tomorrow? That's quick."

"Well, it's the Jewish thing love, you know Grandad had a thing about it."

"It's okay, Dad, I'll cancel obviously." Tara always did the right thing, unlike me.

"No, no, wait till I confirm but if it's tomorrow you can still go on Thursday, what time is your flight?"

"Don't be stupid, Dad, I'm hardly going to be in the mood to party, I want to be around for you and Uncle Mark."

I was now in panic mode and no list was going to help me. "Don't be silly love, do you think Grandad would have ever stopped you having fun, he'd insist you go and enjoy yourself." Despite my devious reasons, it was sort of the truth. God knows I had my angst with my father, but I could never fault him as a Grandad, he worshipped my kids and they worshipped him.

Soon the flat was full of people, the doctor arrived to certify the death, the warden pretended to be upset, Mark entered like he was on a stage, all phoney grief and crocodile tears. Some old bat from next door popped in because she probably realised a fresh demise meant plenty of tea and biscuits. I was relieved when Trudie arrived to say the right things. I enjoyed telling Mrs O'Hara, the warden, that it was in fact my father who threw the deaf old bat's radio out of the window and not me.

I called Jimmy just as Tara arrived, I slipped into the bedroom, locking the door behind me, and sat looking at my dead father.

"Jimmy."

"Sid," he answered.

"My father has just died."

"Jeez, mate, I'm really sorry. When's the funeral?"

"Hopefully tomorrow, it's a Jewish thing."

"I'll be there, mate. Blimey, bad timing eh?"

"I hope not, mate."

"Anyway, Sid, I know you've got a lot on your mind, but could you bring the Glasto tickets to the funeral?" he asked.

"Glasto tickets, why, Jimmy?" I replied, suddenly panicking.

"Well, I guessed this would happen, so I discussed it with Heena and she agreed to come with me if…if your dad died."

My head was spinning, first Tara and the Ibiza business, now this. "Hang on, Jimmy, Heena? Heena hates rock music."

"Yeah I know, Sid, but I told her they have all that healing mumbo jumbo stuff and she said if the worst happens, she knows how much I've been looking forward to it and it might be the last chance I get and all that, she'd come with me."

"Just hang on, if the funeral's tomorrow, I'll be able to take you, mate."

"Don't be ridiculous, Sid, your father's body will still be warm. I understand you don't want to let us down but honestly, I understand there's no way you could come."

"I'll speak to you later, Jimmy." I said, not knowing how to convince him otherwise. I sat staring at the redundant pillow on the floor. I'd done all this plotting so I could take Jimmy to a festival to relive our youth and now he wants me to give him tickets to Glastonbury, which don't exist. Plus, poor Tara wants to cancel her holiday. I should have suffocated the old fucker weeks ago.

My phone buzzed, it was the Rabbi confirming everything was arranged for the next day at two o'clock and all the details will be confirmed when the undertakers collect my father's body.

I spent the rest of the day dealing with the logistics that a death, particularly a Jewish one, involves. Leo eventually surfaced and helped with contacting relatives, friends and hangers on. I climbed into bed just before midnight, utterly drained. Trudie held my hand and looked at me.

"You're going aren't you, Sid?"

"Going where, Trud?"

"With Jimmy, to the festival."

"I know it's wrong, but I don't want to let him down, Trud."

"I know you too well, Sid Levinson, once you have an idea in that strange head of yours nothing can stop you. Besides, Jimmy's looking forward to Glastonbury not the bloody Isle of Wight."

Trudie of course knew me all too well.

36

THE EULOGY

I GOT TO the cemetery nice and early so I could discuss the service with the Rabbi, so he had a flavour of the situation. I'd emailed him a heavily doctored synopsis of his life, bigging up his military service during World War Two and what a great grandad he was. The Rab suggested Mark or I did a eulogy. I didn't think it was a good idea for Mark to do one, I decided to share a story that would sum the old man up.

I was quite surprised at the turnout, seeing that so many of his friends and relatives had already died and that he'd fallen out with so many people. The Rab started his spiel, getting plenty of knowing nods when his war record was mentioned, I looked around the chapel and caught a glimpse of a surprise attendee. There, hanging on to cousin Trevor, was Uncle Martin, who hadn't spoken or seen my father for over twenty years. The lecherous old bugger was 93 and looked it, with his persistent Parkinsons induced head shake.

I stood between Trudie and Tara, whom, along with Mark, intermittently dabbed their faces with their hankies. I saw Jimmy and Heena, Jimmy was looking cool in has new shades. I wondered if he'd packed yet.

"I'd like to invite Sid up to say a few words about his Dad." The Rab gestured for me to approach the microphone. I pulled out my hastily written story about Antonio Rattín, but looking round the room, I didn't think the irony of my father's last words would resonate. I decided at the eleventh hour on a different story.

"My father could be difficult," I started, to a murmuring of agreement. "Trudie once described him as a man who could start a fight in a telephone box, I presume she meant with himself." Another round of knowing nods and twittering. "I'd like to tell you a story about my father that I think sums him up to a tee. I will obviously abbreviate the bad language. In nineteen-nighty-three, I was enjoying one of my mum's legendary Sunday lunches, when quite out of character my father asked me how business was bearing up during what was a bleak recession. I told him it was sh- oops sorry, rubbish, and that it hadn't helped that my main supplier had gone bust. He was genuinely concerned and asked what I planned to do. I explained that I was off the following Thursday to visit a factory in Herne Bay, Kent. Apparently, they'd been specialising in fireplaces for three generations.

"'Can I join you son? I'd love a day out and you know how I love factories,' he asked. I was about to tell him no way, but my mum gave me a pleading look, she was desperate to get rid of him for a day. 'Ok, Dad, but you're not allowed to talk when we get there, okay?' I said to him. 'I won't say a word son, I'll just look and listen,' he replied. Against my better judgment, I picked him up at eight in the morning and, apart from a bit of small talk, we managed to survive the two-hour journey without falling out. We were both really impressed with the factory tour and my father actually asked some impressive technical questions, being an ex-engineer. We ended up in the boardroom where all three generations of directors sat around the most polished mahogany table I've ever seen.

"They watched me study the contract whilst my father sipped his cup of tea. 'Any questions you have, Sid, please do not hesitate to ask,' the CEO said. 'It looks all good to me, I'm happy to sign, the quicker we get your product on display the better,' I confirmed. 'That's great son, you won't regret it,' the eighty-year-old chairman and founder of the company stated from the head of the table. 'Thank you, I'm happy to sign,' I said, picking up a pen with their company logo and crest on it. 'Are you happy with everything, Mr. Levinson?' The CEO respectfully involved my father who'd been on his finest behaviour.

"'It's my son's business,' my father started, 'It's up to him. If he's happy to sign, then fine, but me personally, I wouldn't sign it,' he said. I was poised over the contact and froze as I digested his comments. There were awkward glances amongst the directors. The old Chairman, who reminded me of young Mr Grace in the TV programme *Are You Being Served?*, addressed my old man directly. 'If you find one item sub-standard, Mr. Levinson, write my name on a post-it note and I will personally make sure you receive a replacement within twenty-four hours,' he confirmed. 'I've got no problem with the product, I'm an engineer by trade and although not an expert on the fireplace business, this is one of the best run up-to-date factories I've had the pleasure to visit,' my father responded.

"'So, what's the issue, Mr. Levinson?' The old boy asked. 'Herne Bay,' my father stated, leaving everyone in the room confused. I was beginning to get angry, with no idea of where this was all heading, but realising that bringing my father could be a terrible mistake. 'Herne Bay, Mr. Levinson?' David the Sales Director and the old boy's grandson intervened. David was my initial contact and he'd taken a lot of time explaining to me that the family took great pride in having been not just a big employer in the area but also very involved in many community projects, his father had sat on the council for years and was tipped to be the next mayor.

"'I was sent here in nineteen forty-two, when I joined the Navy to do my basic training. I have very bad memories of how the locals treated us, I wouldn't personally do business with anyone in this town!' my father said. I looked around the room at the shocked faces surrounding me. 'Well I'm more than happy to sign,' I stated, and scribbled my signature in the appropriate places. When we got into my car I was shaking with anger. 'Don't say an effing word!' I screamed at him. He sulked as we headed back to London, just as we got into the Dartford tunnel he swore and cursed, punching the dashboard.

"'What's up with you now?' I shouted, my head throbbing with anger, swearing I'll never talk to him again. 'Eff it!' he shouted repeatedly, before putting his head in his hands for a few seconds and eventually composing himself, declaring, 'I'm an effing idiot, son, it wasn't Herne Bay, it was Weston Super Mare!'"

When the laughter and howls of approval subsided, Mark stepped forward, embraced me and spoke into the microphone.

"I wasn't planning to say anything, and God knows I can't follow Sid's story, but I'd like to think that if I were that teenager struggling with his sexuality today, Dad would have understood."

My brother choked up, as did most of the attendees, Tara stepped forward and held his hand.

"I now realise how difficult it must have been for Sid when I left home, coping with the aftermath. I want to apologise to him for abandoning him way back then and also for leaving him to cope alone in recent years when Mum and then Dad's health failed, whilst I selfishly carried on my life in the Californian sunshine. But...but the truth is, I envy Sid. He has wonderful support in Trudie, Tara here, and Leo and I will try and make it up to them."

Trudie and Leo stepped forward and Mark disappeared in a group hug. Briefly I reflected on how delighted I was when I discovered he'd been kicked out, I moved into his room in literally minutes. I thought he was probably enjoying all this drama, but felt I'd better show some love and join them.

After his command performance, the Rab had organised low chairs as per tradition, where the immediate family sit and are consoled by the other mourners. Mark and I agreed our father would have hated this, as old sweaty hands shook ours and cracked old lips slobbered on our faces. Cousin Trevor led Uncle Martin to us, Trev winked at us as his father took my hand. Usually you simply wish the family a long life, but Uncle Martin took my hand and whispered in my ear.

"Your father was a cunt and so are you."

It reminded me of the assistant head's words to me on leaving school, I wasn't sure if this was a compliment or a gross insult. I pulled him towards me by his lapel and replied.

"Well if anyone is an expert on cunt, it's you Uncle Martin."

* * *

Close friends and family returned to our home to pay respects. Heena led a rather hesitant Jimmy over to me.

"You okay, mate?" He put his hand on my shoulder. "You got the tickets? Heena's joining me," he asked.

I was saved as the Rab addressed everyone from the middle of the room.

"Before I recite the Jewish prayer for the deceased, I'd like to say to the family that everyone deals with their grief in their own personal way and in the coming months, one should make allowances for each other's words and actions, which at times may seem strange but sometimes grief is more powerful than reason."

So that was that, perfectly put. The Rab had given me carte blanche to do what I wanted under the cover of my supposed grief. I turned back to Jimmy and Heena.

"Bloody hell, Jimmy, you didn't think I'd let you down. I'll be round seven tomorrow morning. Have your gear ready."

"Don't be ridiculous, Sid, you can't possibly go." Heena tried to sound serious, whilst secretly relieved that she wouldn't have to suffer festival toilets and screaming guitars, which she once told me was her pet musical hate. "What does Trudie think?" she continued.

"She's not bothered," I shrugged.

I went over to Tara, who was busy helping Trudie with the refreshments. "You haven't cancelled your holiday, have you, Tara?" I tried to sound sincere, but she cut me to the quick.

"It's okay, Dad, Mum told me your plans, you don't have to sound guilty."

I was relieved and then thought about her trip to Ibiza and felt a pang of panic. "Be careful over there, Tara, won't you."

"Yes, Dad, and don't you do anything stupid at the festival. I hear you and Uncle Jimmy have form!"

37

THE ROAD NOT TO GLASTONBURY

(2014)

JIMMY WAS SITTING on his rucksack on the pavement outside his house. I didn't ask if Heena had helped him or if he'd managed himself. It was already twenty degrees, it was going to be a scorcher.

As Jimmy strapped himself in, I considered coming clean on our destination, but he was too quick off the mark.

"Glastonbury here we come!" he bellowed, slapping the car roof through the open window.

We engaged in small talk, mainly about his eye. He told me it was like he was looking through a net curtain, there was just about enough definition to recognise people, but he couldn't read, which he found very frustrating. I was relieved Jimmy couldn't read the road signs as we headed down the M3 towards Portsmouth.

"I take it Heena read the packing list to you?" I asked.

"Yeah, no problem, Heena packed everything. All I added was Smithy's goody bag."

"Goody bag, what goody bag?" I queried.

"Didn't he tell you? He gave me a goody bag at the funeral."

"And what's in the goody bag?"

"He's baked a few cakes, plus there's an envelope that says, 'to be opened at festival', typical Smithy," Jimmy laughed.

"What kind of cakes has the master baker cooked up for us?" I asked.

"Smithy described them as 'Hash cakes with an added kick'."

"What's the kick?" I asked concerned.

"He wouldn't tell me, he just said he'd added a secret ingredient and that we were only to have a little nibble at a time and that one cake would do for the whole weekend."

I wasn't sure if I should be grateful to Smithy or annoyed.

Twenty miles from Portsmouth, Jimmy said he wanted to use the loo, so I pulled into the services. I had to lead Jimmy towards the toilet and felt he'd find life easier with a white stick but could fully understand why he didn't want one. We decided to have coffee and sat among the communal tables, which were full of festival goers. A couple of old hippies sat at the next table.

"Off to the Isle of Wight as well?" One of them tried to make conversation.

"No, Glastonbury, mate," Jimmy replied, with a mixture of excitement and pride.

"Blimey, you're a bit early," the guy looked a bit confused as he knew that Glasto was two weeks away.

"We want to get there early and get set up," I added abruptly, diverting the conversation to how motorway service stations had greatly improved over the years. We finished our coffee and made to leave.

"Enjoy Glastonbury," our neighbour smiled.

"Cheers, mate." I hurriedly ushered Jimmy to the exit.

We'd made good time and got to within a few hundred meters of the ferry terminal surprisingly quickly, but then came to an abrupt halt and didn't move for fifteen minutes.

People started to get out of their cars as a rumour went around that they'd been an incident on the previous ferry. Several police cars and an ambulance whizzed past along the hard shoulder. A youngster who was on Twitter said they'd been a fight between youths from Portsmouth and Southampton, this wasn't a good start. I climbed back into the car and told Jimmy there was an accident up ahead and we could be some time, maybe he should get some shut eye.

As it happened, a few minutes later we started to move and when we eventually entered the ferry, Jimmy was snoring. '*Thank god for that and thank god we've got separate tents,*' I thought. Fortunately, Jimmy slept the entire crossing and only woke up as I joined the crawling traffic heading towards the festival site.

"Where are we, Sid?"

"Almost there, mate."

"What's the time?" he queried.

"Around midday," I confirmed.

"Blimey, you've made good time, mate."

"Cheers, exciting eh?" I chuckled.

We parked up and unloaded the car. I put Jimmy's rucksack on him and tied his pop-up tent to it, before placing various loose items in his hands. I ended up with one free hand to pull the shopping trolley full of beer.

We walked towards the nearest campsite, but the young stewards told us it was full and to keep walking to the next one. It was now over thirty degrees, the next campsite was full, and the growing crowd were getting angry as we were sent in a giant circle. Jimmy was getting frantic, I saw young lady with a walkie talkie and 'Supervisor' on the back of her hi-vis jacket. I told Jimmy to chill for a minute and I approached her. There were a few people angrily swearing at her, as she explained another field would be opened in an hour's time. I waited for them to move on and spoke politely to her.

"Excuse me young lady, this is the situation, we two old boys are struggling, my mate has cancer, get yourself some beers and find us two spaces together for two small pop-up tents," I said as I handed her a twenty-pound note.

"One-minute, sir." She smiled and spoke into her walkie talkie. A minute later she asked us to follow her colleague. "Have a great festival, gentleman." She waved us off as I helped a confused Jimmy over an ocean of guy ropes. We were led to a small clearing in the centre of the campsite, just about big enough to accommodate our tents.

We had the tents up in approximately thirty seconds, which was fifty-nine and a half minutes quicker than it took to assemble the Scout tent at the Weeley Festival, 43 years earlier.

We sorted our stuff out and then sat in the space between our tents, which was just about big enough for our fold up chairs. We cracked open a couple of beers.

"I now declare the festival open," Jimmy toasted, as we clinked bottles.

"Here's to five days of music, footy, beer and freedom," I saluted.

"And cake," Jimmy added.

38

THE RETURN TO WONDERLAND

AFTER A COUPLE of beers, the last few days took their toll on me. I suddenly felt overwhelmed with tiredness. I couldn't remember the last time I had a good night's sleep. Notwithstanding my father's situation, I had my business worries and then the constant nightmares involving Perry. I lay on my freshly inflated airbed stripped to my pants, trying to keep as cool as possible. It suddenly dawned on me that I was free, free of my father, free of financial worries and, if Perry was alive, I could at least pay him off or of course kill him off! My only concern was Jimmy discovering he wasn't at Glastonbury. But now we were here, once the booze and maybe a nibble of cake kicked in, he hopefully wouldn't be bothered.

The music wasn't due to start until 8.00pm that evening in the big tent, but Thursday was generally an arrival day, the calm before the storm. I closed my eyes and slept for eight hours straight. When I woke, there was a note next to me in Jimmy's scrawl, '*See you in the big top*'.

I was concerned Jimmy would struggle on his own. I tried calling him but realised he'd probably not hear his phone if the music had started. I wondered how he'd manage to get about as I navigated the maze of tents, eventually finding the pathway that led to the main arena area. There was a Doors tribute band on in the big tent, Jimmy loved the Doors but I couldn't find him in what was a rapidly growing crowd. I went for a walk around outside the big top, the temperature was now a perfect 22°C. I invested in a pear cider and returned to the big top, where Bruce Foxton's 'From The Jam' was on next.

I knew Jimmy would be down the front somewhere, so I positioned myself about ten people deep from the centre of the stage. They came on to the Batman theme and launched straight into *Eton Rifles*. The crowd went crazy with a mixture of pogoing and moshing. I found myself sucked into the baying mob, a few seconds later my instincts were proven correct when I caught a glimpse of Jimmy right down the front, with his arm around a fellow Jam fan, throwing themselves around like it was 1977 again.

I pushed through the swaying mass of fifty-somethings, eventually coming face to face with my mate.

"Jimmy, it's me!" I screamed, as Foxton's bass thundered a few feet away.

He grabbed me in a bear hug and kissed me on my balding head.

"Sid, this is fucking paradise, mate! What a tune!"

We battled side by side for the next forty-five minutes, reliving our youth. At the end of the set we were out on our feet. I led Jimmy outside, gasping for air. We decided to go and watch the first half of the opening game of the 2014 World Cup on the biggest screen in Europe, before returning to the big top for Boy George, another of Jimmy's favourites.

Jimmy told me he'd had a couple of beers with some young medical students who were in the tent next door, they'd guided him to the big top. We stood by the right-hand support pylon nearest the stage, we'd always stood to the right of the stage at gigs since the seventies. Boy George came on to a great fanfare, but his first words as he gripped the microphone were, "Good evening Isle of Wight! How you all doing?"

"He thinks he's at the Isle of Wight festival Sid!" Jimmy shouted in my ear.

"The poor bastard's mind has been addled by drugs," I replied.

"He doesn't know where he is, Jimmy, remember when we met him?"

"Yes, Sid, the Camden Palace, before he was famous, remember Smithy asking him what he was?"

"I do, Jimmy!" I yelled as his band revelled up. "And I remember Boy George's reply!"

"So do I, 'You'll find out one day sweetheart', and we did find out, I remember when he first appeared on *Top of the Pops*!"

We watched his set, Jimmy loved it, the crowd dispersed slowly as there was a midnight curfew on events because the festival didn't officially start until the next day. There was an atmosphere building amongst the Thursday arrivals, like a medieval army on the eve of a major battle. We headed towards a strip of food stalls that lined the route back to the campsite. We heard the strains of the Sex Pistols *Pretty Vacant* coming from what was called the Hipshaker tent.

I led Jimmy inside, the place was rocking with a crowd mainly approaching our age group. There was a poster on a pylon advertising the three day *'Battle of the Bands'*. I read it aloud to Jimmy.

"Friday, eleven pm, The Specials vs Madness, Saturday, eleven pm, Oasis vs Blur, Sunday, nine pm, The Sex Pistols vs The Clash, eleven, The Stones vs The Who. More to be announced."

"Fucking hell, Sid, what's all this then?"

"Tribute bands, maybe a DJ, we'll check it out tomorrow. I think this should be our HQ, our meeting place," I suggested.

We strolled back slowly taking in the sights (well I was) and sounds, stopping now and again whilst I described the different food and drink stalls to Jimmy, whose sight was much worse at night than in daylight.

"You're making me feel hungry, Sid."

"I'm about to make you feel hungrier, mate," I interrupted, spotting a giant neon sign that simply read '*KEBAB KEBAB*'. There was a hardcore rave beat coming from it. I wondered how Tara was doing, having probably just arrived in Ibiza.

"The festival isn't truly open until we've had a kebab, Sid. I thought the food at Glastonbury would be far more poncey," Jimmy claimed, he was probably right, of course.

"I'm up for one, mate, come on let's check it out."

The choice wasn't difficult to explain to Jimmy. Lamb doner, chicken doner or mixed.

"Got to be a mixed," Jimmy exclaimed.

"Two mixed it is chef." I winked at the Turkish man standing with his mighty kebab slicer in hand. He tossed a couple of giant wraps on the grill before filling them with freshly sliced meats.

"All the salad, geezer?" he enquired.

"Everything, mate!" Jimmy shouted and the fella filled the already bursting wraps, pausing as he picked up the giant squeezy bottle of chilli sauce. I watched him hover the bottle over the wraps, which he held in his other giant hand. He hesitated for a millisecond before addressing me, "I don't even have to ask, do I, mate?" and he squeezed two giant dollops onto our kebabs.

I handed him the dosh. "A work of art, mate," I praised him.

"Enjoy, mate, please, the VIP suite is all yours." He gestured to the small table and benches beside his van.

Jimmy sat down whilst I got a couple of ciders from the conveniently placed bar adjacent to the kebab van. We clinked our plastic cups which had '*IOW 2014*' emblazed on it. Jimmy already had a mouthful of kebab. He went to speak but then put a finger up in a 'one minute' gesture, whilst he finished his mouthful. "I can't believe we're actually here, Sid, the festival has not even really started and I've already seen and heard The Doors, Jam and Culture Club music. I can't wait to get to the Pyramid stage tomorrow, this is fucking wonderland, Sid."

"It certainly is, Jimmy," I concurred, raising my cup. I was just about to confess as to where we actually were when my thoughts were diverted by a couple standing by the vegan stall opposite. There was something familiar about the man talking to a hippy looking Asian women. He was wearing a sort of Russian revolutionary hat, a 'Lenin' cap would be a better description. I could make out a greying ponytail just about creeping out the back of it, but it was his posture, the way he tilted his head that reminded me of an old friend of ours, or adversary would be more like it. I felt a bit foolish, as it certainly wasn't him. Having doubted Jimmy's claims regarding Perry and Tony Beck, I certainly wasn't going to say anything to Jimmy about it. I watched the couple walk off, the guy's strange walking style was so familiar.

"What's the plan tomorrow then, Sid?"

Jimmy broke my concentration and I lost my chance to come clean as to where we were. "I suggest we finish this feast and head back to our tents and have a good night's rest, we've got a big day tomorrow, we need to pace ourselves," I recommended.

"You're right, we've got the whole weekend ahead of us."

We followed the crowds back towards the campsites, eventually seeing an entrance with '*All the young dudes*' written across a wooden arch. I read it aloud to Jimmy.

"Just head for this sign mate and you are at the campsite, if we get split up anytime."

"Got it, and the meeting places, the right-hand pylon in the big top and the hipster tent. A man who fails to plan, plans to fail."

"Spot on, Jimmy, that's why I always have a list," I replied, as I tried to recall exactly where our tents were. It suddenly occurred to me that seeing as we were rushed to our spot after bribing the supervisor and heading to the big top whilst half asleep, I wasn't exactly sure where we pitched our tents. I'd tied an old yellow T-shirt to the top and I did recall seeing a giant orange Dutch flag. I tried to lead Jimmy over the sea of guy ropes, but even with a torch I was struggling, never mind my mate. We stumbled around for a good hour when it dawned on me, we might be in the wrong campsite. We saw two middle-aged women sitting outside their tent with a jug of Pimms.

"Excuse me ladies, are we in the Red campsite?"

"It is, indeed, you're lost I presume?" one of them asked in a strong Scouse accent.

"Yes, seriously lost." I could see they assumed Jimmy was drunk or stoned as he was hanging on to me. "My mate has impaired vision, I need to get him to our tent, it's been a long day."

"Tell us about it, we've come all the way from Liverpool and our mate, who's meant to be in that tent, broke down in Birmingham." She pointed to large empty tent.

"Sorry to hear that. I'm Sid, this is Jimmy."

"We are Pat and Nina, why don't you sit down and have a drink and then gather your wits," Pat offered.

"Nice one," Jimmy replied, basically collapsing beside them.

We told them our back story regarding the eventful Weeley festival, they thought it was wonderful that we were on a reunion trip. I'd guessed they were around ten years younger than us. They were massive fans of the Specials, as was Jimmy, though he'd never seen them live.

"I can't wait to see them on the Pyramid stage on Saturday night," he exclaimed.

"The Pyramid stage?" Nina laughed. "Where do you think you are, Glastonbury?" she added.

Jimmy thought it was a sarcastic response and laughed along with her.

We exchanged gig and festival stories for a good hour before Jimmy declared he needed the loo.

"Listen lads, you're welcome to stay in our empty tent, it doesn't look like our friends are going to make it," Pat offered.

"It will be easier to find your tent in daylight," Nina added.

"That's really kind of you girls, we'll visit the facilities and then take up your offer, eh, Jimmy?"

"Yeah nice one, thanks girls."

Fortunately, the nearest toilet block wasn't too far away from our temporary home. I led Jimmy to one at the end of the block and reached for my side pocket where I kept all my paperwork, tickets, lists etcetera and got out an A4 laminated sheet of paper that I'd printed *Priority Toilet* on and stuck it to the door with blue tack.

"That should keep the scum out for a while," I claimed, and read it to Jimmy who high fived me.

As we returned towards the girls' tent, I caught a glimpse of the orange Dutch flag in the distance, highlighted by the moonlight. "Follow me, Jimmy, I think I've sussed out where our tents are." A few minutes later we were home at last.

"What about the girls?" Jimmy asked.

"We'll go and see them in the morning, take them some booze as a thank you."

* * *

One of the reasons I was delighted to find our tents was that Trudie had bought us two soup containers each from the pound shop. They were bright yellow and had screw-on tops so made for ideal 'piss pots'. Bearing in mind Jimmy and I averaged five visits a night, each container could accommodate at least three efforts each. This would save us a lot of clambering around tents in the dark.

I don't think I could have got more than three hours sleep, the tent was like an oven. I'd planned to have a decent lie-in, but it was only 7.30am and there were a lot of raised voices and joviality outside. I peered through the tent flap and there was Jimmy, slumped on a blow up lilo surrounded by our medical student neighbours, who were pouring beer into a funnel with a plastic tube attached to my mate's mouth.

"Come and join us for breakfast," a very posh young man said to me.

"Morning, Sid!" Jimmy shouted looking wide awake, despite his dark glasses.

There were at least ten revellers who all were students at Guys. "We've examined your mate thoroughly and can confirm he is a certified 'Cyclops'," another one laughed, as did Jimmy. They threw me a can of cider and Jimmy beckoned me to join him on the inflatable chair.

"Don't forget, we're supposed to be pacing ourselves today," I reminded him.

"Yeah I know, mate, but the sun woke me up at six and I had the munchies, so I've had a bit of cake." Jimmy was talking at 100 miles an hour.

"How much cake?" I enquired.

"Just a nibble," he answered defensively.

"Let's have a look, Jimmy." I must have sounded like a schoolteacher as he pulled a small clingfilm ball out of his short's pocket and handed it to me. I pulled out the cake, there was at least a quarter bitten out of it.

"That's a bit more than a nibble, remember Smithy warned us to go steady."

"I know, Sid, but fuck, I could be fucking totally blind or even dead this time next year!"

His words struck a chord, I thought about the last few weeks, I'd received a text from Mark chastising me for disappearing straight after the funeral. "Oh well, Jimmy, breakfast is served." I bit another chunk out the cake, washing it down with a gulp of cider.

After regaling the youngsters with our tales from Weeley, we made our way to the Scouse girls tent with our thank you present. The girls were right, it was much easier to find our way around in daylight. The girls it seems were also early risers, as their tent was unoccupied and padlocked shut. We managed to squeeze the beers under the flap, hoping they'd realise who they were from.

We visited our 'Priority' toilet. My sign was still attached and whilst there were queues three deep outside the others, Jimmy went straight into ours. We got someone to take a picture of us under the *'All the young dudes'* arch, as we headed to the epicentre of the festival. We stopped for a breakfast bap and a coffee, but I don't know what Smithy's secret ingredient was, both of us were buzzing and talking ten to the dozen.

"We didn't have grub like this at Weeley, did we?" I reminisced.

"I wouldn't know, Sid, I had to make do with hospital food, didn't I?"

"Shit, I forgot, well you've lasted a lot longer this time and so have our tents!"

"You're right there, I didn't even see one band."

I felt guilty, as I always have, that I had so many memories from Weeley and Jimmy didn't. "That was a fucking palaver with the old bill and our parents," I mentioned.

"You're right, but can you imagine if that had happened nowadays, there would have been enquiry after enquiry," Jimmy stated.

We carried on chatting about the aftermath of Jimmy's injury as we made our way to HQ, the Hipshaker tent. We sat in some comfortable chairs, reminding each other we were going to pace ourselves. It was only 10.30am, the first band weren't due on till 4.00pm.

"So, what happened about the Hells Angel that was murdered?" I'd always been curious but never discussed it with Jimmy.

"As far as I know, nobody was ever charged over his murder, the police thought I'd been through enough and Mum was happy because she got a cheque from the local roundtable for dropping legal claims."

"What a fuck up," I said, looking at a lady erecting a sign advertising Northern Soul lessons at 11.00am.

"Are you boys going to join us?" she asked us.

"No thanks, we missed the Northern Soul era by a few years," I stated.

"You're never too old for Northern Soul dancing," she replied.

"We're waiting for the pogo class," Jimmy exclaimed. "So, what's the plan, Sid?"

"Well I think we should refrain from drinking until the music starts, I suggest we have a good look around the whole festival site, rest up for a couple of hours and…" I got my line-up list out and studied the red asterisks I'd placed next to the bands I wanted to see, "and then we kick off at four thirty in the big tent with Sam Fox."

"Sam Fox, the actual Sam Fox, as in Page Three Sam Fox?" Jimmy shouted excitedly.

"Yes, that Sam Fox," I confirmed.

"I'll be right down the front, Sid, I've got to get the best possible view, even a blurry Sam Fox has to be seen."

"What was the name of her hit?" I asked, knowing Jimmy would know the answer.

"Touch me, I want your body," Jimmy even knew the tune.

Just then a fella in a Charlton Athletic football shirt, our age but with rock star hair, asked if he could sit in a spare chair at our table. I gestured that it was free. Jimmy moved closer to him, peering at the red shirt, eventually taking his shades off. The fella could see Jimmy squinting and held the club badge closer to him.

"Yep, Charlton Athletic Football Club, you a fellow Addick pal?" the fella asked.

"No, mate, we're Chels, but I lived in Charlton up until the age of eleven, always my second team," Jimmy replied.

"Shame about that, mate. Anyway, I'm Ricky, excuse me while I take a slurp of my breakfast." He knocked back at least a third of his pint.

Jimmy and Ricky reminisced about the Charlton legends for a few minutes before two young boys, who'd I'd spotted running around, came over to Ricky.

"Can we have some money to get some crisps?"

He gave them a fiver and told them to behave. He told us they were eight and ten, we guessed their mother was Thai from the look of them. He told us he had three older children from three previous marriages and that his partner was working here at the festival in the well-being tent. Him and the two boys followed her around all summer as she worked at all the top festivals.

"What's your favourite then, Ricky?" Jimmy asked.

"Glastonbury, I suppose, though I like Latitude, much more intimate and chilled."

"Do you remember that winger Colin Powell?" I quickly changed the subject.

"Yeah, of course he made the big match goal of the season for Derek Hales, he was an underrated player." He took another huge gulp of his beer and stood up. "Fancy a beer, lads?" he asked.

"You're alright, we're pacing ourselves, long day ahead," I replied.

"Come on, lads, I thought you Chelsea boys were made of tougher stuff than that," Ricky teased us.

"Two ciders then please," Jimmy requested.

That was it, our plan went out the window, as soon as we'd finished those pints. I was honour bound to get another round. By midday, we'd had four pints, plus the cake, and we were rocking. We even tried our hand at the Northern Soul lesson with Ricky's kids, but basically just made fools of ourselves.

I was thinking about moving on when Ricky's phone buzzed. After a brief conversation he asked us if we could just keep an eye on his kids while he 'went to see a man about a dog' just across at the big top centre. He'd be five minutes, he said.

"Okay." We both shrugged as the boys sat a few feet from us on their phones playing a game.

"Here, don't know if you're interested." Ricky turned to us as he was leaving. "I'm going to score some MDMA, shall I get some extra for you?"

"Thanks, Ricky, but not our thing," I replied.

"I understand, Chelski lightweights," he teased us.

"We're on the cake pal," Jimmy patted his pocket.

"I thought you were on something lads," he laughed and was gone.

We discussed what we should do once Ricky returned and whether it was a good idea for him to be pill popping whilst with his kids.

"Bit of lad is Ricky," I observed.

"Typical South East Londoner like me," Jimmy added.

A good twenty minutes went past and there was no sign of Ricky.

"Fancy another cider?" Jimmy asked.

"No thanks, mate, I thought we were pacing ourselves."

"How about a short, a nice little scotch?" he persisted.

"Oh, go on then," I relented.

I made sure the boys were ok, but they were too engrossed in their games to even acknowledge me.

"Large ones," Jimmy boasted on his return from the bar.

"Where the fuck is Ricky?" I asked, checking my phone, noting it was now about forty minutes since he left his kids in our care.

"Maybe he's been hospitalised by a Hells Angel," Jimmy quipped.

"Oi, boys!" I shouted, feeling very pissed all of sudden as the scotch blended with the cider and cake. "Where's your dad? We've got things to do."

They reluctantly came over, the older one spoke up, "You mean Ricky?"

"Yeah, your dad."

"He's not our dad, he's our dad's mate," he sniggered.

Jimmy and I looked at each other. "Your dad's mate?" I repeated, making sure I wasn't that drunk that I'd misheard.

"Yeah, Earth is our dad."

"Earth," Jimmy chipped in

"Yes, Earth, he runs the wellbeing tent with my mum," the boy confirmed.

"And Ricky's looking after you today," I queried.

"Yes, he's a friend of my mum and dad. Can we carry on with our game please, mister?" And off they went back to where they were sitting by an amplifier.

"That's fucking weird," Jimmy stated, and I concurred. We talked about another disastrous festival we went to as seventeen-year-olds somewhere in Wiltshire. We'd hitchhiked there, took a whole day. It was supposed to be a free festival with smaller bands like Stray, Blodwyn Pig, the Pink Fairies and the Groundhogs, but when we eventually got there, everyone was leaving as the stage had been destroyed in a fire. We were jinxed but we decided to hang around and an hour later, a lorry turned up with Edgar Broughton band playing on the back of it. They played nonstop for eighteen hours.

"Out Demons Out!" Jimmy yelled, recalling the band's signature track.

"That fucker has been gone an hour Jimmy," I exclaimed.

"Fuck him, let's just fuck off. Those little runts won't even miss us, let's leg it."

I agreed.

* * *

So much for pacing ourselves, we both leaned against a giant oak tree that was strategically placed near the big top and crashed out for at least three hours. I was woken by Jimmy shaking me. "Sid, what time is it? We haven't missed Sam, have we?"

I'd not seen Jimmy this excited in years. "Got twenty minutes before she comes on, let's get you down the front."

I underestimated how popular this eighties icon was. There was a crowd three deep already assembled at the front barrier. I managed to usher Jimmy to the front and wedge him between a couple of very camp fellas dressed in nothing but hot pants.

"I'll go get us a couple of beers and meet you at the end of her set by our pylon."

Jimmy gave me a thumbs up, oblivious to the crowd I'd left him with. I went to the bar thinking about the morning's events. I decided to quickly check out the Hipshaker tent, just in case they were still there. There was no sign of them, so I made my way out of curiosity to the wellbeing tent, which was a good ten-minute walk away. The tent looked very alternative, with a blackboard advertising their services: Reflexology, Aromatherapy, meditation, Reiki, Massage and Tarot readings.

As I got closer, I saw a youngish Thai woman giving a bloke, sitting in what looked like a dentist chair, a head massage. That must be the boys' mum, I thought, but there was no sign of them or Ricky. Just then I saw an attractive mature lady arrive and a tent flap opened behind the massage chair, a familiar face welcome her inside. It was the guy I saw by the vegan van last night with the 'Lenin' cap and the funny little ponytail. I had a strange feeling about the guy…it couldn't be, I told myself.

I returned to the big top still clutching the beers. I got back just as Sam Fox concluded her set with her big hit, her only hit. I plotted up by our pylon, the crowd excitedly singing and dancing along. I was hoping she hadn't acknowledged where she was. We'd been at the Isle of Wight festival for thirty-six hours and Jimmy was still convinced he was at Glastonbury! Forty-three years since Weeley and I was still the master of deceit.

She finished her set to excited yelping, I stood by our pylon as the crowd dispersed, I was keen to find Jimmy and get to the main stage as soon as possible to see the wonderful Starsailor, whose first album *Love is Now* is one of my favourites. The crowd completely dispersed, save for one or two who remained at the barrier, but there was no sign of Jimmy. I waited a few minutes, thinking he'd gone for a slash, but ten minutes went past and there was still no sign of him.

I'd downed my pint and was still holding Jimmy's as I headed back to the Hipshaker tent, but he wasn't there either. I tried phoning him but that was a waste of time as there was very little signal. I made my way to the main stage and tried to forget about my mate and enjoy Starsailor, who didn't disappoint under the clear blue late afternoon sky.

I studied my line up list, guessing the bands Jimmy was likely to see. The big top was packed for The Selecter, who were definitely one of Jimmy's must see bands. I stood by the pylon and then shuffled backwards and forwards through the crowd, who were very lively during the hi-tempo 40-minute set. I then legged it to see a bit of Rudimental, an exciting band that Jimmy raved about. There was no chance I'd find him among the fifty thousand revellers, so I headed back to the Hipshaker where the Ramonas, a female Ramones tribute band, were in the middle of an electrifying version of *Blitzkrieg Bop*, in front of an enthusiastic throng of pogoers. I forgot about Jimmy and joined them for the rest of their breath-taking set.

By the time I'd watched the brilliant headliners Biffy Clyro on the main stage, I thought I'd better make a concerted effort to find Jimmy, as it was now eleven and very dark. It didn't take long. I took a look in the big top where the weird and wonderful Polyphonic Spree, all fourteen of them dressed in white robes, were making a splendid racket. The singer jumped into the sparse crowd and offered the microphone to a crowd of fans to sing the chorus. I was watching the action on the big screen and suddenly there was Jimmy in full voice. I made my way through the crowd and there he was being held up by the Scouse girls we'd met last night, Pat and Nina.

"Jimmy!" I shouted, and he grabbed onto me, absolutely off his nut.

The girls and I dragged him outside.

"We found him staggering around the big top after The Selecter, I thought we'd better look after him," Pat explained.

"It's Smithy's fault, Sid, I don't know what that extra ingredient was, but it's fucked me right up," Jimmy slurred.

"You ate the rest of the cake you idiot," I chastised him.

"And the other one," he confessed.

39

AKA 'EARTH'

PAT AND TINA insisted they put the now semi-conscious Jimmy in their spare tent, where they could keep an eye on him. Seeing as they were both nurses, it made sense. We sat outside drinking the thank you beers I'd left the girls earlier.

"From what you've told us, you two shouldn't be allowed anywhere near a festival together," Tina laughed.

"It's not me, it's Jimmy, he's a magnet for trouble," I retorted. "Anyway, The Specials tomorrow night, it's going to be a long day so I'm going to retire. I'll swing by in the morning and make sure he's still alive."

"Okay, Sid, we'll keep an eye on him," Pat reassured me.

"Oh, by the way girls, he thinks he's at Glastonbury," I whispered.

"What? Why?" both girls replied in tandem.

"It's a long story." I sighed and spent five minutes giving them the edited highlights, before checking on Jimmy. He looked very content in the girls' spare tent, which was bigger than both ours put together. He was snoring as usual and then I noticed, well I couldn't really miss it, he had a massive hard on. I thought that was a bit strange but hey ho, I left him in the girls hopefully capable hands.

I made my way to my tent via our 'priority' toilet. I was delighted to see my A4 sign was still attached and the actual toilet was still completely unscathed! I managed to find my tent straight away this time, but curiosity got the better of me and I decided to have a look in Jimmy's tent and see what exactly was in Smithy's goody bag.

It took some finding, I looked through his rucksack, his various plastic bags, before finding a Lidl bag in a wellington boot. I emptied the contents onto his sleeping bag.

"The cunning bastard." I laughed as six of Smithy's cakes rolled around. He told me there were only two. I'd forgotten to ask him what was in the envelope that was marked '*Open at Glastonbury*', but he'd obviously already opened it. There was a small cellophane bag with two strange yellow tablets in it and a packet of ten gels, which had been opened, there were only eight inside. "What's Jimmy taken?" I asked myself, studying the splurge. Each gel was a different flavour, banana, lemon, raspberry, rhubarb etc. I started to laugh uncontrollably as I realised they were Viagra gels, Jimmy had obviously had a couple not knowing what they were. Hence his massive erection.

I fell asleep still smiling but was disturbed in the small hours by someone trying to get into my tent. I fumbled for my torch and shone it on the flap but whoever was out there was trying to cut a hole in the side of the tent. I saw a pair of decorating scissors jabbing in and out creating a hole. I reached for the mallet that I'd used to bang in the metal pegs, but it was too late, as a pair of hands reached in and started strangling me!

I knew it was Perry, I knew he'd find me eventually. I surrendered, knowing resistance was futile.

I woke in a sweat, relieved it was only my recurring nightmare.

Once again, the sun made a lie-in impossible. I jumped out the tent with the intention of having a much-needed shower. The medical students were already drinking and partying.

"Where's Cyclops?" one asked. Jimmy had obviously warmed to them.

"He pulled a couple of milfs," I joked, before heading to the communal showers.

I felt a lot cleaner as I made my way find Jimmy. The girls were just waking up when I arrived.

"You alright, girls?" I whispered by their entrance flap.

"Hi, Sid, come in," Pat invited me. I kneeled between their sleeping bags.

"We're suffering this morning because of your mate," Tina moaned.

I dreaded what he'd been up to.

"After you left, we thought we'd better check he was ok and well…" They both laughed trying to tell me what I already suspected.

"His erection," I interrupted.

"Blimey it's usual is it?!" Pat bellowed.

I took a gel out of my pocket and threw it to her. "I don't know what he thought they were, but he had a couple."

"Well that explains it, we just thought we had that effect on him," Tina stated with a smile.

"He gave us a hash cake, blimey it was lethal," Pat confirmed.

"I'd better check he's still alive girls."

"Tell me something, Sid, is Jimmy happily married?" Tina asked with a hint of guilt.

"Married yes, happily is not a description I'd use," I replied truthfully, as I backed out of the tent.

I looked in the spare tent, it was empty. *Fuck it*, I thought, *where the fuck has he gone now?*

* * *

258

It was still ridiculously early, today was going to be the hottest day of the year. I made my way to the festival food area and decided on a full English breakfast. The hot weather had certainly woken everyone up and there was already a buzz about the place with the tables full of early risers. I was halfway through my breakfast, thinking about looking for Jimmy when I just thought, '*Fuck it, I nearly fucking killed my father to get here, I'm going to enjoy myself. Jimmy's a big boy, besides I'll run into him somewhere.*'

I pushed my breakfast aside and decided on a livener and went and got myself a pear cider. I found the tree where I'd dozed yesterday afternoon and leaned against it watching the world go by. There was a smooth stump perfectly placed to put my beer on. I reached into the zipped pocket in my shorts and pulled out a cake I'd taken from the goody bag. I took a small bite and then another, soon I'd eaten half.

I laughed aloud thinking about Jimmy's hard on, he probably thought he was taking ecstasy or something. Heena would kill him. I suspect he'd returned to his tent and was having a wanking session! For some strange reason, maybe the cake made me a bit nostalgic, but I thought about what a great time we had in 1977 and then him going missing in early '78 before phoning me and asking to meet me in the *Lemon Tree Arms*, a pub he always called poncey.

* * *

When I arrived, Jimmy was sitting in an alcove having already got the drinks in, he looked even paler than normal.

"It's a large one," he pointed at my scotch and lemonade. "You're going to need it," he added seriously.

"Sounds ominous, mate, where you been for the last three months, a new woman I take it?" I guessed.

"Not exactly." He took a gulp of his larger.

"I'll come straight to the point, Sid, and I'll understand if you never want to see me again, but all these years we've been drinking, stinking, going to gigs and Chelsea, you've been bests mates with a Leeds United supporter."

I'd be readying myself for some kind of confession that he'd been seeing one of my ex-girlfriends, I was confused. "What the fuck are you on about, Jimmy?"

"I'm from fucking Leeds. I was born in Leeds," he confessed, as if he was a war criminal. "That's why I've been elusive, a woman from social services has been investigating who my real parents are, and they are from Leeds!"

I knew Jimmy had been taking an interest in his past since he was eighteen, it was only natural, I was certain Alice knew the day would come. "Does Alice know about all this?" I asked.

"Not yet, I'll tell her when I'm a hundred percent certain."

"So, it's not confirmed?"

"The social worker is in Leeds right now and I'm meeting her next week, she reckons she will have all the documentation."

"But maybe Alice knows all this, maybe she could help?" I questioned him.

"I know but I couldn't bring myself to ask her, Sid, you know what she's done for me and my sister. She fostered twenty-five kids and chose me and Lily. How could I ask her for fucks sake."

I shrugged and took a long sip of my drink. "So, what do you know so far?" I asked.

"I know that I was born in Leeds, but my mother moved to somewhere near Kings Cross shortly after I was born and a few months later she handed me over for adoption."

"Sounds quite a story, mate, I suppose if she came down to London by train, Kings Cross is where she'd arrive," I considered.

"Exactly, seems she left in a hurry, people didn't move from their hometown unless they had a good reason in those days."

It didn't sound like there would be a happy ending and of course there wasn't.

"So, I might be a dirty Leeds supporter, if you want to leave now," Jimmy said seriously. Indeed, all Chelsea fans hated Leeds United in the '70s and they hated us. It all stemmed from 1970 FA cup final. Don Revie regarded us as soft southern dandies. We had Chopper Harris, but they had eleven hard northern bastards in their team. Both teams had large hooligan elements, of which Jimmy was one.

"It's okay, Jimmy, I think you've proved your allegiance to the blues, remember that brick you lobbed at the Leeds fans at Earls Court Station!"

"I suppose you're right, Sid, I'm going to hate Leeds even more if it turns out my father was a wrongun."

I went and got the drinks in and when I returned, I clinked glasses with Jimmy. "Well good luck to you, mate, if there's anything I can do," I offered.

"Maybe you can come and give me some moral support when I eventually tell Alice."

"No problem, mate."

"There is one positive thing to have come out of this Sid, the social worker."

"What about her, Jimmy?"

"We've sort of hit it off."

"Really, how old is she?"

"Twenty-five."

"Fucking hell, you're a toy boy."

"There's only four and a half years difference," he said defensively.

"How did this happen then?"

"She lives in Leeds but since she started working on my case, she has fallen in love with London and spent some weekends here and well, someone had to show her the sights," Jimmy boasted.

* * *

The cake had really kicked in, I decided to go and check out the wellbeing tent, check out the dude in the Lenin hat. I thought I'd pop into our HQ, the Hipshaker tent, just in case

Jimmy was about. I got another cider and sat on one of the sofas, sod it, why not. I'd been through a shitstorm and I'll be returning to it in a couple of days. I ate the rest of the cake.

* * *

I didn't see Jimmy again for four months after the Lemon Tree meet up. I ran into Alice at the local butchers, she told me Jimmy had moved in with his girlfriend.

"Girlfriend?" I queried.

"Indian girl, social worker," she confirmed, and then gave me his phone number. I called him and he invited me round to their tiny Islington bedsit.

I took an instant disliking to Heena, I found her very arrogant and she seemed hell bent on turning Jimmy into something he wasn't. Maybe I was jealous, I admit that, but looking round the walls they were full of her posters and artwork. There was no sign of Jimmy's signed photo of the Chelsea cup winning team or his 'Who Live at Leeds' poster, despite the Leeds connection. It had transpired that his father had joined the merchant navy and disappeared when he impregnated Jimmy's mother. Her family had decided she was too young at 17 to cope with a baby and would put the baby up for adoption immediately. But his mum was desperate to keep him and fled to London before her family could intervene. She naturally struggled to survive the mean streets of Kings Cross and reluctantly gave Jimmy up after a few months and returned to Leeds. That's where the story was left, until the internet made life's jigsaws easier to solve.

I knew at the first meeting Heena would tame and capture my mate. Heena fell pregnant a few months later and Jimmy proposed, despite her family's objections. They married at Greta Green. Whilst on honeymoon in Whitley Bay, Heena fell ill, she lost the baby and her fallopian tubes. Jimmy was devastated, because of his past he was desperate for his own happy family. He was lost to me for a few years as Heena tried to create a new lifestyle for them. I had my own distractions, namely the stalking, wooing and courting of Trudie. Then the kids, mortgage etcetera, the wilderness years as I called them.

We'd meet up every blue moon to see a gig, normally Lou Reed, or the very occasional Chelsea game. Then in the early nineties he asked me to meet him in the *Lemon Tree Arms* for a crisis meeting. I told Trudie that he was going to tell me he was leaving Heena, but I was wrong. Same alcove, same large scotch and lemonade.

Jimmy got down to business. "Remember Ibiza, Sid?"

"Summer of '77, how could I forget."

"Remember Club Galaxy, we all met up in there after you'd gone missing after the boat trip and I'd been nicked."

"Yes, and Clive got engaged to that little fat ugly rich bird," I laughed.

"Caroline, Sid, Clive's on wife number three now."

"I hear that's on the rocks," I replied.

"Anyway, Sid, the two girls you brought with you who looked after you when you were off your nut."

"The two Geordie birds?" I remembered. "You disappeared with one if I recall, Jimmy."

"Mary," Jimmy interrupted.

"We spent the last couple of days together. I wanted to see her again but she confessed she was engaged and that was it, just a brief two night stand."

"And?" I pressed.

"Apparently I got her pregnant."

"You what?"

"I'm a fucking father, Sid."

"She had it?"

"Yes, she married her bloke and he naturally assumed he was the father until they split up when the kid was eight, and he got himself checked out because him and his new missus struggled to have a kid. Turned out he was a 'Jaffa', couldn't have kids."

"Fucking hell, Sid, that couldn't have gone down well."

"No, it didn't. Mary decided to make a new life for herself and moved down to South London."

"And?" I asked again.

"And last month, Mary tracked me down and introduced me to my sixteen-year-old daughter Molly."

"Fucking hell, Jimmy, does Heena know?"

"We've all met up, Mary is in a steady relationship living in Streatham, she just wanted Molly to know the truth. I've since met up with Molly and she's coming to stay with us this weekend, I'd like you and Trudie and the kids to meet her."

"Wow, of course. I can't believe it. And Heena?"

"It's early days, we're all coming to terms with the situation. It's not easy for Heena obviously, what with what happened, you know."

"Yeah, yes, Jimmy, I understand. Wow," I said, gobsmacked.

"I'm a dad." Jimmy grabbed my arm.

"I'm delighted for you!"

"Thanks, Sid, me of all people realise I've got to do the right thing. Here, look at this." He passed me a photo of her in her school uniform.

"Molly is definitely your daughter, Jimmy," I confirmed, to Jimmy's delight.

"Thanks, Sid, but there's more."

"More what?"

"More family," he boasted.

"What do you mean?"

"Apparently I'm going to be a grandfather!"

* * *

The walk from the Hipshaker to the wellbeing tent seemed to take forever as I had trouble walking in a straight line, I kept veering to the right. Eventually I got there, I saw the Thai woman preparing the area under the canopy. I leaned against the side of a burger van, almost opposite and I saw the two boys who Jimmy and I abandoned the day before.

A couple of minutes later, Ricky, the guy claiming to be their father, arrived this time sporting an England shirt. It reminded me they were playing Italy that night in the World Cup, but it clashed with the Red Hot Chilli Peppers. I stumbled over to them feeling like I was being controlled by a puppet master.

"How you doing man?" I tapped Ricky on the arm. "Remember me?" I asked.

"Yes, I do, you were supposed to look after the kids yesterday," he grunted.

"Hey fuck you, you're not even their father," I retorted, but it was like someone else was making me belligerent.

"I never said I was but you just left them there," he accused me.

I was now in his face. "You said you'd be ten minutes, but you were gone for over an hour, you idiot!" I shouted.

He grabbed me by my T-shirt. I pushed back and he fell over a chair and dragged me down with him.

The kids ran over, as did the Thai woman, who jumped on my back. One or two people passing by looked on in amazement at us. Suddenly the tent flap opened and the man in the Lenin hat jumped out, pulling the woman off and then standing between Ricky and I as we stood up.

"Everyone calm down," he demanded, in an almost hushed vicar-like tone.

"Sorry, Earth." Ricky stepped back a few paces. This middle-aged hippy type turned towards me and was about to speak but hesitated as we both recognised each other at the same time.

"Sid?" he queried, softly placing his hand on my shoulder.

I couldn't really address him by his old nickname, so I replied addressing him by his proper name. "Michael," I almost whispered, the high from the cake extinguished by my surprise.

"You know this man, Earth?" the Thai woman asked.

"Yes love, this is Sid, he's an old friend of mine, we were at school together. This is my partner, Tulip," he introduced her, though I doubt it was her real name. "What you doing here, Sid?"

"I'm with…I'm with friends for the festival," I hesitated, just in time thinking it best not to mention Jimmy's name.

"Come inside. Tulip will make us some tea? We've got a lot of catching up to do Havn't we Sid?"

I followed him into what was a giant Wigwam, there were Persian rugs on the floor and lots of colourful cushions. There was a harp placed beside what was basically a throne without legs. My host sat on it crossed legged, looking like a guru, which perhaps he was, but to me he was and always will be Ink Bat.

40

ENGLAND VS. THE CHILLI PEPPERS

I DIDN'T KNOW 'Earth', I knew and despised Michael James, Ink Bat. The teenager I knew was a stirrer and squealer. He stood by when I got thumped by Grant Bishop. He was sarcastic and just totally unlikeable, excommunicated from the Third Tree Club. He moved to Brighton with his family when he was sixteen. He wasn't missed by anybody, especially me. Maybe once or twice we would wonder, '*What ever happened to that idiot Ink Bat?*', but he didn't register in our lives for 25 years, until I was summoned to the Lemon Tree Arms.

This time I guessed correctly that Jimmy had a problem with Heena. He explained that she'd been dabbling in Eastern mysticism, which given her ethnicity was not totally surprising, but she'd then got obsessed with Yoga and various alternative lifestyle pastimes. This culminated in leaving Jimmy a note that she was going away for a while to find herself. Jimmy interpreted this as another, more subtle, way of her telling him that she's having an affair with her yoga teacher. He was spot on. He then went on to tell me that he'd followed her to a class and guess who her teacher was, Ink Bat. I couldn't believe it.

Jimmy took me to a converted farmhouse in Essex a couple of days later, and I saw for myself it was indeed our old adversary.

"I'm going to kill him," Jimmy announced on the drive home.

"Leave it to me," I demanded. "You'll be the main suspect, I'll sort it. Trust me, I'm an expert." Ink Bat was suddenly on my kill list.

"Can you kill Heena as well?" he casually added as an afterthought.

"Are you sure, Jimmy?"

"Definitely", he confirmed, but I wasn't sure he meant it.

A few weeks later Trudie told me Heena had called her trying to involve her in one of these pyramid scams that came around every 20 years. Heena was officially placed on my kill list.

I got to an advanced planning stage, when a few months later Jimmy phoned me and told me Heena was back.

"She's found herself then, that was quick," I stated.

"No, Sid, seems Ink Bat has found himself a younger model and fucked off to France."

"So, you don't want them killed, Jimmy?" I asked for confirmation.

"Not Heena, but if I ever see that fucking cunt Ink Bat anywhere, I'll fucking kill him myself. Not only did he steal my missus, he fleeced her for three grand as well," Jimmy exclaimed.

So I took Heena off the list but kept Ink Bat on it.

* * *

What was worrying me was that after sitting down chewing the fat with the new Ink Bat for an hour or so, I quite liked him. Of course, the cake might have had something to do with it.

He admitted he was a pain in the arse as a teenager. He blamed his over strict parents and told me he left home at eighteen and went to live on a kibbutz in Israel, where he reinvented himself and started to look at alternative lifestyles. He travelled around India and Nepal and came back to live in London, where he started his own retreat specialising in whatever the new fad was. He confessed to me that he was never a man's man, not gay, quite the opposite, he preferred the company of women. I was surprised when he confessed that a lot of his treatments and ideas are 'mumbo jumbo' but are a great way to impress women!

"So, I'm confused, are you married to Tulip?" I asked.

"No, she's my partner and the mother of my children. She's married to Ricky technically but we all enjoy an open relationship."

I was still confused. "What about Heena?" I pressed.

"Heena?" He looked puzzled.

"Jimmy's wife, Heena, Indian girl," I added.

"Yes, I remember Heena, but you're telling me she was married to Jimmy Faulkner?" He looked completely taken aback.

"They're still married," I confirmed.

"Shit, I had no idea. Jimmy must hate me."

"He wanted to kill you, but you disappeared."

"I went to France and then Spain, I was living off money I'd fleeced off some of my clients, I'm afraid to say."

"The pyramid scam?" I reminded him.

"Shit, Sid, I hope your wife wasn't drawn in."

"Almost, I wasn't happy."

"Not my finest moment for sure. How do you think Jimmy feels about me now?"

"Probably still wants to kill you," I replied honestly.

"I'd like to meet him, I'm sorry to hear about his eye problems, maybe we could make a fresh start."

* * *

I spent the rest of the day stage hopping and drinking, taking a break in the big tent for some shut eye during Dappy's unbelievably shit set. I decided to head back to the campsite to see if Jimmy was there. I wasn't worried, just curious to what he'd been up to. *Should I tell him about Ink Bat?*

He wasn't in his tent, but neither was the goody bag. This worried me.

I stopped off at the girls' tent, I could hear hysterical laughing coming from inside. I coughed but it made no difference. I heard a familiar voice.

"Girls, seriously, my penis is killing me!" I heard Jimmy yell. "Nurse, do something!" he cried out, followed by another crescendo of laughter.

"I'm trying, I'm trying!" Nina, I think, screamed out.

I stood there, my mind racing. I knew if I entered the tent it would literally be sex, drugs and rock n roll. Those girls were fit and definitely game. I thought about Trudie, we'd had our blips but without her support and understanding, I would have been back home pretending to grieve. My father only died four days ago, maybe an orgy was a step too far!

I climbed into the spare tent, I could still hear everything. I spotted the goody bag discarded on the sleeping bag Jimmy had made his home. Two more gels and two more cakes had gone. I made a mental list. Half a cake, a wank, an hour's kip, The Specials, Red Hot Chilli Peppers and then England v Italy. *Could life be any better?* I suppose, I could be Jimmy right now.

"Keep going girls, it's got to go down eventually!" he cried.

* * *

I ticked off the first things on my list and peeped into the girl's tent. The girls were sparko, Jimmy was curled up in the foetal position snoring like a goodun. I couldn't see if he still had an erection, but he had a smile on his face.

I left a note on the goody bag, '*Gone to eat, then Specials. Will be on right hand side of the stage. P.S. Keep off the gels!*'.

I sat by my usual tree eating Thai green curry, followed by half a cake, and washed down with a pear cider. I wondered what Smithy's extra ingredient was. I felt uneasy about Jimmy and the girls but seeing as he recently told me they hadn't had sex for over two years and given Heena's transgression with Michael/Ink Bat/Earth, who could blame him. Over forty hours and he was still enjoying his Glastonbury experience! I was beginning to think I might just pull off my greatest ever deception, it was unlikely Terry Hall would shout out 'Isle of Wight make some noise!'.

I walked around the different venues, feeling the most relaxed I had in probably years.

The music, pear cider and cake all working their magic as I got into position near the front of the main stage. The teenagers that had been screaming at The 1975 were swiftly replaced by an expectant mob of fifty somethings. Pork pie hats, braces and Dr Martens were all on display, strangers reminiscing about where they saw them back in the day. A massive geezer in a Coventry shirt was given due respect for actually hailing from the original Ghost Town.

Suddenly, I got a tap on the shoulder, Pat and Nina were guiding Jimmy through the throng.

"You're still alive then!" I yelled above the spasmodic cries of *Rude Boy* from the crowd around us.

"Blimey, Sid, what a day! What a festival! I love Glasto!"

"It's something else isn't it?!" I replied ironically.

"What we going to watch after the Specials, Sid? The Chilli Peppers or the football?"

"Tough call, Jimmy, bit of both maybe."

"I've asked the girls to take me to the legendary Glastonbury 'healing fields' after, you up for it?"

"Defo," I replied, slightly concerned.

"I might be fucking healed," Jimmy laughed.

"Still on the cake, Jimmy?" I enquired.

"Oh yes, but I've given the gels away, they were a bit of an error. I thought they were Amyl nitrite or something."

"Thank fuck."

He put his arm around me and kissed me on the head. "Thanks for this, Sid, this is a fucking wonderland, thanks, mate!"

I was elated by his sincerity, I'm sure it wasn't just the cake talking.

The Specials didn't disappoint. An hour of all their classic hits and it was great to see Jimmy skanking with the best of them. As they broke into a finale of *Ghost Town* and *Too Much too Young*, the crowd got very lairy and Jimmy lost his footing and slipped under the swaying crowd.

I tried to pull Jimmy up but couldn't get a grip on him. Suddenly, a proper old school Rude Boy pushed the surrounding crowd away and yanked Jimmy up.

"My glasses, my glasses!" Jimmy yelled, feeling his eyes. The geezer screamed at the crowd to move away.

"This blokes in trouble, step away whilst I find his glasses!"

The crowd parted like the Red Sea and within seconds he'd retrieved Jimmy's shades.

"Cheers pal," I patted him on the back. "My mate has impaired vision."

"No worries, I'll stand behind him make sure he's ok," the kind stranger, now Jimmy's minder, reassured.

In the melee we'd lost the girls. The Specials amazing set came to an end, the rude boys and girls immediately drifted away to be replaced by rockers, ready for the Red Hot Chilli Peppers headline set.

"Cheers, mate," I thanked our rescuer.

"No worries. I've lost my mates, I'm going to head to the football, see if I can find them," he stated.

"Good idea, mate. Come on, Sid," Jimmy agreed.

"What about the Chillis?" I protested.

"We can catch them after the game." Jimmy didn't seem too bothered about one of the best live bands I've ever seen. Our new mate saw me hesitate.

"I'll keep your mate company pal," he offered reassuringly.

"Cheers, I'm Sid, this is Jimmy. He gets very excitable watching football," I joked.

"I'm Eric, who's your team?"

"We're Chels," Jimmy stated.

"Oh dear." Eric showed us his Millwall Lion tattoo.

"Well, at least none of us are dirty Leeds," I laughed.

"That's true," Eric confirmed.

"How about we meet in the Hipshaker tent at eleven-thirty for the Pistols verses the Clash," I suggested.

"Nice one, I'm a Clash man myself. You don't half look familiar Sid, I'm sure we've met before," he said, as he led Jimmy off through the crowd.

I shared the same feeling that our paths had crossed before.

* * *

I'd put the Red Hot Chilli Peppers in the top five live bands on the planet. I took Tara and Leo to see them at the V festival when they were fifteen and fourteen. It was a priceless moment seeing their faces as *Under the Bridge* was played as the sun set. Not quite the same as my first festival experience!

I was torn between the Isle of Wight headliners and the football, which both started at the same time. Within seconds of Anthony Kiedis taking to the stage, I knew I'd made the correct decision. Dressed just in shorts and trainers he bounced around the stage like a whirling Dervish, driving the crowd into a frenzy. Four songs in there was a short pause between songs and we heard an almighty roar emit from the football stage. I hesitated, a brief memory of the Rattín incident flickered in my head.

I started to jostle through the crowd, I had to get to the football despite the Chilli's best efforts. It wasn't long before the biggest screen in Europe came into view, the booming commentary clashed with the wonderful noise coming from the main stage. Just as I joined the excited crowd singing 'It's coming home', Italy scored to go into a 2-1 lead.

'*All my fault*', I thought and decided I'd jinxed England. So I joined a few thousand others, who decided to return to the Chilli Peppers.

* * *

I was relieved to see Jimmy and his new minder Eric at the bar in the Hipshaker tent, as arranged. The Scouse girls turned up at the same time and now they were joined by their friend Laura, who had broken down on the way on Thursday and whose tent Jimmy had been dossing in.

England had lost, so we decided to drink away our disappointment. Some people behave irrationally when there's a full moon, I turn into a complete lunatic every four years during the World Cup. I use the whole month to escape from the realities of life. Back in '66 I was starstruck and believed England would win the cup every four years but was crushed with disappointment at my father's complete disinterest. In 1990, Gazza's tears deflected me from the imminent threat of bankruptcy. This time round, the competition would shield me from the inevitable repercussions of my selfishness in going to a music festival the day after my father's funeral.

"Fucking useless," Jimmy moaned.

"To think we gave up the Red Hot Chilli Peppers for that shower of shite," Eric chipped in.

"Early days yet, I'm sure we'll beat Uruguay," I said, more in hope than expectation. "Thanks for keeping an eye on my mate, no pun intended," I added, noticing Jimmy had found the girls.

"No problem pal, your mate's a fucking legend, told me all about Weeley, we reckon we probably punched each other in a Millwall Chelsea scrap at London Bridge back in the day."

"Yeah, I remember it well, we'd lost four nil to Charlton at the Valley. Set the turnstiles on fire and then your lot were waiting at London Bridge. I legged it but Jimmy was right in the thick of it, great times."

"The best, mate, loved it! The Den, the Clash, Sham 69, fucking loved it!" Eric slapped him on the back as a Sex Pistols tribute band sprang into action on the small stage.

"We'll have to have a beer sometime, I hope Jimmy will be okay."

"Yes defo, I hope so. Give me your number, I'll be in touch."

I put his number in my phone. "Blimey, I've already got an Eric in my address book," I laughed.

"Not Clapton?" he replied.

"No, a client of mine. What shall I put you under?"

"I'm known throughout London as Eric the locksmith, so that will do."

"Eric the locksmith!" I exclaimed. "That's where I know you from! You came to the flat I was renting out about five years ago, you tried to barge the bathroom door open and this mad naked bird opened it."

"Yes, I remember. You were trying to get rid of a tenant. What a fucking small world eh?!"

I updated him about Perry, claiming he was no longer a problem.

"Cheers for the cake geezer," he exclaimed.

Jimmy offered a thumbs up.

We watched the Pistols and Clash tribute bands battle it out and then Jimmy decided a midnight trip to Glastonbury's legendary healing field was in order. I tried to talk him out of it, but he was insistent.

"You never know, Sid, I might actually be healed," he said half serious.

Pat whispered they'd take him down to the 'village', where there was a small cluster of alternative lifestyle tents, including Ink Bat's.

I asked him to go steady with the goody bag. He said there were only two cakes left, plus the two mysterious yellow tablets. He never mentioned the gels.

I had a few more beers with Eric and his mates who turned up, all drunk as skunks before deciding to call it a day.

I staggered back to my tent stopping at 'our' toilet, but sadly we'd been rumbled. My laminated A4 *'Priority Toilet'* sign was no more. I looked inside and it was well and truly soiled. I decided to take advantage of the piss pot Trudie had got me from the pound shop instead. I made sure the lid was clasped firmly shut but I had to clamber out of my sleeping bag just half an hour later for effort number two. An hour after that, effort number three was a long one, I guessed there was just about room for one more effort.

I dreamt about Perry again, he was alive and well and living in my garden shed. None of the family knew he was there, and he was blackmailing me. I woke in a sweat and dying for a piss. My phone said it was 5.15am, I fumbled for my torch but couldn't find it. I burst out of my sleeping bag and looked around for the piss pot, which I positioned between the end of my blow-up mattress and the front flaps. I managed to get the lid off and started to urinate into the void, whilst kneeling.

I got terrible cramp in my calf and struggled to finish the job. I was in agony and started to worry I'd over fill the piss pot, but the seal had been broken so I took my chances in the darkness. It wasn't easy scrabbling around looking for the lid and as I felt it beside me, I thought of how difficult it must be for poor Jimmy. Suddenly my whole leg went into spasm and I kicked out in pain, instantly kicking the piss pot into the air! The lid flew off and the contents of a day's drinking lined the whole tent. My sleeping bag was completely saturated, as was my rucksack.

I opened the flap and crawled out cursing. Fortunately, it was still really warm, so I stripped off to my pants. I heard a wolf whistle and saw some of the young medical students sitting outside their tent sharing a spliff.

"Kicked my piss pot over," I grumbled.

"Shit, you'll have to leave your tent here, they are going send them to Syria," he informed me.

276

"Blimey, I feel sorry for the poor souls that get mine," I laughed. I climbed into Jimmy's empty piss free tent and crashed out on his nice dry sleeping bag.

"What the fuck!" I heard a cry and then felt the weight of a fourteen stone man lying on me.

"Jimmy!" I yelled, as he rolled off me.

"What the fuck you doing in my tent, Sid?"

I started to explain but Pat the Scouse girl who'd guided Jimmy back interrupted. "You alright in there Jimmy, you sure this is your tent?"

"It's ok Pat, thanks, it's only Sid."

I explained what happened, Jimmy nearly wet himself laughing.

"So, what happened to you?" I enquired.

"Well, I thought I was having an interesting time in the legendary Glastonbury healing fields, but it turns out this is the Isle of Wight."

I sat up, Jimmy had clambered onto the pillow end of his bed. It was getting lighter, I could just about make out his frame. I guessed this was how Jimmy saw everything.

"What you on about, Jimmy?" I guessed the game was up, I'd done well to keep up the charade for so long. "Jimmy, I-" I started to explain, wondering how he finally found out, probably a performer shouting out 'Isle of Wight make some noise' or something similar, but he cut me short.

"Listen, Sid, never mind all that. You'll never guess who I ran into in a so called 'wellbeing' tent?"

I decided to play dumb. "Who?"

"Well the girls dragged me into this place and explained to this fucking healing man called Earth or something about my eye and he took me into this sort of room and put fucking weird music on and told me he would do some reiki shit on me, told me he was a reiki master and that if I completely blotted everything out of my mind, he could work wonders. Anyway, there was something about his voice I recognised, but before I knew it, we had complete silence and he placed his hands on my head and neck. After a few minutes, I could feel real heat around these areas and he then placed his fingers over my eyes, both of them, and it was like they were on fire. And then suddenly for a brief second, I had perfect vision! I saw this Earth's face and you won't believe this Sid; I'd recognised the voice and my brief view of his face confirmed who it was."

"Who was it?" I interrupted, claiming ignorance.

"Fucking Ink Bat," Jimmy confirmed.

"Ink Bat, as in Michael James?" I feigned surprise.

"Yes, fucking Ink Bat is here, he's a fucking healer or something, calls himself Earth."

"Did you confront him?"

"No, I'm sure he knew who I was, but he didn't let on and I decided not to let on either."

"So, what did he say? What happened?" I enquired.

"Well, he told me he goes around the festivals during the summer and then puts on wellbeing workshops around the UK. I asked him whether this was his favourite festival and he said no, Glastonbury was. I told him this was Glastonbury and he laughed and explained where we were."

"Typical Ink Bat, he's still obviously a stirring cunt," I protested. "I'm sorry, Jimmy. I didn't know how to tell you mate. If it wasn't for that cunt, you'd have fully enjoyed the Glasto experience."

"Don't worry about it, Sid, this is fucking wonderland, it's heaven on Earth mate. Best weekend of my life and it ain't over by a long shot, got another day yet."

I was flushed with relief and really looking forward to a full day not having to worry about the Glastonbury charade.

"You didn't feel tempted to chin the wanker?" I probed.

"Yes, but I don't know what came over me, I suddenly felt a wave of euphoria and forgiveness and just went with the flow."

I suspected it was the guilt of him getting up to no good with the girls that concentrated his mind, rather than any magic from the charlatan hands of Ink Bat.

"So how did it end up?" I asked.

"Well, I realised I had no money and the cunt wanted fifty fucking quid, so I gave him the remains of the goody bag."

"What was left in it?" I enquired, secretly relieved it was gone.

"One and a half cakes and those two mystery yellow tablets," Jimmy confirmed.

41

DEATH IN WONDERLAND

I'D ONLY GOT a couple of hours sleep since returning to my tent, where my only option was to turn over my piss saturated sleeping bag. The medical students next door were continuing their non-stop party. I heard Jimmy's voice among the revellers. I crawled out and saw him sharing an early morning spliff with the crowd of youngsters. I desperately needed a shower, but Jimmy seemed hell bent on enjoying every second of his last day in 'wonderland'.

We shared stories of gigs in the '70s with the kids, I felt very old but at the same time, very privileged. Jimmy then ushered me away back to our tents, something was on his mind.

"Fuck it, I should have lumped that Ink Bat last night, the least we can do is go and confront the cunt, he was responsible for the Heena episode," Jimmy snarled.

I tried to calm him down, but he got up to go by himself.

"Hang on, Jimmy, I've got a confession to make." I stopped him in his tracks and told him about my meeting with him and suggested maybe it's time to let bygones be bygones.

"I just want to embarrass him, Sid, nothing more," he said and off we went. If only I'd sorted him out back in the day.

As we walked across the festival site, my anger grew as I reminisced about how Ink Bat stood there laughing when Grant Bishop smashed me in the nose.

We stopped for an early livener at a bar and sat at a table talking about the past. Jimmy suddenly went quiet, he took off his shades. "This is it, Sid, this could be my last fucking day at a festival, the Kings of Leon could be the last band I ever see mate. You've been on the net, you know this thing could kill me."

"Yeah, I've researched it all, Jimmy. I know the worst-case scenario, but science is finding new cures all the time, you've got to stay positive mate. Besides, the Kings of Leon won't be the last band you see, Travis are closing the big top and finish half an hour after them. Believe me, they are fantastic live." I reminded Jimmy about seeing them kick off the V festival in the early noughties, along with Coldplay, Snow Patrol and Muse, who are now all headliners.

"Do you ever think about Weeley?" Jimmy interrupted.

"Nearly every day, Jimmy, it changed my life."

"And mine, Sid, literally!"

I felt guilty having such different memories of it. "I know, mate." I put my hand on his shoulder.

"Did you know it was that fucking cunt Ink Bat that started my Cyclops nickname?" Jimmy exclaimed.

"He was always a fucking nuisance," I mumbled, thinking about the bus stop incident.

"Then he fucked up my relationship with Heena," Jimmy spat.

"Drink up, Sid, let's go and pay the cunt a visit."

I led my pal through the festival site, which was coming alive on yet another beautiful day. Suddenly we heard a shout, "Morning lads, how you doing?!"

It was Eric the locksmith carrying four pints.

We went over and started to discuss the night before and were introduced to his mates. We were discussing the day's line-up when I noticed Jimmy had slipped off in the direction of the wellbeing tent. He was zig zagging in the general direction.

"Is Jimmy okay?" Eric asked.

"Why's he holding a knife?" Eric's mate interrupted.

"What?!" I exclaimed.

"Yeah, he pulled a blade out of his coat pocket and strolled off."

"Shit!" I cried, realising Jimmy's intentions, given his state of mind and body. I started to leg it as fast as I could in his direction. I shouted to him as I lost my footing on the ridge of a slope that led down to the wellbeing area. I saw the solid frame of Eric hurdle over me and then noticed Jimmy had stopped still.

A few seconds later, Eric rugby tackled Jimmy, sending him crashing to the ground and losing his grip on the knife. I managed to catch up and picked up the knife and threw it into a nearby recycling bin. It was then I noticed the ambulance and police car parked outside Ink Bat's wellbeing tent.

"What the fuck?" I exclaimed, as Eric helped Jimmy up, explaining the situation in front of us.

"You'd better get down there and check out what's going on," Jimmy whispered.

I nodded and took a couple of steps down the slope, before stopping. "Not sure it's a good idea either of us getting involved, maybe you could go down there Eric, you've got no history with them."

We watched our new friend stroll towards the scene of the crime, disappearing behind the ambulance as I gave Jimmy a running commentary.

* * *

Eric returned half an hour later, after I'd explained to Jimmy that I'd seen a covered body being loaded into the back of the ambulance.

"Who is it, what happened?" I asked frantically.

"I'll explain over a beer, let's go to the Hipshaker," Eric suggested. We made our way through the excited Sunday mid-morning crowd. I got the beers in, Eric and Jimmy found a quiet corner.

"Who has died?" Jimmy wasted no time.

"Some bloke called Earth, apparently," Eric confirmed.

"Ink Bat," Jimmy and I answered together.

"I take it he's the geezer you wanted to kill, mate?" Eric addressed Jimmy.

"The very one. What happened?" Jimmy replied.

"Seems he had a massive heart attack, six this morning."

I looked at Jimmy, who took his shades off and blinked.

"You thinking what I'm thinking, Sid?"

"The yellow tablets," I whispered.

"Exactly," Jimmy concurred.

"What tablets?" Eric interrupted.

"He tried to sell us these yellow tablets, said they were strong stuff," I lied beautifully.

"So, you obviously had beef with this geezer?" Eric guessed correctly.

"He stole my wife!" Jimmy yelled.

"He was a complete cunt," I added.

"Well, it looks like a win-win situation then, let's drink to that." Eric raised his plastic cup of beer.

I pondered on whether Jimmy had indirectly killed Ink Bat and for a brief second thought about the coincidences involving his death and my father's just a few days before.

God certainly works in mysterious ways.

42

THE LAST DAY IN WONDERLAND

WE SAT ON the dry sun-baked grass in the main arena, enjoying the chilled acoustic tunes of Passenger. We had decided to spend our last day listening to some great music and enjoying a few beers, without any more shenanigans.

"Well that was quite a morning," Jimmy laughed.

"It's been quite a weekend," I added.

"Best fucking weekend of my life, mate," Jimmy replied back with a smile on his face.

"Even if it's not Glastonbury?" I chanced.

"Well it was Glastonbury until fucking Ink Bat spoilt it for me, I reckon you might have got away with it if that cunt hadn't fucking put his oar in."

"He did it on purpose, Jimmy. I told him about my ruse, he was a shit stirrer to his dying day."

Jimmy started to laugh uncontrollably, he was trying to tell me something, but he couldn't get the words out for all his laughter. Eventually he composed himself.

"We're averaging one dead body per festival, Sid, and this one ain't over yet," he managed to blurt out.

"Yeah, one Hells Angel and one healer," I spat out, as we burst into more laughter.

The beer, sun and mellow music had the inevitable effect of inducing an afternoon nap. I felt a wave of contentment that Jimmy was having such a great time, despite the Glasto ruse. Yes, I'd face some stick on my return but hopefully the sale of the old man's property would ease my financial worries. Above all, I was convinced my serial killer days were over.

We both slept through the entire Fall Out Boy set, I fetched us a couple of beers as we eagerly awaited the next band Suede.

"Are we going to tell Smithy he might be responsible for Ink Bat's death," Jimmy asked seriously.

"Let's just ask him what those yellow tablets were?" I suggested.

"Talking of tablets, fancy trying one of these?" Jimmy produced a couple of small off-white tablets with a smiley face on it.

"Are these what I think they are?" I muttered. "Where the fuck did you get them?"

"I dipped that cunt Ricky's pocket when I visited Ink Bat's tent."

"Ricky?"

"Yes, Ricky, that cunt that left the Thai bird's kids with us when he went off to get his pills."

"Oh yes, the geezer that was married to Ink Bat's partner?" I still found the love triangle confusing.

"Yeah, well, I managed to nick a couple of pills and a twenty pound note off him with my heightened sense of touch. Besides, the cunt owed us for child minding services." Jimmy was laughing again.

"What about those poor orphans?" I pondered.

"I suspect there will be a lot of orphans dotted across the globe," Jimmy guessed, probably correctly.

"Well, are we? Shall we?" Jimmy displayed the two E's in the palm of his hand.

"I've never tried one before," I confessed.

"Neither have I," he concurred.

I thought about Trudie, the kids, the business, my father and Jimmy's eye problems. "Fuck it, Jimmy! We're in wonderland! Let's do this!"

With that, he swallowed his and handed me mine, which I gulped down with my pear cider. At that very moment, one of the young medical students, who were our neighbours at the camp site, walked past us.

"Hi old timers, how you doing this fine day?" He slapped us both on the back, he was clearly stoned.

"Aghh the good doctor to be, pray tell us what are the effects of us old timers taking an E?"

"You naughty boys, you're fucking legends! Have you really?"

We both nodded in unison. "Speed and weed were our drug back in the day, but never tried MDMA."

"Think speed on steroids," the young man laughed. "You'll be raving all night and telling each other all your secrets. You'll be in love with the world! Have a great day. Last night party later if you old timers are still high."

"Oh well, Sid, best fasten our seat belts."

* * *

Within a few minutes we made our way to the front of the stage. It's was funny that Suede, an iconic '90s band, took to the stage just as the iconic '90s drug was kicking in. The crowd around us all seemed to be around the forty mark, and all seemed up for it. Neither of us were great fans but knew the hits, and when they finished with *The Beautiful Ones,* we were in a huddle with some new friends we'd never met or spoken to before.

I felt a feeling of total euphoria. The music, the crowd, the sun, the booze and obviously the E, brought us to a moment where life could not be any better. As Suede ended their magnificent set, we returned to the back of the main arena and collapsed in a joyful heap.

"I'm fucking buzzing, Sid."

"Likewise, I'll get us another beer in a minute."

"No rush, Sid, let's just enjoy the moment."

"Good idea, Jimmy."

"I was just thinking, here we are, the two of us in our fifties, at a festival enjoying a weekend of sex, drugs and rock n roll!"

"Not the sex bit for me."

In the forty plus years I'd been besties, the subject of infidelity had never been discussed, save for the Heena business. I waited for Jimmy to continue.

"You're not cross with me are you, Sid?"

"About what?" I acted dumb.

"The Scouse girls."

I shrugged my shoulders, not knowing what to say because I didn't know how I felt. I couldn't blame him, but I felt awkward with it.

"Fucking hell, Heena and me haven't had sex in two, three years, in fact it may be longer."

"I'm sorry Jimmy, that's tough."

"Heena is at it again with one of her 'spiritual' friends but to be honest I don't give a shit."

I suspected as much, I'm sure she was only sticking with Jimmy because of his health problems.

"Well, I can't blame you, mate. I hope everything works out."

"Well the fact that fucking Ink Bat is dead means one less cunt to worry about."

"So, who is this bloke seeing Heena? Do you want me to-"

"I'm past caring. Besides, I've got a guilty secret," Jimmy interrupted.

"Really, what's that?"

"Remember Julie O'Neill?" he whispered.

"How could I forget the O'Neills," I exclaimed, recalling the Third Tree Club living in fear of them and then Terry O'Neill questioning whether his circumcision would hurt. Ironically, it was Terry and his brother that helped me get Perry out of the flat above my shop.

"Well, I ran into her last year working on a supermarket till and to cut a long story short, I pop round to her gaff every now and again for a bit of slap and tickle," Jimmy confessed.

"Wasn't she married to that lunatic Clem Johnson?" I enquired, recalling her marrying the infamous North Londoner gangster.

"She still is, but he's halfway through a ten year stretch for attempted murder," Jimmy whispered.

"Fucking hell, Jimmy, you don't half pick em!"

"Well we both have simple needs, there's nothing serious between us."

I nodded, seeing the benefits of this relationship. "Do any of the O'Neill's know about it?"

"Nope."

"Best keep it that way," I advised.

There was a brief pause before Jimmy surprised me. "What about you, Sid?"

"What about me?" I asked.

"Have you ever played away?"

"Have I what?" I snapped.

"Had an affair, you know what I'm asking."

"No," I answered defensively. "Why do you ask?"

"We've taken a 'truth serum', I'm curious that's all."

"So, do you believe me?" I tried to put Jimmy on the back foot.

"I do, but if you had strayed, I wouldn't judge you."

"You won't believe me because I'm a serial liar, as you know."

"One of the best, I mean I spent three days in Glastonbury," he laughed.

"I'm flattered, but no. I've been one hundred percent faithful since I married Trudie," I answered honestly, but was frustrated I couldn't read his eyes, as there was something in his voice, his questioning, that I was uncomfortable with. I had a hunch I knew what was coming next and I was right.

"And Trudie?"

I had the feeling this was a question Jimmy had wanted to ask me for years, but it took an E to give him the courage.

"You know, don't you?" I felt as if Jimmy could sense the pain his question caused me.

"I know, Sid," he confirmed.

I swallowed hard, a part of me wanting to run off and get a drink, but the MDMA was in control of my conscience. "It was few years ago, water under the bridge," I stated matter-of-factly. Jimmy was quiet, tempting me to elaborate. "How much do you know?"

"Only that there was a rumour Trudie had a brief dalliance with Clive."

Suddenly, it was as if someone had put their hand inside my brain and pulled out all the data in the section marked 'Supressed info'.

"He was decorating our house, the one in Pullman Road. You know Clive, a serial offender and too fucking good looking for his own good." I wanted to close my eyes, but I couldn't, the scene was as vivid as it was when I popped home early to pick up my passport fifteen years ago. "I came home early to get my passport as I needed ID to take to the bank to make a large cash withdrawal and…and there was Trudie and Clive on the sofa."

There were a few seconds silence, broken by the Kings of Leon road crew tuning their instruments.

"I'm looking forward to this lot," Jimmy tried to change the subject, but I couldn't help myself, I needed to tell Jimmy everything.

"I didn't realise it was Clive at first, but then I saw his decorating whites on the floor.

"The bastard," Jimmy interrupted.

I ignored him. "And you know what I did, Jimmy?"

"What, Sid?"

"Nothing, absolutely nothing, I just stood there," I recalled. "Trudie's face was a mixture of total panic and ecstasy. I just stood there watching them. I felt nothing, no hatred or anything."

"You must have been angry, surely?"

"No, Jimmy, I wasn't. Surprised, yes, but not angry or even jealous."

"Wow, Sid."

"I know what you're thinking, how could this be given the fact I was so jealous of that cunt Roland during our courtship."

"Yeah, you were off your nut with jealousy, we were all concerned that you would do something stupid."

"And I did, Jimmy."

"Did what?"

"Did something stupid, very stupid."

"How stupid, Sid?"

"Tried to kill him stupid." I was past caring.

"You tried to kill Roland?" Jimmy whispered, as the crowd started to swell around us in readiness for the headliners.

"I sort of did kill Roland, if I'd been caught, I'd have done time for attempted murder for sure." I proceeded to tell the whole story to Jimmy.

"You we're actually going to smash his skull in with a hammer?" he exclaimed, as the crowd roared Kings of Leon onto the stage.

I nodded and then we turned our attention to the headliners but not before I had the last word. "And you were going to stab Ink Bat!"

* * *

Great musicians and some great tunes, but when you grew up with the likes of Bowie, Freddie, Alex Harvey, Rod, The Who, The Jam, and obviously Mott, Kings of Leon looked very lame.

Twenty minutes into their set, I persuaded Jimmy to follow me to the big top to see Travis. Compared to the aforementioned list of the best live acts I'd seen, Travis would seem very tame indeed, but in Fran Healy they possess one of the most engaging front men I've seen, and we weren't to be disappointed. The tent was packed to the rafters, but I managed to get us to our normal pillar and joined the crowd as they sang along to hit after hit, climaxing with an epic *Why Does it Always Rain on M*e.

After, we made our way to the Hipshaker tent, where there was a Ska cover band and a very lively crowd.

"What do you reckon, Jimmy?" I yelled.

"Well, if Travis is the last band I ever see, it will be a great memory," he confirmed.

The effects of the E certainly seemed to be long lasting, as Jimmy and me skanked around like whirling Dervishes to covers of Specials, Madness and Bad Manners.

Suddenly, there was a crowd of about ten teenagers aggressively pushing and shoving a crowd of older fellas dancing beside us. Words were exchanged and a huge gap appeared between the two groups. It turned out the teenagers were from Portsmouth and the older crowd from rival Southampton.

"Just like the old days," Jimmy laughed.

But back in the old days he would have been happy to dive in and throw the first punch, now he wanted peace and love to prevail and stepped into the void, appealing to everyone to calm down.

"Come on lads, we've had a fantastic festival. Let's all have another beer together," he preached to the mob.

"Get out the fucking way, Grandad." The leader of the teenage gang stepped forward.

"You're right, mate, I'm a grandad and I'm half blind, but I'd still put you on the floor sonny."

The guy moved forward, I knew what was coming and seconds later Jimmy threw himself at the idiot with a flurry of punches and all hell broke loose. For a few seconds a Wild West brawl broke out, I dived in to back up Jimmy but fortunately security quickly intervened, ejecting the teenage Portsmouth crew. A few minutes later Jimmy was being feted with beers from the Saints mob.

The DJ put *Too Much Too Young* on and peace and love was restored, as the whole tent sang along and danced to this Ska classic. We danced our way till the last tune, I was wondering if I'd feel the effects of the E forever. I couldn't see Jimmy's eyes behind his shades, but I detected a sadness that the festival was coming to an end.

We made our way back to the campsite, it was quieter than the previous three nights, as the revellers had either ran out of steam or were resting up before the journey home. The effects of the stolen drugs were beginning to wear off as I led Jimmy through the now familiar maze of guy ropes, collapsible chairs and the odd prostate human. Suddenly Jimmy stopped, placing his hand on my shoulder.

"Sid, I have to ask you a personal question. How did you resolve your issues with Trudie?"

"What issues?" I replied, knowing full well what he meant.

"You know, the Clive business?"

"What about it?"

"Well, how did you and Trudie deal with it?"

"We didn't."

"What do you mean you didn't?"

"I knew she knew I was there when Roland was killed, I was always sure of it and this was probably a revenge fuck."

"So, you just carried on with life?"

"Yep."

"And Clive, did he apologise?"

"Apologise for what?"

"You know, don't make me spell it out, Sid."

"Well he spent another week decorating the house and he never gave me a bill, so I suppose that was sort of an apology."

"So that was it?"

"That was it," I lied. "Come on, I've got a long drive tomorrow, I need some sleep." I took my mate's arm and started to lead him toward our tents.

"Let's go via the Scouse girls' tents, I just want to say goodbye," Jimmy requested.

When we got there, we could hear laughter inside. Jimmy peered through the flap and said, "Hi girls, it's us, came to say goodbye."

Nina opened the flap, they were high and pissed, beckoning us in for a party. I knew what was likely to happen. Jimmy threw himself on top of them, they were laughing hysterically. I hesitated outside, Pat opened the flap, I could see she was only wearing knickers.

"Come and join the fun, Sid." She winked invitingly.

I mumbled an embarrassed apology and legged it to my tent, which reeked of piss, so I climbed into Jimmy's. I reckoned he'd be gone all night. I lay there thinking what I'd just ran away from.

At first, I laughed to myself thinking about Jimmy having to perform without the assistance of the Viagra gels. I then thought about my confession about Trudie and Clive and questioned whether a one-off indiscretion on my part would be forgivable. I had given Jimmy the false impression that the Trudie/Clive thing was a one off, but I had my doubts.

I'd collected my passport and left them dressing in the living room. I came home that evening and Leo and Tara had friends round, so nothing was said. It was surreal at dinner time when the kids started commenting on the decorating. Leo said that Clive was doing a very thorough job, Trudie and I exchanged the briefest of glances.

It was a couple of days later that we were alone. "We need to talk," I suggested.

"Yes, we should," Trudie agreed, pouring us both a glass of wine. Trudie lounged on the sofa I sat in my armchair and turned the TV off.

"Was that the first time?" I asked, having wondered about this question since I left the house after interrupting them.

"No," Trudie answered honestly.

"So, tell me all," I sighed.

"I don't want to hurt you, Sid, it was just sex. I'm not about to run off with him."

"I know, Trudie, but I just need to know."

"The sordid details?" she teased.

"Exactly."

"No, it wasn't the first time. The first time was at Smithy's party, you'd passed out and Clive followed me to bathroom .

I recalled the party, I got hammered on his homemade cider. It was fancy dress, Clive was the Incredible Hulk and Trudie was dressed as a schoolgirl and I have to say she did look hot.

"And since then?" I enquired matter-of-factly.

"We've fucked every lunchtime since he started decorating our house," she confessed nonchalantly.

I quickly worked out he'd been here eleven days. "Today?" I mumbled.

She nodded.

"Fucking hell, Trudie, you're like rabbits."

"Well *we* hardly ever do it, do we?" she sniped.

And she was right of course but I was always shattered after work. "What about tomorrow?" I chanced.

"I'm out with the girls tomorrow."

"The future?"

"It's just animal, Sid, Clive is a stud. I love you, not him. It's just sex."

I refilled our glasses. "So, what happens when he finishes the job?"

Trudie gave an ambiguous shrug. "You don't seem too bothered, Sid."

I paused before answering. "You know, don't you, Trudie?"

She nodded.

I was about to clarify we were on the same wavelength and mention Roland's name for the first time in our married life, when she got up and took my hand.

"Come on, Sid, let's go to bed."

43

THE DAY AFTER WONDERLAND

IT WAS A noble act by the Isle of Wight festival organisers to send all the tents that were left behind to a Syrian refugee camp, but even those wretched souls wouldn't appreciate my piss-covered canvas. I decided to leave everything and just go in the clothes I was wearing from the day before. I managed to collapse Jimmy's tent and pack his stuff. I sat his rucksack up, waiting for him to return.

"Fancy a farewell spliff old timer?" one of the medical students offered.

"Cheers, mate, but I'm driving home, best not and hey, a little less of the 'old timer' if you don't mind," I replied.

"Only joking, you and your mate Jimmy are legends," he laughed, drawing on his joint.

I sat there for half an hour surveying the festival reluctantly closing shop. The campsite resembled the aftermath of a monumental battle, Agincourt sprung to mind. I assumed Jimmy must be struggling with exhaustion and went to fetch him, but the girls, their tents and Jimmy were nowhere to be seen. I went back to Jimmy's stuff and waited another hour in the hope he'd gone to get breakfast. Eventually, I made an executive decision and decided to lug Jimmy's rucksack to the car, leaving his pop-up tent to the Syrians.

I checked my phone as I reached the car park but there was still no signal. Eventually I spotted my 'old man's' car, as my kids called it, and immediately noticed a note had been left under my wind screen wiper.

Sid,

I'll never be able to thank you enough for my weekend in wonderland and if it's the last one then rest assured this weekend will occupy my last thoughts! Maybe I'm not thinking straight, what with the illness and the weekend's excesses, but I can't face going back to Heena. I'm going to Liverpool with the girls for a few days to carry on the party. Don't worry, they will look after me! Once again Sid, a thousand thank yous, Glasto, Isle of Wight, whatever, this was fucking paradise mate.

Jimmy.

P.S. there's something for you in the exhaust!

I read the note again, threw his gear in the boot and felt in the exhaust. There was a small cellophane pouch and in it was a huge spliff.

"The bugger." I laughed out as I climbed in the car and put the packet in the glove compartment.

As I joined the queue for the ferry, my phone pinged into life for the first time since arriving. There were umpteen messages. Tara and Leo were pretty negative about my disappearance to the festival, as was Mark. There was only one from Trudie, it was from the morning before asking if I was still alive and was she right in expecting me home today. I text her back: '*Still alive, waiting for ferry*'.

There was also a message from Heena: '*I haven't heard a word from Jimmy, is he ok? When are you back?*'

I chose to ignore it, what could I say. But I did message Jimmy: '*Got your note. Good luck mate! Heena wants to know when we are back, what shall I tell her?*'

I was almost home when Jimmy replied: '*I'll call her but if she calls you, tell her the truth Sid*'.

The truth, not my strongest skill.

* * *

I parked up and saw the living room awash with light, I'd received a message that the kids would be home for dinner, I wasn't in the mood for happy families. I opened the glove compartment and picked up the spliff, I was tempted but Trudie would smell the weed. I decided to hide it under the spare tyre, maybe save it for the next time I saw Jimmy.

My family were in the middle of dinner when I came in the front door. I stood in the dining room doorway having not showered for thirty-six hours and not shaved for five days.

"Blimey, Sid, we smelt you coming down the road, the state of you," Trudie laughed.

"Bloody hell, Dad, you look like you've been in a war zone," Tara added.

"I'm going to have a shave and bath," I declared.

"Good idea," Leo concurred.

I felt reborn as I lay in the bubble filled bath, having washed away five days of festival grime. The spliff would have been the icing on the cake but it would have to stay hidden. I'd agreed to give up the Speed back when Trudie moved in with me, besides I didn't need it anymore, I had what I wanted. I'd enjoyed the very odd puff of weed when offered over the years, but this weekend was something else.

Trudie crept into the bathroom. "Heena is after you, she's phoned three times and text you asking if you're anywhere near home."

I guessed Jimmy hadn't called her. "I'll call her when I get out."

"So, where is he?"

"Wonderland," I laughed.

"Where?" Trudie looked confused.

"I'm not sure, Trudie, maybe Liverpool."

"Liverpool?" she said, shocked.

"It's a long story, Trudie, he just didn't want the weekend to end, he can't face Heena and a return to the constant worry about his health."

Trudie sat on the laundry box. "So how was Glastonbury?" she asked with a wry smile.

"Well, we enjoyed Glastonbury until Sunday morning and then loved the Isle of Wight for the last day." I told her about the near misses, the 'Isle of Wight make some noise' moments. "How's things been around here?" I thought I'd better ask.

"Well, I've spent the weekend covering your arse Sid. Your brother is incandescent, you best add him to the list of phone calls, he's returning to the States in a couple of days."

She re-joined the kids, I wanted to stay in the lovely warm bath and soak forever. I recalled my mum marching me up to the bathroom when I returned from Weeley. I didn't have a clue what had happened to Jimmy back then and forty-something years later, history had repeated itself.

I eventually dragged myself out the bath. I sat on the bed, counted to ten and called Heena. "Hi, Heena."

"Are you home, Sid? Where the fuck is he?" She sounded royally pissed off.

I thought about claiming ignorance but remembered Jimmy's instruction to tell her the truth. I tried.

"I think he's gone to Liverpool for a few days."

"What? Why the fuck would he go to Liverpool?" she snapped.

"He made some friends at the festival from there, he's gone to stay up there for a few days." I tried to sound casual, like it was no big deal.

"What the fuck are you telling me, Sid? He can hardly fucking see, he's got a hospital appointment next week." Heena was seething.

"He had such a wonderful time, he didn't want it to end," I interjected.

"Sid, you were supposed to be looking after him, I want to know exactly where he is."

"I genuinely don't know, Heena."

"What fucking happened at your stupid festival. Don't tell me he met someone."

I was about to tell her the truth about Pat and Nina but decided to hit her with another truth. "Things got a bit weird, Heena."

"What the fuck are you on about, what was weird?"

"We ran into an old friend of yours."

"What old friend?!" she shouted.

"Ink Bat," I whispered.

"Who?"

"Earth."

"Who the fuck is Earth?"

"Michael, Michael James," I confirmed.

I was met with silence.

"He died on Sunday, drug induced heart attack," I added.

"I'll call you back," she blabbed, obviously shocked to both hear he was at the festival and that he had died.

I called Mark straight after, that didn't go well either. He called me a "selfish, unfeeling cunt" for running off to the Isle of Wight festival whilst our father's body was still warm. I wanted to ask him where he was when I was running around for years sorting out my parent's problems, whilst he was living it up in sun kissed LA. But I took my chastisement and wished him a pleasant flight.

I joined the family in the living room, Trudie lightened my mood. "Sid, where's your tent, sleeping bag, rucksack, may I ask?"

Leo chipped in before I could muster an excuse. "You knocked the piss pot over, didn't you, Dad?" he guessed correctly.

"Spot on, son," I laughed.

Tara, sun kissed from her short break In Ibiza however, wasn't laughing, she was clearly disappointed with me as she left the room. I understood her feelings, whilst I had my issues with my father, I was planning to kill him for God's sake, I would agree he was a fantastic grandfather to Tara and Leo. They loved him unconditionally.

An hour later Heena called me back, she had been drinking heavily.

"Have you heard anything from Jimmy yet?" I enquired.

"Not a fucking word, did he talk to Michael?" There was desperation in her voice.

"Yes, I believe he did, why?"

"Was Jimmy upset?"

"He wasn't too happy," I confirmed.

"Did he upset Michael? I know how angry Jimmy can get."

Despite Jimmy suggesting I tell the truth, it was a case of what happened in Vegas, stays in Vegas.

"If you hear from Jimmy, let me know won't you, Sid?"

"Of course, Heena, and likewise."

Later, I lay next to Trudie, it was a joy to be in my own bed. I thought about my confession to Jimmy, Clive's name hadn't been mentioned in at least four years. I hoped it was all history between them, but I wasn't sure.

"Trudie, can I ask you something?"

"Sure, Sid, what is it?"

"Nevermind, it doesn't matter."

44

A SONG FOR JIMMY

(2019)

HEENA CALLED ME a week later and informed me Jimmy had turned up looking and feeling awful. He told her he'd had an unbearable headache for three days and couldn't sleep. She'd called the doctor the next morning, who in turn called an ambulance. I asked Heena to keep me updated and to her credit, she called me every day.

A few days after he was admitted. Heena called me in tears explaining that's Jimmy's eye cancer had spread to his brain and was inoperable and that he was being moved to a hospice.

Jimmy passed just seven weeks after our weekend at the Isle of Wight. I realised this had been a slow process and explained his behaviour. Tony Beck having Jimmy's Mott album and his supposed sighting of Perry were almost certainly part of his condition, my nightmares about Perry ceased.

I visited him every day in the hospice, he went totally blind and lost his speech, but I'd talk about gigs and football games we'd shared and, now and again, he'd squeeze my hand in approval.

I wanted '*All the Young Dudes*' to be played at his cremation but Heena had her own plans. So, a couple of weeks later, on the August Bank holiday weekend, I made my own tribute to my pal. I left home in the darkness at 4.00am and drove two hours towards the east coast, eventually coming to the village sign as dawn broke, '*Weeley (Please drive slowly)*'.

I parked up, opened the boot and took out a fold-up camp chair. I then lifted the floor, exposing the spare tyre, I felt for and found the kick ass spliff Jimmy had left in the exhaust. I walked down a footpath, eventually climbing into a field, which I hoped was the festival site. The heavens opened and it started to bucket it down, I opened up the camp chair I was carrying and sat facing where I guessed the stage had been all those years before.

I could hardly see for the rain, I sat there until 6.30am, the exact time Mott the Hoople had come on stage exactly forty-three years previously. I slowly enjoyed the spliff, reminiscing about the incredible weekend that changed our lives. Jimmy, of course, would have been in Colchester hospital at this time with his life changing injury, but I stood up and sung every word of '*All the Young Dudes*' in the pouring rain.

I realised Mott the Hoople's biggest hit hadn't even been written in 1971, David Bowie was still a one hit wonder back then. But I recalled Jimmy and I's excitement when we sat in his living room two years later watching our heroes on *Top of the Pops*.

I folded up the chair, returned to my car and drove home. I've not repeated the pilgrimage since, I don't need to, I think of Jimmy every day.

I'm a grandad now, banned by Trudie and my doctors from 'mosh pits' due to my dangerously high blood pressure. I destroyed my kill list, though I still think about Erika and the humiliation on the odd occasion. It's fair to say that my serial killing days, like my 'pogoing', are well and truly over.

Having said that, I'm off to see The Stranglers next week.

ALSO BY SIMON LYONS

How to Kidnap a String Quartet

ABOUT THE AUTHOR

Having left his North London sink comprehensive at the age of fifteen with few qualifications, Simon travelled extensively before settling down to family life and 'blagging' a living. A ferocious gig and festival goer, he always felt he had a story to tell and How to Kidnap a String Quartet, his debut novel, is an expression of his varied experiences of life and wild and whacky imagination. The follow up The Good Poison Club is an exciting thriller set in a London NHS hospital.

www.simonlyonsauthor.com
Facebook: simonlyonsauthor
Twitter: @simonlyonsbooks
Instagram: simonlyonsauthor